THE SAINT CLOSES
THE CASE

FOREWORD BY STEVE BAILIE

THE ADVENTURES OF THE SAINT

THE SAINT
CLOSES THE
CASE

LESLIE CHARTERIS

SERIES EDITOR: IAN DICKERSON

fTHOMAS & MERCER

Text copyright © 2014 Interfund (London) Ltd.
Foreword © 2014 Steve Bailie
Preface © 1964 Interfund (London) Ltd.
Publication History and Author Biography © 2014 Ian Dickerson

Published by Thomas & Mercer, Seattle

www.apub.com

ISBN-13: 9781477842621
ISBN-10: 1477842624

Cover design by David Drummond, www.salamanderhill.com

Printed in the United States of America.

To Jean and Jeannine,
From whom I have learned so much

Paris, January 1930

PUBLISHER'S NOTE

The text of this book has been preserved from the original edition and includes vocabulary, grammar, style, and punctuation that might differ from modern publishing practices. Every care has been taken to preserve the author's tone and meaning, allowing only minimal changes to punctuation and wording to ensure a fluent experience for modern readers.

FOREWORD TO THE
NEW EDITION

It's midnight. I'm in Paris. It's a hot summer evening. The windows are open, the cafés in the Place du Tertre below are still buzzing, and I have just finished rereading *The Saint Closes the Case* for maybe the sixth or seventh time in my life, polished off the vin rouge, and come upstairs to write these words while the experience is still fresh in my mind.

There is a direct link between the first reading and this latest one and why I am in Paris. I shall explain.

The Saint Closes the Case was first published in 1930, under its far superior—and more accurate—title, *The Last Hero*. It was the second of Charteris's Saint adventures to be published.

I first read the novel as a teenager in Belfast in the early 1970s, a grey and forbidding city at that time, overrun by the madness of what we called "The Troubles." I always found The Troubles to be a wholly inaccurate name for what was damn as near a full civil war at times, but it takes more than a few bombs and bullets before the Irish will declare a situation a war, an attitude which demonstrates a certain stoicism and optimism almost worthy of Simon Templar himself.

In that gloomy era one of the great highlights of my week—having run the gauntlet of a particular prescribed path home which avoided certain street corners—was to get back from school in time to catch afternoon reruns of the 1960s Saint television series. The TV show led me to hunt down the books, and I still treasure, amongst many other volumes, a copy of *Send for the Saint* which I've been meaning to return to the public lending library for a few decades now.

If your image of Simon Templar is conditioned by Sir Roger Moore's witty and charming television performance, then the Saint of *The Last Hero* will add some interesting colour to the character. This Saint is not a solitary international playboy; rather, he is a cold-blooded killer, by knife, by gun, by bomb.

He is the leader of a gang of fellow "Saints": the equally dashing Roger Conway and Norman Kent, and the faithful ex-sergeant major cum housekeeper Orace. And perhaps most surprisingly of all— Templar has a steady girl, Patricia Holm, whom he met in his first published adventure.

Patricia Holm embodies a certain type of woman—the cliché would be English rose: the well-bred, plucky heroine standing fast by her man's side, unfazed by guns and bullets, supremely confident in her lover's ability to cope with whatever danger comes their way.

Although the Saint makes light of their relationship late in the novel, there is no doubt that this is a young couple in love. And when Patricia is kidnapped by the novel's villain, the physically giant warmonger Rayt Marius, he unleashes a rage in Templar that has never been portrayed on screen. This Saint will kidnap, torture, and cold-bloodedly murder the Ungodly in his quest to save Patricia.

Much of this was a surprise to me when I undertook that first reading of the novel. The television Saint would only use a gun if he took it from a bad guy. He most certainly never carried a knife, let alone fetishised them by giving them names, as he does in early Saint books.

But in the Belfast of the 1970s, Charteris's writing was a great source of joy—comfort even—to a young man trying to make sense of the daily evils that were happening in his hometown. The Saint articulated what we all knew—that evil men did exist, that they were often beyond redemption, and that sometimes justice needed to step in where The Law could not.

The books and TV episodes opened up new worlds to me. Somewhere off the shores of Ireland there were other countries. They had beautiful landscapes and beautiful food and beautiful women. I wanted to go see them for myself.

I was less keen on getting into punch-ups, however. So I transferred those energies to the written word, and my earliest fumblings with pen and ink were juvenile rip-offs of Saint stories, lovingly handwritten in exercise books.

Somewhere over the years that became a career, and here I am in Paris, where tomorrow we shall be filming a scene in a TV series I've been writing for, wherein a lone hero dismantles four bad guys single-handedly, then drives off into the night with a beautiful mademoiselle by his side. Exactly the kind of thing I've been wanting to write since the Saint first brightened a day for me. Even now, I can identify a fellow Saint fan by his writing style, pick up the small subtle influences that I know originated from a love of the character. I doubt the writers of *Leverage*, *Burn Notice*, or *Hustle* among many others would disagree with me.

So as I sit here tonight I know for sure that Charteris's Saint stories impacted on my adolescent development and sent me in search of a life of the sort that leads a man to be writing in a Parisian apartment under the shadow of the Sacré-Cœur in the wee small hours.

Two things from this book lived on in my head right from that very first reading, some thirty-odd years ago now. To this day I can quote a passage verbatim, as the author, then Templar himself, espouse the Saint's basic philosophy:

> *He believed that life was full of adventure and he went*
> *forth in the full blaze and surge of that belief* . . . *"Into*
> *battle, murder and sudden death, Good Lord, deliver me up*
> *to the neck!"*

But what lived with me even more is the ending of *The Last Hero*. I will give no spoilers here, but it is as powerful and noble a final few pages as I have read in any of the great romantic adventures.

So I hand you over to Leslie Charteris himself for your further reading. This is an embryonic Saint, a young man living beyond his means, crackling with youthful energy, but already on the path he has chosen himself for life. In later books you will find a more polished Saint, but in this novel the sheer *joie de vivre* of Simon Templar's thirst for adventure is impossible to resist.

And as soon as you have finished it, go straight to *The Avenging Saint*, which picks up three months after *The Last Hero* ends. Then read *The Saint's Getaway*. Together, all three volumes make up one of the Saint's biggest and greatest adventures.

—*Steve Bailie*

THE SAINT CLOSES
THE CASE

PREFACE

This was the first "big" Saint novel—that is, the first story in which he went up against king-size international dragons, as against the ordinary leeches, rats, skunks, and other vermin of the Underworld—and it still seems to be one of the prime favorites of those loyal readers who have followed his adventures almost from the beginning.

For the benefit of those who may be taking up the series so much later, however, I feel it may be necessary to slip in this reminder that the book was written in 1929, when the world was politically, technologically, and temperamentally a totally different place from the one we live in today.

In those days, there was a genuine widespread suspicion, which I was inclined to share with a great many of my generation, that modern wars were plotted and deliberately engineered by vast mysterious financial cartels for their own enrichment. There was also a vague idea that fighting, itself, was still a fairly glamorous activity, or would be if the scientists would leave it alone. No doubt there were romantics in other periods who thought it was more sporting to be shot at with arrows than with bullets, and they were followed by others who thought that rifles were more fun than machine-guns and howitzers, and after them came those who thought that poison gas was the last step to reducing glorious war to sordidness.

This book is based on the Saint's accidental discovery that the usual slightly goofy scientist has dreamed up something called an "electron cloud," a sort of extension of the gas horror with radioactive overtones, and his decision that it should not only be kept out of the hands of the stateless war-mongers, but for the good of humanity should be suppressed altogether, on the theory that this would still leave heroes happily free to enjoy the relatively good clean fun of air raids and ordinary mustard gas. (The original title of the book was *The Last Hero*, and in it the Saint first expounded his philosophy of "battle, murder, and sudden death" as a joyous form of self-expression.)

Well, this was an attitude of youth which of course I shared with him, or he got from me. And in those days there were no mushroom clouds on the horizon to make even Vargan's electron cloud look like a comparatively harmless toy. But this should not for a moment be taken to imply that either of us, today, would be supporters of the "Ban the Bomb" kind foggy-minded idealism. There are many things which seemed like eternal truths to both of us in those days, which no longer look so immutable. In fact, I myself am often tempted now to lean with the optimists who think that the Bomb may actually achieve what the moralists failed to do, and abolish major warfare by making it impossible for anyone, financier or despot, to hope to profit by it.

Be tolerant, then, of one or two outworn ideas, and enjoy it simply as a rattling good adventure story of its time, which I think it still is.

—Leslie Charteris (1964)

PRELUDE

It is said that in these hectic days no item of news is capable of holding the interest of the public for more than a week; therefore journalists and news editors age swiftly, and become prematurely bald and bad-tempered, Tatcho and Kruschen availing them naught. A new sensation must be provided from day to day, and each sensation must eclipse its predecessor, till the dictionary is bled dry of superlatives, and the imagination pales before the task of finding or inventing for tomorrow a story fantastic and colossal enough to succeed the masterpiece of yesterday.

That the notorious adventurer known as the Saint should have contrived to keep in the public eye for more than three months from the date of his first manifestation, thereby smithereening all records of that kind, was due entirely to his own energy and initiative. The harassed sensationalists of Fleet Street welcomed him with open arms. For a time the fevered hunt for novelty could take a rest. The Saint himself did everything in that line that the most exacting editor could have asked for—except, of course, that he failed to provide the culminating sensation of his own arrest and trial. But each of his adventures was more audacious than the last, and he never gave the interest aroused by his latest activity time to die down before he burst again upon a startled public with a yet more daring coup.

And the same enterprising lawlessness continued for over three months, in the course of which time he brought to a triumphant conclusion some twenty raids upon the persons and property of evildoers.

Thus it came to pass that in those three months the name of the Saint gathered about itself an aura of almost supernatural awe and terror, so that men who had for years boasted that the law could not touch them began to walk in fear, and the warning of the Saint—a ridiculous picture of a little man with one-dimensional body and limbs, such as children draw, but wearing above his blank round head an absurd halo such as it rarely occurs to children to add to their drawings—delivered to a man's door in plain envelope, was found to be as fatal as any sentence ever signed by a Judge of the High Court. Which was exactly what the Saint himself had desired should happen. It amused him very much.

For the most part, he worked secretly and unseen, and his victims could give the police nothing tangible in the way of clues by which he might have been traced. Yet sometimes it was inevitable that he should be known to the man whose downfall he was engineering, and, when that happened, the grim silence of the injured party was one of the most surprising features of the mystery. Chief Inspector Teal, after a number of fruitless attempts, had resigned himself to giving up as a bad job the task of trying to make the victims of the Saint give evidence.

"You might as well try to get a squeak out of a deaf-and-dumb oyster in a tank of chloroform," he told the Commissioner. "Either the Saint never tackles a man on one count unless he's got a second count against him by which he can blackmail him to silence, or else he's found the secret of threatening a man so convincingly that he still believes it the next day—and all the days after that."

His theory was shrewd and sound enough, but it would have been shrewder and sounder and more elaborate if he had been a more imaginative man; but Mr Teal had little confidence in things he could not see and take hold of, and he had never had a chance of watching the Saint in action.

There were, however, other occasions when the Saint had no need to fall back upon blackmail or threats to ensure the silence of those with whose careers he interfered.

There was, for instance, the case of a man named Golter, an anarchist and incorrigible firebrand, whose boast it was that he had known the inside of every prison in Europe. He belonged to no political faction, and apparently had no gospel to forward except his own mania for destruction, but he was anything but a harmless lunatic.

He was the leader of a society known as the Black Wolves, nearly every member of which had at some time or another served a heavy sentence for some kind of political offence—which, more often than not, consisted of an attempted assassination, usually by bomb.

The reason for such societies, and the mentality of their adherents, will always provide an interesting field of speculation for the psychiatrist, but occasions will arise when the interest ceases to be the abstract diversion of the scientist and becomes the practical problem of those whose business it is to keep peace under the law.

The law awoke to this fact, and simultaneously to a rather alarmed recognition of the existence of the Black Wolves, after a week in which two factories in the North of England were the scenes of explosions which resulted in no little loss of life, and the bullet of an undiscovered sniper actually grazed across the back of the Home Secretary as he stepped into his car outside the House of Commons.

The law found Golter, but the man who had been detailed to follow him and report on his movements somehow contrived to lose him on the afternoon in which a Crown Prince drove in state through the streets of London on his way to a luncheon given by the Lord Mayor.

The procession was arranged to pass by way of the Strand and Fleet Street to the City. From a tiny office which he had rented for the purpose in Southampton Row, of which the police knew nothing, Golter had found an easy way to the roofs of the houses on the north side of Fleet Street. He sat there, in a more or less comfortable position, among the chimney-stacks, from which he could look down and see the street below, while armed men scoured London for a trace of him, and a worried Commissioner ordered a doubling of the plain-clothes detectives stationed along the route.

Golter was a careful and a thoughtful man, and he had a fair grounding in the principles of dynamics. He knew to an inch how high he was from the ground, and he had calculated exactly how many seconds a bomb would take to fall to the street; the fuses of the Mills bombs in his pockets were adjusted accordingly. Again, in Fleet Street, a little farther down towards the Strand, he had measured the distance between two lamp-posts. With the aid of a stop-watch he would discover how long the leading car took to pass between them; then, by consulting an elaborate chart which he had prepared, he would be able to learn at once, without further calculation, exactly at what instant he had to launch his bombs so that they would fall directly into the back of the Crown Prince's car as it passed. Golter was proud of the scientific precision with which he had worked out every detail.

He smoked a cigarette, drumming his heels gently against the leads. It was fifteen minutes before the procession was due to arrive at that point, according to the official time-table, and already the street below was packed with a dense crowd which overflowed the pavements and wound hampering tentacles into the stream of traffic. The mass of people looked like ants, Golter thought. Bourgeois insects. He amused himself by picturing the ant-like confusion that would follow the detonation of his three bombs . . .

"Yes, it should be an interesting spectacle."

Golter's head snapped round as though it had been jerked by an invisible wire.

He had heard nothing of the arrival of the man who now stood over him, whose gentle, drawling voice had broken into his meditations far more shatteringly than any explosion could have done. He saw a tall, trim, lean figure in a grey fresco suit of incredible perfection, with a soft grey felt hat whose wide brim shaded pleasant blue eyes. This man might have posed for any illustration of the latest and smartest effort of Savile Row in the way of gents' natty outfitting—that is, if he could have been persuaded to discard the automatic pistol, which is not generally considered to form an indispensable adjunct to What the Well-Dressed Man will Wear this Season.

"Extraordinarily interesting," repeated the unknown, with his blue eyes gazing down in a rather dreamy way at the throng a hundred feet below. "From a purely artistic point of view, it's a pity we shan't be able to watch it."

Golter's right hand was sliding towards a bulging pocket. The stranger, with his automatic swinging in a lazy arc that centred over Golter's stomach, encouraged the movement.

"But leave the pins in, Beautiful," he murmured, "and pass 'em to me one by one . . . That's a good boy!"

He took the bombs in his left hand as Golter passed them over, and handed them to someone whom Golter could not see—a second man who stood behind a chimney-stack.

A minute passed, in which Golter stood with his hands hanging loosely at his sides, waiting for a chance to make a grab at the gun which the stranger held with such an affectation of negligence. But the chance never came.

Instead, came a hand from behind the chimney-stack—a hand holding a bomb. The stranger took the bomb and handed it back to Golter.

"Put it in your pocket," he directed.

The second and third followed, and Golter, with his coat once again dragged out of shape by the weight, stood staring at the stranger, who, he thought, must be a detective, and who yet behaved in such an incomprehensible manner.

"What did you do that for?" he demanded suspiciously.

"My own reasons," answered the other calmly. "I am now leaving you. Do you mind?"

Suspicion—fear—perplexity—all the emotions chased and mingled with one another over Golter's unshaven face. Then inspiration dawned in his pale eyes.

"So you aren't a busy!"

The stranger smiled.

"Unfortunately for you—no. You may have heard of me. I am called the Saint . . ."

His left hand flashed in and out of his coat pocket in a swift movement, and Golter, in the grip of a sudden paralysis of terror, stared as if hypnotised while the Saint chalked his grotesque trade-mark on the chimney-stack.

Then the Saint spoke again.

"You are not human. You are a destroyer—an insane killer without any justification but your own lust for blood. If you had any motive, I might have handed you over to the police, who are at this moment combing London for you. I am here not to judge any man's creed. But for you there can be no excuse . . ."

He had vanished when Golter looked round for him, wondering why the condemnation did not continue, and the roof was deserted. The Saint had a knack of disappearing like that.

The procession was approaching. Golter could hear the cheering growing rapidly louder, like the roar of many waters suddenly released from burst flood-gates. He peered down. A hundred yards away he could see the leading car crawling through the lane of human ants.

His brain was still reeling to encompass the understanding of what the Saint had come to do. The Saint had been there, accusing—and then he had gone, giving Golter back his bombs. Golter could have believed himself to have been the victim of an hallucination. But the fantastic sketch on the chimney-stack remained to prove that he had not been dreaming.

With an hysterical sweep of his arm, he smeared his sleeve over the drawing, and took from his pocket his stop-watch and the time-chart he had made. The leading car had just reached the first of the two lamp-posts on which he had based his calculations. He watched it in a kind of daze.

The Crown Prince drove in the third car. Golter recognised the uniform. The Prince was saluting the crowd.

Golter found himself trembling as he took the first bomb from his pocket and drew the pin, but he threw it on the very instant that his stop-watch and chart indicated.

"The true details of the case," wrote *The Daily Record*, some days later, "are likely to remain a mystery for ever, unless the Saint should one day elect to come out into the open and elucidate them. Until then the curiosity of the public must be satisfied with the findings of the committee of Scotland Yard experts who have been investigating the affair—that in some way the Saint succeeded in so tampering with the fuses of the Mills bombs with which Golter intended to attempt the life of the Crown Prince that they exploded the moment he released the spring handle, thereby blowing him to pieces . . ."

"Whatever the opinions which may be expressed concerning the arrogance of this gentleman who presumes to take the law into his own lawless hands, it cannot be denied that in this case his intervention undoubtedly saved the life of our royal guest, and few will be found to deny that justice was done—though perhaps it was justice of too poetic a character to be generally accepted as a precedent . . ."

With this sensational climax, which put the name of the Saint on the lips of every man and woman in the civilised world, came the end of a clearly defined chapter in his history.

The sensation died down, as the most amazing sensations will die down for lack of re-stimulation. In an open letter which was published in every newspaper throughout Europe, the Crown Prince offered his thanks to the unknown, and promised that the debt should not be forgotten if at any time the Saint should stand in need of help from high places. The British Government followed almost immediately with the offer of a free pardon for all past offences on condition that the Saint revealed himself and took an oath to turn his energy and ingenuity into more legitimate channels. The only answer was a considered letter of acknowledgment and regretful refusal, posted simultaneously to all the leading news-agencies.

"Unfortunately," wrote the Saint, "I am convinced, and my friends with me, that for us to disband at the very moment when our campaign is beginning to justify itself in the crime statistics of London—and (which is even more important) in those more subtle offences against the moral code about which there can be no statistics—would be an act of indefensible cowardice on my part. We cannot be tempted by the mere promise of safety for ourselves to betray the motive which brought us together. The game is more than the player of the game . . . Also, speaking for myself, I should find a respectable life intolerably dull. It isn't easy to get out of the rut these days: you have to be a rebel, and you're more likely to end up in Wormwood Scrubs than Westminster Abbey. But I believe, as I have never believed anything before, that I am on the right road. The things of value are the common, primitive things. Justice is good—when it's done fanatically. Fighting is good—when the thing you fight for is simple and sane and you love it. And danger is good—it wakes you up, and makes you live ten times more keenly. And vulgar swashbuckling may easily be the best of all— because it stands for a magnificent belief in all those things, a superb faith in the glamour that civilisation is trying to sneer at as a delusion and a snare . . . As long as the ludicrous laws of this country refuse me these, I shall continue to set those laws at defiance. The pleasure of applying my own treatment to the human sores whose persistent festering offends me is one which I will not be denied . . ."

And yet, strangely enough, an eagerly expectant public waited in vain for the Saint to follow up this astonishing manifesto. But day after day went by, and still he held his hand, so that those who had walked softly, wondering when the uncanny omniscience of the Unknown would find them out, began to lift up their heads again and boast themselves with increasing assurance, saying that the Saint was afraid.

A fortnight grew into a month, and the Saint was rapidly passing into something like a dim legend of bygone days.

And then, one afternoon in June, yelling newsboys spread a special edition of *The Evening Record* through the streets of London, and men and women stood in impatient groups on the pavements and read the most astounding story of the Saint that had ever been given to the Press.

It was the story that is told again here, as it has already been retold, by now, half a hundred times. But now it is taken from a different and more intimate angle, and some details are shown which have not been told before.

It is the story of how Simon Templar, known to many as the Saint (plausibly from his initials, but more probably from his Saintly way of doing the most un-Saintly things), came by chance upon a thread which led him to the most amazing adventure of his career. And it is also the story of Norman Kent, who was his friend, and how at one moment in that adventure he held the fate of two nations, if not of all Europe, in his hands; how he accounted for that stewardship; and how, one quiet summer evening, in a house by the Thames, with no melodrama and no heroics, he fought and died for an idea.

1

HOW SIMON TEMPLAR WENT FOR A DRIVE, AND SAW A STRANGE SIGHT

Simon Templar read newspapers rarely, and when he did read them he skimmed through the pages as quickly as possible and gleaned information with a hurried eye. Most of the matter offered in return for his coppers was wasted on him. He was not in the least interested in politics; the announcement that the wife of a Walthamstow printer had given birth to quadruplets found him unmoved; articles such as "A Man's Place Is in the Home" (by Anastasia Gowk, the brilliant authoress of *Passion in Pimlico*) left him completely cold. But a quarter-column, with photograph, in a paper he bought one evening for the racing results chanced to catch his roving gaze and roused a very faint flicker of attention.

Two coincidences led him from that idly assimilated item of news to a red-hot scent, the fascination of which for him was anything but casual.

The first came the next day, when, finding himself at Ludgate Circus towards one o'clock, it occurred to him to call in at the Press Club in the hope of finding someone he knew. He found Barney Malone, of *The Clarion*, and was promptly invited to lunch, which was exactly what he had been looking for. The Saint had an ingrained prejudice against lunching alone.

Conversation remained general throughout the meal, except for one bright interlude.

"I suppose there's nothing new about the Saint?" asked Simon innocently, and Barney Malone shook his head.

"He seems to have gone out of business."

"I'm only taking a rest," Simon assured him. "After the calm, the storm. You wait for the next scoop."

Simon Templar always insisted on speaking of the Saint as if he himself was that disreputable outlaw. Barney Malone, for all his familiarity with Simon's eccentric sense of humour, was inclined to regard this affectation as a particularly aimless pleasantry.

It was half an hour later, over coffee, that the Saint recalled the quarter-column which had attracted his attention, and asked a question about it.

"You may be quite frank with your Uncle Simon," he said. "He knows all the tricks of the trade, and you won't disappoint him a bit if you tell him that the chief sub-editor made it up himself to fill the space at the last moment."

Malone grinned.

"Funnily enough, you're wrong. These scientific discoveries you read about under scare headlines are usually stunt stuff, but if you weren't so uneducated you'd have heard of K. B. Vargan. He's quite mad, but as a scientist his class is A1 at the Royal Society."

"So there may be something in it?" suggested the Saint.

"There may, or there may not. These inventions have a trick of springing a leak as soon as you take them out of the laboratory and try using them on a large scale. For instance they had a death-ray years ago that would kill mice at twenty yards, but I never heard of them testing it on an ox at five hundred."

Barney Malone was able to give some supplementary details of Vargan's invention which the sub-editor's blue pencil had cut out as unintelligible to the lay public. They were hardly less unintelligible to Simon Templar, whose scientific knowledge stopped a long way short of Einstein, but he listened attentively.

"It's curious that you should refer to it," Malone said, a little later, "because I was only interviewing the man this morning. He burst into the office about eleven o'clock, storming and raving like a lunatic because he hadn't been given the front page."

He gave a graphic description of the encounter.

"But what's the use?" asked the Saint "There won't be another war for hundreds of years."

"You think so?"

"I'm told so."

Malone's eyebrows lifted in that tolerantly supercilious way in which a journalist's eyebrows will sometimes lift when an ignorant outsider ventures an opinion on world affairs.

"If you live for another six months," he said, "I shall expect to see you in uniform. Or will you conscientiously object?"

Simon tapped a cigarette deliberately on his thumb-nail.

"You mean that?"

"I'm desperately serious. We're nearer to these things than the rest of the public, and we see them coming first. In another few months the rest of England will see it coming. A lot of funny things have been happening lately."

Simon waited, suddenly keyed up to interest, and Barney Malone sucked thoughtfully at his pipe, and presently went on:

"In the last month, three foreigners have been arrested, tried, and imprisoned for offences against the Official Secrets Act. In other words, espionage. During the same period, four Englishmen have been similarly dealt with in different parts of Europe. The foreign governments concerned have disowned the men we've pinched, but since a government always disowns spies as soon as they get into trouble, on principle, no one ever believes it. Similarly, we have disclaimed the four Englishmen, and, naturally, nobody believes us either—and yet I happen to know that it's true. If you appreciate really subtle jokes, you might think that one over, and laugh next time I see you."

The Saint went home in a thoughtful mood.

He had a genius that was all his own—an imaginative genius that would take a number of ordinary facts, all of which seemed to be totally unconnected, and none of which, to the eye of anyone but himself, would have seemed very remarkable, and read them into a signpost pointing to a mystery. Adventure came to him not so much because he sought it as because he brazenly expected it. He believed that life was full of adventure, and he went forward in the full blaze and surge of that belief. It has been said of a man very much like Simon Templar that he was "a man born with the sound of trumpets in his ears"; that saying might almost equally well have been said of the Saint, for he also, like Michael Paladin, had heard the sound of the trumpet, and had moved ever afterwards in the echoes of the sound of the trumpet, in such a mighty clamour of romance that at least one of his friends had been moved to call him the last hero, in desperately earnest jest.

"'From battle, murder, and sudden death, Good Lord, deliver us!'" he quoted once. "How can any live man ask for that? Why, they're meat and drink—they're the things that make life worth living! Into battle, murder, and sudden death, Good Lord, deliver me up to the neck! That's what I say . . ."

Thus spoke the Saint, that man of superb recklessness and strange heroisms and impossible ideals, and went on to show, as few others of his age have shown, that a man inspired can swashbuckle as well with cloak and stick as any cavalier of history with cloak and sword, and there can be as much chivalry in the setting of a modern laugh as there can ever have been in the setting of a medieval lance, that a true valour and venture finds its way to fulfilment, not so much through the kind of world into which it happens to be born, as through the heart with which it lives.

But even he could never have guessed into what a strange story this genius and this faith of his were to bring him.

On what he had chanced to read and what Barney Malone had told him, the Saint built in his mind a tower of possibilities whose magnitude, when it was completed, awed even himself. And then, because he had the priceless gift of taking the products of his vivid imagination at their practical worth, he filed the fancy away in his mind as an interesting curiosity, and thought no more about it.

Too much sanity is sometimes dangerous.

Simon Templar was self-conscious about his imagination. It was the one kind of self-consciousness he had, and certainly he kept it a secret which no one would have suspected. Those who knew him said that he was reckless to the point of vain bravado, but they were never more mistaken. If he had chosen to argue this point, he would have said that his style was, if anything, cramped by too much caution.

But in this case caution was swept away, and imagination triumphantly vindicated by the second coincidence.

This came three days later, when the Saint awoke one morning to find that the showery weather which had hung over England for a week had given place to cloudless blue skies and brilliant sunshine.

He hung out of his bedroom window and sniffed the air suspiciously, but he could smell no rain. Forthwith he decided that the business of annoying criminals could be pardonably neglected while he took out his car and relaxed in the country.

"Darling Pat," said the Saint, "it'd be a crime to waste a day like this!"

"Darling Simon," wailed Patricia Holm, "you know we'd promised to have dinner with the Hannassays."

"Very darling Pat," said the Saint, "won't they be disappointed to hear that we've both been suddenly taken ill after last night's binge?"

So they went, and the Saint enjoyed his holiday with the comfortable conviction that he had earned it.

They eventually dined at Cobham, and afterwards sat for a long time over cigarettes and coffee and matters of intimate moment which have no place here. It was eleven o'clock when the Saint set the long nose of his Furillac on the homeward road.

Patricia was happily tired, but the Saint drove very well with one hand.

It was when they were still rather more than a mile from Esher that the Saint saw a light, and thoughtfully braked the car to a standstill.

Simon Templar was cursed, or blessed, with an insatiable inquisitiveness. If ever he saw anything that trespassed by half an inch over the boundaries of the purely normal, and commonplace, he was immediately fired with the desire to find out the reason for such erratic behaviour. And it must be admitted that the light had been no ordinary light.

The average man would undoubtedly have driven on somewhat puzzledly, would have been haunted for a few days by a vague and irritating perplexity, and would eventually have forgotten the incident altogether. Simon Templar has since considered, in all sober earnestness, what might have been the consequences of his being an average man at that moment, and has stopped appalled at the vista of horrors opened up by the thought.

But Simon Templar was not an average man, and the gift of minding his own business had been left out of his make-up. He slipped into reverse and sent the car gently back a matter of thirty yards to the end of a lane which opened off the main road.

A little way down this lane, between the trees, the silhouette of a gabled house loomed blackly against the star-powdered sky, and it was in an upper window of this house that the Saint had seen the light as he passed. Now he skilfully lighted a cigarette with one hand, and stared down the lane. The light was still there. The Saint contemplated it in silence, immobile as a watching Indian, till a fair, sleepy head roused on his shoulder.

"What is it?" asked Patricia.

"That's what I'd like to know," answered the Saint, and pointed with the glowing end of his cigarette.

The blinds were drawn over that upper window, but the light could be clearly seen behind them—a light of astounding brilliance, a blindingly white light that came and went in regular, rhythmic flashes like intermittent flickers of lightning.

The night was as still as a dream, and at that moment there was no other traffic on that stretch of road. The Saint reached forward and switched off the engine of the Furillac. Then he listened—and the Saint had ears of abnormal sensitiveness—in a quiet so unbroken that he could even hear the rustle of the girl's sleeve as she moved her arm.

But the quiet was not silence—it was simply the absence of any isolated noise. There was sound—a sound so faint and soothing that it was no more than a neutral background to a silence. It might have been a soft humming, but it was so soft that it might have been no more than a dim vibration carried on the air.

"A dynamo," said the Saint, and as he spoke he opened the door of the car and stepped out into the road.

Patricia caught his hand.

"Where are you going, Saint?"

Simon's teeth showed white in the Saintly smile.

"I'm going to investigate. A perfectly ordinary citizen might be running a dynamo to manufacture his own electric light—although this dynamo sounds a lot heavier than the breed you usually find in home power plants. But I'm sure no perfectly ordinary citizen uses his dynamo to make electric sparks that size to amuse the children. Life has been rather tame lately, and one never knows . . ."

"I'll come with you."

The Saint grimaced.

Patricia Holm, he used to say, had given him two white hairs for every day he had known her. Ever since a memorable day in Devonshire, when he had first met her, and the hectic days which followed, when she had joined him in the hunting of the man who was called the Tiger, the Saint had been forcing himself to realise that to try to keep this girl out of trouble was a hopeless task. By this time he was getting resigned to her. She was a law unto herself. She was of a mettle so utterly different to that of any girl he had ever dreamed of, a mettle so much finer and fiercer, that if she had not been so paradoxically feminine with it he would have sworn that she ought to have been a man. She was—well, she was Patricia Holm, and that was that . . .

"O.K., kid," said the Saint helplessly.

But already she was standing beside him. With a shrug, the Saint climbed back into his seat and moved the car on half a dozen yards so that the lights could not be seen from the house. Then he rejoined her at the corner of the lane.

They went down the lane together.

The house stood in a hedged garden thickly grown with trees. The Saint, searching warily, found the alarm on the gate, and disconnected it with an expert hand before he lifted the latch and let Patricia through to the lawn. From there, looking upwards, they could see that queer, bleak light still glimmering behind the blinds of the upper window.

The front of the house was in darkness and the ground-floor windows closed and apparently secured. The Saint wasted no time on those, for he was without the necessary instrument to force the catch of a window, and he knew that front doors are invariably solid. Back doors, on the other hand, he knew equally well are often vulnerable, for the intelligent foresight of the honest householder frequently stops short of grasping the fact that the best-class burglar may on occasion stoop to using the servants' entrance. The Saint accordingly edged round the side of the house, Patricia following him.

They walked over grass, still damp and spongy from the rain that had deluged the country for the past six days. The humming of the dynamo was now unmistakable, and with it could be heard the thrum and whir of the motor that drove it. The noise seemed, at one point, to come from beneath their feet.

Then they rounded the second corner, and the Saint halted so abruptly that Patricia found herself two paces ahead of him.

"This is fun!" whispered the Saint.

And yet by daylight it would have been a perfectly ordinary sight. Many country houses possess greenhouses, and it is even conceivable that an enthusiastic horticulturist might have attached to his house a greenhouse some twenty-five yards long and high enough to give a tall man some four feet headroom.

But such a greenhouse brightly lighted up at half past eleven at night is no ordinary spectacle. And the phenomenon becomes even more extraordinary—to an inquisitive mind like the Saint's—when the species of vegetable matter for which such an excellent illumination is provided is screened from the eyes of the outside world by dark curtains closely drawn under the glass.

Simon Templar needed no encouragement to probe further into the mystery, and the girl was beside him when he stepped stealthily to a two-inch gap in the curtains.

A moment later he found Patricia Holm gripping his arm with hands that trembled ever so slightly.

The interior of the greenhouse was bare of pots and plants; for four-fifths of its length it was bare of anything at all. There was a rough concrete floor, and the concrete extended up the sides of the greenhouse for about three feet, thus forming a kind of trough. And at one end of the trough there was tethered a goat.

At the other end of the building, on a kind of staging set on concrete pillars, stood four men.

The Saint took them in at a glance. Three of them stood in a little group—a fat little man with a bald head and horn-rimmed spectacles, a tall, thin man of about forty-five with a high, narrow forehead and iron-grey hair, and a youngish man with pince-nez and a notebook. The fourth man stood a little apart from them, in front of a complicated switchboard, on which glowed here and there little bulbs like the valves used in wireless telegraphy. He was of middle height, and his age might have been anything from sixty to eighty. His hair was snow-white, and his clothes were shapeless and stained and shabby.

But it was on nothing human or animal in the place that the Saint's gaze concentrated after that first swift survey.

There was something else there, on that concrete floor, between the four men and the goat at the other end. It curled and wreathed sluggishly, lying low on the ground and not rising at all, and yet, though the outside of it was fleecily inert, it seemed as if the interior of the thing whirled and throbbed as with the struggling of a tremendous force pent up in ineffectual turmoil. This thing was like a cloud, but it was like no cloud that ever rode the sky. It was a cloud such as no sane and shining sky had ever seen, a pale violet cloud, a cloud out of hell. And here and there, in the misty violet of its colour, it seemed as if strange little sparks and streaks of fire shot through it like tiny comets, gleamed momentarily, and were gone, so that the cloud moved and burned as with an inner phosphorescence.

It had been still when the Saint first set eyes on it, but now it moved. It did not spread aimlessly over the floor; it was creeping along purposefully, as though imbued with life. The Saint, afterwards, described it as like a great, ghostly, luminous worm travelling sideways. Stretched out in a long line that reached from side to side of the greenhouse, it humped itself forward in little whirling rushes, and the living power within it seemed to burn more and more fiercely, until the cloud was framed in a faint halo of luminance from the whirl of eye-searing violet at its core.

It had seemed to be creeping at first, but then the Saint saw that that impression had been deceptive. The creeping of the cloud was now the speed of a man running, and it was plain that it could have only one objective. The goat at the end of the trough was cringing against the farthest wall, frozen with terror, staring wild-eyed at the cloud that rolled towards it with the relentlessness of an inrushing tide.

The Saint flashed a lightning glance back at the staging, and divined, without comprehending, why the cloud moved so decisively. The white-haired man was holding in one hand a thing of shining metal rather like a small electric radiator, which he trained on the cloud, moving it from side to side. From this thing seemed to come the propulsive force which drove the cloud along as a controlled wind might have done.

Then the Saint looked back at the cloud, and at that instant the foremost fringe of it touched the petrified goat.

There was no sound that the Saint could hear from outside. But at once the imprisoned power within the cloud seemed to boil up into a terrible effervescence of fire, and where there had been a goat was nothing but the shape of a goat starkly outlined in shuddering orange-hued flame. For an instant, only the fraction of a second, it lasted, that vision of a dazzling glare in the shape of a goat, and then, as if the power that had produced it was spent, the shape became black. It stood of itself for a second; then it toppled slowly and fell upon the concrete. A little black dust hung in the air, and a little wreath of bluish smoke drifted up towards the roof. The violet cloud uncoiled slothfully, and smeared fluffily over the floor in a widening pool of mist.

Its force was by no means spent—that was an illusion belied by the flickering lights that still glinted through it like a host of tiny fireflies. It was only that the controlling rays had been diverted. Looking round again, Simon saw that the white-haired man had put down the thing of shining metal with which he had directed the cloud, and was turning to speak to the three men who had watched the demonstration.

The Saint stood like a man in a dream.

Then he drew Patricia away, with a soft and almost frantic laugh.

"We'll get out of here," he said. "We've seen enough for one night."

And yet he was wrong, for something else was to be added to the adventure with amazing rapidity.

As he turned, the Saint nearly cannoned into the giant who stood over them, and, in the circumstances, Simon Templar did not feel inclined to argue. He acted instantaneously, which the giant was not expecting. When one man points a revolver at another, there is, by convention, a certain amount of back-chat about the situation before anything is done, but the Saint held convention beneath contempt.

Moreover, when confronted by an armed man twice his own size, the Saint felt that he needed no excuse for employing any damaging foul known to the fighting game, or even a speciality of his own invention.

His left hand struck the giant's gun arm aside, and at the same time the Saint kicked with one well-shod foot and a clear conscience.

A second later he was sprinting, with Patricia's hand in his.

There was a car drawn up in front of the house. Simon had not noticed it under the trees as he passed on his way round to the back, but now he saw it, because he was looking for it, and it accounted for the stocky figure in breeches and a peaked cap which bulked out of the shadows round the gate and tried to bar the way.

"Sorry, son," said the Saint sincerely, and handed him off with some vim.

Then he was flying up the lane at the girl's side, and the sounds of the injured chauffeur's pursuit were too far behind to be alarming.

The Saint vaulted into the Furillac, and came down with one foot on the self-starter and the other on the clutch pedal.

As Patricia gained her place beside him he unleashed the full ninety-eight horse-power that the speedster could put forth when pressed.

His foot stayed flat down on the accelerator until they were running into Putney, and he was sure that any attempt to give chase had been left far astern, but even during the more sedate drive through London he was still unwontedly taciturn, and Patricia knew better than to try to make him talk when he was in such a mood. But she studied, as if she had never seen it before, the keen, vivid intentness of his profile as he steered the hurtling car through the night, and realised that she had never felt him so sheathed and at the same time shaken with such a dynamic savagery of purpose. Yet even she, who knew him better than anyone in the world, could not have explained what she sensed about him. She had seen, often before, the inspired wild leaps of his genius, but she could not know that this time that genius had rocketed into a more frantic flight than it had ever taken in all his life. And she was silent.

It was not until they were turning into Brook Street that she voiced a thought that had been racking her brain for the past hour.

"I can't help feeling I've seen one of those men before—or a picture of him . . ."

"Which one?" asked the Saint, a trifle grimly. "The young secretary bird—or Professor K. B. Vargan—or Sir Roland Hale—or Mr Lester Hume Smith, Her Majesty's Secretary of State for War?"

He marked her puzzlement, turning to meet her eyes. Now Patricia Holm was very lovely, and the Saint loved her. At that moment, for some reason, her loveliness took him by the throat.

He slipped an arm around her shoulders and drew her close to him.

"Saint," she said, "you're on the trail of more trouble. I know the signs."

"It's even more than that, dear," said the Saint softly. "Tonight I've seen a vision. And if it's a true vision it means that I'm going to fight something more horrible than I've ever fought before, and the name of it may very well be the same as the name of the devil himself."

2

HOW SIMON TEMPLAR READ
NEWSPAPERS, AND UNDERSTOOD
WHAT WAS NOT WRITTEN

Here may conveniently be quoted an item from one of the stop press columns of the following morning.

> The Clarion *is officially informed that at a late hour last night Mr Lester Hume Smith, the Secretary for War, and Sir Roland Hale, Director of Chemical Research to the War Office, attended a demonstration of Professor K. B. Vargan's "electron-cloud." The demonstration was held secretly, and no details will be disclosed. It is stated further that a special meeting of the Cabinet will be held this morning to receive Mr Hume Smith's report, and, if necessary, to consider the Government's attitude towards the invention.*

Simon Templar took the paragraph in his stride, for it was no more than a confirmation and amplification of what he already knew.

This was at ten o'clock—an extraordinary hour for the Saint to be up and dressed. But on this occasion he had risen early to break the habits of a lifetime and read every page of every newspaper that his man could buy.

He had suddenly become inordinately interested in politics; the news that an English tourist hailing from Manchester and rejoicing in the name of Pinheedle had been arrested for punching the nose of a policeman in Wiesbaden fascinated him; only such articles as "Why Grandmothers Leave Home" (by Ethelred Sapling, the brilliant author of *Lovers in Leeds*) continued to leave him entirely icebound.

But he had to wait for an early edition of *The Evening Record* for the account of his own exploit:

> . . . *From footprints found this morning in the soft soil, it appears that three persons were involved—one of them a woman. One of the men, who must have been of exceptional stature, appears to have tripped and fallen in his flight, and then to have made off in a different direction from that taken by his companions, who finally escaped by car.*
>
> *Mr Hume Smith's chauffeur, who attempted to arrest these two, and was knocked down by the man, recovered too late to reach the road in time to take the number of their car. From the sound of the exhaust, he judges it to have been some kind of high-powered sports model. He had not heard its approach or the entrance of the three intruders, and he admits that when he first saw the man and the woman he had just woken from a doze.*
>
> *The second man, who has been tracked across two fields at the back of Professor Vargan's house, is believed to have been picked up by his confederates farther along the road. The fact of his presence was not discovered until the arrival*

of the detectives from London this morning.

Chief Inspector Teal, who is in charge of the case, told an Evening Record representative that the police have as yet formed no theory as to what was the alarm which caused the hurried and clumsy departure of the spies. It is believed, however, that they were in a position to observe the conclusion of the experiment . . .

There was much more, stunted across the two middle columns of the front page.

This blew in with Roger Conway, of the Saint's very dear acquaintance, who had been rung up in the small hours of that morning to be summoned to a conference, and he put the sheet before Simon Templar at once.

"Were you loose in England last night?" he demanded accusingly.

"There are rumours," murmured the Saint, "to that effect."

Mr Conway sat down in his usual chair, and produced cigarettes and matches.

"Who was your pal—the cross-country expert?" he inquired calmly.

The Saint was looking out of the window.

"No one I know," he answered. "He kind of horned in on the party. You'll have the whole yarn in a moment. I phoned Norman directly after I phoned you; he came staggering under the castle walls a few seconds ago."

A peal on the bell announced that Norman Kent had reached the door of the apartment, and the Saint went out to admit him. Mr Kent carried a copy of *The Evening Record*, and his very first words showed how perfectly he understood the Saint's eccentricities.

"If I thought you'd been anywhere near Esher last night . . ."

"You've been sent for to hear a speech on the subject," said the Saint.

He waved Norman to a chair, and seated himself on the edge of a littered table which Patricia Holm was trying to reduce to some sort of order. She came up and stood beside him, and he slid an arm around her waist.

"It was like this," he said.

And he plunged into the story without preface, for the time when prefaces had been necessary now lay far behind those four. Nor did he need to explain the motives for any of his actions. In clipped, slangy, quiet, and yet vivid sentences he told what he had seen in the greenhouse of the house near Esher, and the two men listened without interruption.

Then he stopped, and there was a short silence.

"It's certainly a marvellous invention," said Roger Conway at length, smoothing his fair hair. "But what is it?"

"The devil."

Conway blinked.

"Explain yourself."

"It's what *The Clarion* called it," said the Saint; "something we haven't got simple words to describe. A scientist will pretend to understand it, but whether he will or not is another matter. The best he can tell us is that it's a trick of so modifying the structure of a gas that it can be made to carry a tremendous charge of electricity, like a thunder-cloud does—only it isn't a bit like a thunder-cloud. It's also something to do with a ray—only it isn't a ray. If you like, it's something entirely impossible—only it happens to exist. And the point is that this gas just provides the flimsiest sort of sponge in the atmosphere, and Vargan knows how to saturate the pores in the sponge with millions of volts and amperes of compressed lightning."

"And when the goat got into the cloud . . ."

"It was exactly the same as if it had butted into a web of live wires. For the fraction of a second that goat burnt like a scrap of coal in a blast furnace. And then it was ashes. Sweet idea, isn't it?"

Norman Kent, the dark and saturnine, took his eyes off the ceiling. He was a most unsmiling man, and he spoke little and always to the point.

"Lester Hume Smith has seen it," said Norman Kent. "And Sir Roland Hale. Who else?"

"Angel Face," said the Saint; "Angel Face saw it. The man our friend Mr Teal assumes to have been one of us—not having seen him wagging a Colt at me. An adorable pet, built on the lines of something between Primo Carnera and an overgrown gorilla, but not too agile with the trigger finger—otherwise I mightn't be here. But which country he's working for is yet to be discovered."

Roger Conway frowned.

"You think . . ."

"Frequently," said the Saint. "But that was one think I didn't need a cold towel round my head for. Vargan may have thought he got a raw deal when they missed him off the front page, but he got enough publicity to make any wide-awake foreign agent curious."

He tapped a cigarette gently on his thumb-nail and lighted it with slow and exaggerated deliberation. In such pregnant silences of irrelevant pantomime he always waited for the seeds he had sown to germinate spontaneously in the brains of his audience.

Conway spoke first.

"If there should be another war . . ."

"Who is waiting for a chance to make war?" asked Norman Kent.

The Saint picked up a selection of the papers he had been reading before they came, and passed them over. Page after page was scarred with blue pencillings. He had marked many strangely separated things—a statement by Kruschev, the speech of a French delegate before the United Nations, the story of a break in the Oil Trust involving the rearrangement of two hundred million pounds of capital, the announcement of a colossal merger of chemical interests, the latest movement of warships, the story of an outbreak of rioting in India, the story of an inspired bull raid on the steel market, and much else that he had found of amazing significance, even down to the arrest of an English tourist hailing from Manchester and rejoicing in the name of Pinheedle, for punching the nose of a policeman in Wiesbaden. Roger Conway and Norman Kent read, and were incredulous.

"But people would never stand for another war so soon," said Conway. "Every country is disarming . . ."

"Bluffing with everything they know, and hoping that one day somebody'll be taken in," said the Saint. "And every nation scared stiff of the rest, and ready to arm again at any notice. The people never make or want a war—it's sprung on them by the statesmen with the business interests behind them, and somebody writes a 'We-Don't-Want-to-Lose-You-but-We-Think-You-Ought-to-Go' song for the brass bands to play, and millions of poor fools go out and die like heroes without ever being quite sure what it's all about. It's happened before. Why shouldn't it happen again?"

"People," said Norman Kent, "may have learnt their lesson."

Simon swept an impatient gesture.

"Do people learn lessons like that so easily? The men who could teach them are a past generation now. How many are left who are young enough to convince our generation? And even if we are on the crest of a wave of literature about the horrors of war, do you think that cuts any ice? I tell you, I've listened till I'm tired to people of our own age discussing those books and plays—and I know they cut no ice at all. It'd be a miracle if they did. The mind of a healthy young man is too optimistic. It leaps to the faintest hint of glory, and finds it so easy to forget whole seas of ghastliness. And I'll tell you more . . ."

And he told them of what he had heard from Barney Malone.

"I've given you the facts," he said. "Now, suppose you saw a man rushing down the street with a contorted face, screaming his head off, foaming at the mouth, and brandishing a large knife dripping with blood. If you like to be a fool, you can tell yourself that it's conceivable that his face is contorted because he's trying to swallow a bad egg, he's screaming because someone has trodden on his pet corn, he's foaming at the mouth because he's just eaten a cake of soap, and he's just killed a chicken for dinner and is tearing off to tell his aunt all about it. On the other hand, it's simpler and safer to assume that he's a homicidal maniac. In the same way, if you like to be fools, and refuse to see a complete story in what spells a complete story to me, you can go home."

Roger Conway swung one leg over the arm of his chair and rubbed his chin reflectively.

"I suppose," he said, "our job is to find Tiny Tim and see that he doesn't pinch the invention while the Cabinet are still deciding what they're going to do about it?"

The Saint shook his head.

For once, Roger Conway, who had always been nearest to the Saint in all things, had failed to divine his leader's train of thought, and it was Norman Kent, that aloof and silent man, who voiced the inspiration of breath-taking genius—or madness—that had been born in Simon Templar's brain eight hours before.

"The Cabinet," said Norman Kent, from behind a screen of cigarette smoke, "might find the decision taken out of their hands . . . without the intervention of Tiny Tim . . ."

Simon Templar looked from face to face.

For a moment he had an odd feeling that it was like meeting the other three again for the first time, as strangers. Patricia Holm was gazing through the window at the blue sky above the roofs of Brook Street, and who is to say what vision she saw there? Roger Conway, the cheerful and breezy, waited in silence, the smoke of his neglected cigarette staining his fingers. Norman Kent waited also, serious and absorbed.

The Saint turned his eyes to the painting over the mantelpiece, and did not see it.

"If we do nothing but suppress Tiny Tim," he said, "England will possess a weapon of war immeasurably more powerful than all the armaments of any other nation. If we stole that away, you may argue that sooner or later some other nation will probably discover something just as deadly, and then England will be at a disadvantage."

He hesitated, and then continued in the same quiet tone.

"But there are hundreds of Tiny Tims, and we can't suppress them all. No secret like that has ever been kept for long, and when the war came we might very well find the enemy prepared to use our own weapon against us."

Once again he paused.

"I'm thinking of all the men who'll fight in that next war, and the women who love them. If you saw a man drowning, would you refuse to rescue him because, for all you know, you might only be saving him for a more terrible death years later?"

There was another silence, and in it the Saint seemed to straighten and strengthen and grow, imperceptibly and yet tremendously, as if something gathered about him which actually filled every corner of the room and made him bulk like a preposterously normal giant. And, when he resumed, his voice was as soft and even as ever, but it seemed to ring like a blast of trumpets.

"There are gathered here," he said, "three somewhat shop-soiled musketeers—and a blessed angel. Barring the blessed angel, we have all of us, in the course of our young lives, broken half the Commandments and most of the private laws of several countries. And yet, somehow, we've contrived to keep intact certain ridiculous ideals, which to our perverted minds are a justification for our sins. And fighting is one of those ideals. Battle and sudden death. In fact, we must be about the last three men in the wide world who ought to be interfering with the making of a perfectly good war. Personally, I suppose we should welcome it—for our own private amusement. But there aren't many like us. There are too many—far too many—who are utterly different. Men and boys who don't want war. Who don't live for battle, murder, and sudden death. Who wouldn't be happy warriors, going shouting and singing and swaggering into battle. Who'd just be herded into it like dumb cattle to the slaughter, drunk with a miserable and futile heroism, to struggle blindly through a few days of squalid agony and die in the dirt. Fine young lives that don't belong to our own barbarous god of battles . . . And we've tripped over the plans for the next sacrifice, partly by luck and partly by our own brilliance. And here we are. We don't give a damn for any odds or any laws. Will you think me quite mad if I put it to you that three shabby, hell-busting outlaws might, by the grace of God . . ."

He left the sentence unfinished, and for a few seconds no one spoke.

Then Roger Conway stirred intently.

"What do you say?" he asked.

The Saint looked at him.

"I say," he answered, "that this is our picnic. We've always known— haven't we?—at the back of our minds, dimly, that one day we were bound to get our big show. I say that this is the cue. It might have come in any one of a dozen different ways, but it just happens to have chosen this one. I'll summarise . . ."

He lighted a fresh cigarette and hitched himself farther on to the table, leaning forward with his forearms on his knees and the fine, rake-hell, fighting face that they all knew and loved made almost supernaturally beautiful with such a light of debonair dare-devilry as they had never seen before.

"You've read the story," he said. "I'll grant you it reads like a dime novelette, but there it is, staring you in the face, just the same. All at once, in both England and America, there's some funny business going on in the oil and steel and chemical trades. The amount of money locked up in those three combines must be nearly enough to swamp the capitals of any other bunch of industries you could name. We don't know exactly what's happening, but we do know that the big men, the secret moguls of Wall Street and the London Stock Exchange, the birds with the fat cigars and the names ending in -heim and -stein, who juggle the finances of this cockeyed world, are moving on some definite plan. And then look at the goods they're on the road with. Iron and oil and chemicals. If you know any other three interests that'd scoop a bigger pool out of a really first-class war, I'd like to hear of them . . . Add on Barney Malone's spy story. Haven't you realised how touchy nations are, and how easy it really would be to stir up distrust? And distrust, sooner or later, means war. The most benevolent and peaceful nation, if it's continually finding someone else's spies snooping round its preserves, is going to make a certain song and dance about it. Nobody before this has thought of doing that sort of thing on a large scale—trying to set two European Powers at each other's throats with a carefully wangled quarrel—and yet the whole idea is so gloriously simple. And now it's happened—or happening . . . And behind it all is the one man in the world with the necessary brain to conceive a plot like that, and the influence and qualifications to carry it through. You know who I mean. The man they call the Mystery Millionaire. The man who's supposed to have arranged half a dozen wars before, on a minor scale, in the interests of high finance. You've seen his name marked in red in those newspapers every time it crops up. It fits into the scheme in a darn sight too many ways—you can't laugh that off. Dr Rayt Marius . . ."

Norman Kent suddenly spun his cigarette into the fireplace.

"Then Golter might fit in . . ."

Conway said, "But the Crown Prince is Marius's own Crown Prince!"

"Would that mean anything to a man like Marius?" asked the Saint gently. "Wouldn't that just make things easier for him? Suppose . . ."

The Saint caught his breath, and then he took up his words again in a queerly soft and dreamy voice.

"Suppose Marius tempted the Crown Prince's vanity? The King is old, and there have been rumours that a young nation is calling for a young leader. And the Prince is ambitious. Suppose Marius were able to say, 'I can give you a weapon with which you can conquer the world. The only price I make is that you should use it . . .'"

They sat spellbound, bewildered, fascinated. They wanted to laugh that vision away, to crush and pulverise and annihilate it with great flailing sledge-hammers of rational incredulity. And they could find nothing to say at all.

The clock ticked leaden seconds away into eternity.

Patricia said breathlessly, "But he couldn't . . ."

"But he could!"

Simon Templar had leapt to his feet, his right arm flung out in a wild gesture.

"It's the key!" he cried. "It's the answer to the riddle! It mayn't be difficult to nurse up an international distrust by artificial means, but a tension like that can't be as fierce as a genuine international hatred. It'd want a much bigger final spark to make it blaze up. And the Crown Prince and his ambitions—and Vargan's invention—they'd make the spark! They're Marius's trump card. If he didn't bring them off his whole scheme might be shipwrecked. I know that's right!"

"That man in the garden," whispered Patricia. "If he was one of Marius's men . . ."

"It was Marius!"

The Saint snatched a paper from the table, and wrung and smashed it out so that she could see the photograph.

Bad as had been the light when they had found themselves face to face with the original, that face could never have been mistaken anywhere—that hideous, rough-hewn nightmare, expressionless like the carved stone face of a heathen idol.

"It was Marius . . ."

Roger Conway came out of his chair.

"If you're right, Saint—I'll believe that you didn't dream last night—"

"It's true!"

"And we haven't all suddenly got softening of the brain—to be listening to these howling, daft deductions of yours . . ."

"God knows I was never so sure of anything in my life."

"Then . . ."

The Saint nodded.

"We have claimed to execute some sort of justice," he said. "What is the just thing for us to do here?"

Conway did not answer, and the Saint turned to meet Norman Kent's thoughtful eyes, and then he knew that they were both waiting for him to speak their own judgment.

They had never seen the Saint so stern.

"The invention must cease to be," said Simon Templar.

"And the brain that conceived it, which could recreate it—that also must cease to be. It is expedient that one man should die for many people . . ."

3

HOW SIMON TEMPLAR RETURNED TO ESHER, AND DECIDED TO GO THERE AGAIN

This was on the 24th of June—about three weeks after the Saint's reply to the offer of a free pardon.

On the 25th, not a single morning paper gave more than an inconspicuous paragraph to the news which had filled the afternoon editions of the day before, and thereafter nothing more at all was said by the Press about the uninvited guests at Vargan's demonstration. Nor was there more than a passing reference to the special Cabinet meeting which followed.

The Saint, who now had only one thought day and night, saw in this unexpected reticence the hand of something dangerously like an official censorship, and Barney Malone, appealed to, was so uncommunicative as to confirm the Saint in his forebodings.

To the Saint it seemed as if a strange tension had crept into the atmosphere of the season in London. This feeling was purely subjective, he knew, and yet he was unable to laugh it away. On one day he had walked through the streets in careless enjoyment of an air fresh and mild with the promise of summer, among people quickened and happy and alert; on the next day the clear skies had become heavy with the fear of an awful thunder and a doomed generation went its way furtively and afraid.

"You ought to see Esher," he told Roger Conway. "A day away from your favourite bar would do you good."

They drove down in a hired car, and there the Saint found further omens.

They lunched at the Bear, and afterwards walked over the Portsmouth Road. There were two men standing at the end of the lane in which Professor Vargan lived, and the two men broke off their conversation abruptly as Conway and the Saint turned off the main road and strolled past them under the trees. Farther down, a third man hung over the garden gate sucking a pipe.

Simon Templar led the way past the house without glancing at it, and continued his discourse on the morrow's probable runners, but a sixth sense told him that the eyes of the man at the gate followed them down the lane, as the eyes of the two men at the corner had done.

"Observe," he murmured, "how careful they are not to make any fuss. The last thing they want to do is to attract attention. Just quietly on the premises, that's what they are. But if we did anything suspicious we should find ourselves being very quietly and carefully bounced towards the nearest clink. That's what we call Efficiency."

A couple of hundred yards farther on, on the blind side of a convenient corner, the Saint stopped.

"Walk on for as long as it takes you to compose a limerick suitable for the kind of drawing-room to which you would never be admitted," he ordered. "And then walk back. I'll be here."

Conway obediently passed on, carrying in the tail of his eye a glimpse of the Saint sidling through a gap in the hedge into the fields on the right. Mr Conway was no poet, but he accepted the Saint's suggestion, and toyed lazily with the lyrical possibilities of a young lady of Kent who whistled wherever she went. After wrestling for some minutes with the problem of bringing this masterpiece to a satisfactory conclusion, he gave it up and turned back, and the Saint returned through the hedge, a startlingly immaculate sight to be seen coming through a hedge, with a punctuality that suggested that his estimate of Mr Conway's poetical talent was dreadfully accurate.

"For the first five holes I couldn't put down a single putt," said the Saint sadly, and he continued to describe an entirely imaginary round of golf until they were back on the main road and the watchers at the end of the lane were out of sight.

Then he came back to the point.

"I wanted to do some scouting round at the back of the house to see how sound the defences were. There was a sixteen-stone seraph in his shirtsleeves pretending to garden, and another little bit of fluff sitting in a deck-chair under a tree reading a newspaper. Dear old Teal himself is probably sitting in the bathroom disguised as a clue. They aren't taking any more chances!"

"Meaning," said Conway, "that we shall either have to be very cunning or very violent."

"Something like that," said the Saint.

He was preoccupied and silent for the rest of the walk back to the Bear, turning over the proposition he had set himself to tackle.

He had cause to be—and yet the tackling of tough propositions was nothing new to him. The fact of the ton or so of official majesty which lay between him and his immediate objective was not what bothered him; the Saint, had he chosen to turn his professional attention to the job, might easily have been middleweight champion of the world, and he had a poor opinion both of the speed and fighting science of policemen. In any case, as far as that obstacle went, he had a vast confidence in his own craft and ingenuity for circumventing mere massive force. Nor did the fact that he was meddling with the destiny of nations give him pause: he had once, in his quixotic adventuring, run a highly successful one-man revolution in South America, and could have been a fully accredited Excellency in a comic-opera uniform if he had chosen. But this problem, the immensity of it, the colossal forces that were involved, the millions of tragedies that might follow one slip in his enterprise . . . Something in the thought tightened tiny muscles around the Saint's jaw.

Fate was busy with him in those days.

They were running into Kingston at the modest pace which was all the hired car permitted, when a yellow sedan purred effortlessly past them. Before it cut into the line of traffic ahead, Conway had had indelibly imprinted upon his memory the bestial, ape-like face that stared back at them through the rear window with the fixity of a carved image.

"Ain't he sweet?" murmured the Saint.

"A sheik," agreed Conway.

A smile twitched at Simon Templar's lips.

"Known to us," he said, "as Angel Face or Tiny Tim—at the option of the orator. The world knows him as Rayt Marius. He recognised me, and he's got the number of the car. He'll trace us through the garage we hired it from, and in twenty-four hours he'll have our names and addresses and YMCA records. I can't help thinking that life's going to be very crowded for us in the near future."

And the next day the Saint was walking back to Brook Street towards midnight, in the company of Roger Conway, when he stopped suddenly and gazed up into the sky with a reflective air, as if he had thought of something that had eluded his concentration for some time.

"Argue with me, Beautiful," he pleaded. "Argue violently, and wave your hands about, and look as fierce as your angelic dial will let you. But don't raise your voice."

They walked the few remaining yards to the door of the Saint's apartment with every appearance of angry dissension. Mr Conway, keeping his voice low as directed, expatiated on the failings of the Ford car with impassioned eloquence. The Saint answered, with aggressive gesticulations.

"A small disease in a pot hat has been following me half the day. He's a dozen yards behind us now. I want to get hold of him, but if we chase him he'll run away. He's certain to be coming up now to try and overhear the quarrel and find out what it's about. If we start a fight we should draw him within range. Then you'll grab him while I get the front door open."

"The back axle . . ." snarled Mr Conway.

They were now opposite the Saint's house, and the Saint halted and turned abruptly, placed his hand in the middle of Conway's chest, and pushed.

Conway recovered his balance and let fly. The Saint took the blow on his shoulder, and reeled back convincingly. Then he came whaling in and hit Mr Conway on the jaw with great gentleness. Mr Conway retaliated by banging the air two inches from the Saint's nose.

In the uncertain light it looked a most furious battle, and the Saint was satisfied to see Pot Hat sneaking up along the area railings only a few paces away, an interested spectator.

"Right behind you," said the Saint softly. "Stagger back four steps when I slosh you."

He applied his fist caressingly to Conway's solar plexus, and broke away without waiting to see the result, but he knew that his lieutenant was well trained. Simon had just time to find his key and open the front

49

door. A second later he was closing the door again behind Conway and his burden.

"Neat work," drawled the Saint approvingly. "Up the stairs with the little darling, Roger."

As the Saint led the way into the sitting-room Conway put Pot Hat down and removed his hand from the little man's mouth.

"Hush!" said Conway in a shocked voice, and covered his ears.

The Saint was peering down through the curtains.

"I don't think anyone saw us," he said. "We're in luck. If we'd planned it we might have had to wait years before we found Brook Street bare of souls."

He came back from the window and stood over their prisoner, who was still shaking his fist under Conway's nose and burbling blasphemously.

"That'll be all from you, sweetheart," remarked the Saint frostily. "Run through his pockets, Roger."

"When I find a pleeceman," began Pot Hat quiveringly.

"Or when a policeman finds what's left of you," murmured Simon pleasantly. "Yes?"

But the search revealed nothing more interesting than three new five-pound notes—a fortune which such a seedy-looking little man would never have been suspected of possessing.

"So it will have to be the third degree," said the Saint mildly, and carefully closed both windows.

He came back with his hands in his pockets and a very Saintly look in his eyes.

"Do you talk, Rat Face?" he asked.

"Wotcher mean—talk? Yer big bullies—"

"Talk," repeated the Saint patiently. "Open your mouth, and emit sounds which you fondly believe to be English. You've been tailing me all day, and I don't like it."

"Wotcher mean?" demanded the little man again, indignantly. "Tailing yer?"

The Saint sighed, and took the lapels of the little man's coat in his two hands. For half a hectic minute he bounced and shook the little man like a terrier shaking a rat.

"Talk," said the Saint monotonously.

But Pot Hat opened his mouth for something that could only have been either a swear or a scream, and the Saint disapproved of both. He tapped the little man briskly in the stomach, and he never knew which of the two possibilities had been the little man's intention, for whichever it was died in a choking gurgle. Then the Saint took hold of him again.

It was certainly very like bullying, but Simon Templar was not feeling sentimental. He had to do it, and he did it with cold efficiency. It lasted five minutes.

"Talk," said the Saint again, at the end of the five minutes, and the blubbering sleuth said he would talk.

Simon took him by the scruff of his neck and dropped him into a chair like a sack of peanuts.

The story, however, was not very helpful.

"I dunno wot 'is name is. I met 'im six months ago in a pub off Oxford Street, an' 'e gave me a job to do. I've worked for 'im on an' off ever since—followin' people an' findin' out things about 'em. 'E allus paid well, an' there wasn't no risk—"

"Not till you met me," said the Saint. "How do you keep in touch with him if he hasn't told you his name?"

"When 'e wants me, 'e writes to me an' I meet 'im in a pub somewhere, an' 'e tells me wot I've got to do. Then I let 'im know wots 'appening by telephone. I got 'is number."

"Which is?"

"Westminster double-nine double-nine."

"Thanks," said the Saint. "Good-looking man, isn't he?"

"Not 'arf! Fair gives me the creeps, 'e does. Fust time I sore 'im—"

The Saint shouldered himself off the mantelpiece and reached for the cigarette-box.

"Go home while the going's good, Rat Face," he said. "You don't interest us any more. Door, Roger."

"'Ere," whined Pot Hat, "I got a wife an' four children—"

"That," said the Saint gently, "must be frightfully bad luck on them. Give them my love, won't you?"

"I bin assaulted. Supposin' I went to a pleeceman—"

The Saint fixed him with a clear blue stare.

"You can either walk down the stairs," he remarked dispassionately, "or you can be kicked down by the gentleman who carried you up. Take your choice. But if you want any compensation for the grilling you've had, you'd better apply to your handsome friend for it. Tell him we tortured you with hot irons and couldn't make you open your mouth. He might believe you—though I shouldn't bet on it. And if you feel like calling a policeman, you'll find one just up the road. I know him quite well, and I'm sure he'd be interested to hear what you've got to say. Good night."

"Callin' yerselves gentlemen!" sneered the sleuth viciously. "You—"

"Get out," said the Saint quietly.

He was lighting his cigarette, and he did not even look up, but the next thing he heard was the closing of the door.

From the window he watched the man slouching up the street. He was at the telephone when Conway returned from supervising the departure, and he smiled lazily at his favourite lieutenant's question.

"Yes, I'm just going to give Tiny Tim my love . . . Hullo—are you Westminster double-nine double-nine? . . . Splendid. How's life, Angel Face?"

"Who is that?" demanded the other end of the line.

"Simon Templar," said the Saint. "You may have heard of me. I believe we—er—ran into each other recently." He grinned at the stifled exclamation that came faintly over the wire. "Yes, I suppose it is a pleasant surprise. Quite overwhelming . . . The fact is, I've just had to give one of your amateur detectives a rough five minutes. He's walking home. The next friend of yours I find walking on my shadow will be removed in an ambulance. That's a tip from the stable. Pleasant dreams, old dear!"

He hung up the receiver without waiting for a reply.

Then he was speaking to Inquiry.

"Can you give me the name and address of Westminster double-nine double-nine? . . . What's that? . . . Well, is there no way of finding out? . . . Yes, I know that, but there are reasons why I can't ring up and ask. Fact is, my wife eloped yesterday with the plumber, and she said if I really wanted her back I could ring her up at that number, but one of the bath-taps is dripping, and . . . Oh, all right. Thanks very much. Love to the supervisors."

He put down the instrument and turned to shrug at Conway's interrogatively raised eyebrows.

"'I'm sorry—we are not permitted to give subscribers' names and addresses,'" he mimicked. "I knew it, but it was worth trying. Not that it matters much."

"You might," suggested Conway, "have tried the directory."

"Of course. Knowing that Marius doesn't live in England, and that therefore Westminster double-nine double-nine is unlikely to be in his name . . . Oh, of course."

Conway grimaced.

"Right. Then we sit down and try to think out what Tiny Tim'll do next."

"Nope," contradicted the Saint cheerfully. "We know that one. It'll either be prussic acid in the milk tomorrow morning, or a snap shot from a passing car next time I walk out of the front door. We can put our shirts on that, and sit tight and wait for the dividends. But suppose we didn't wait . . ."

The emphatic briskness of his first words had trailed away while he was speaking into the gentle dreamy intonation that Conway knew of old. It was the sign that the Saint's thoughts had raced miles ahead of his tongue, and he was only mechanically completing a speech that had long since become unimportant.

Then for a little while he was silent, with his cigarette slanting between his lips, and a kind of crouching immobility about his lean body, and a dancing blue light of recklessness kindling in his eyes. For a moment he was as still and taut as a leopard gathering itself for a spring. Then he relaxed, straightening, and smiled, and his right arm went out in one of those magnificently romantic gestures that only the Saint could make with such a superb lack of affectation.

"But why should we wait?" he challenged.

"Why, indeed?" echoed Conway vaguely. "But—"

Simon Templar was not listening. He was already back at the telephone, calling up Norman Kent.

"Get out your car, fill her up with gas, and come right round to Brook Street. And pack a gun. This is going to be a wild night!"

A few minutes later he was through to his bungalow at Maidenhead—to which, by the grace of all the Saint's gods, he had sent his man down only that very day to prepare the place for a summer tenancy that was never to materialise as Simon Templar had planned it.

"That you, Orace? . . . Good. I just phoned up to let you know that Mr Kent will be arriving in the small hours with a visitor. I want you to get the cellar ready for him—for the visitor, I mean. Got me?"

"Yessir," said Orace unemotionally, and the Saint rang off.

There was only one Orace—late sergeant of Marines, and Simon Templar's most devoted servant. If Simon had said that the visitor would be a kidnapped President of the United States, Orace would still have answered no more than the gruff, unemotional "Yessir!"—and carried on according to his orders.

Said Roger Conway, climbing out of his chair and squashing his cigarette end into an ash-tray, "The idea being—"

"If we leave it any longer one of two things will happen. Either (a) Vargan will give his secret away to the Government experts, or (b) Marius will pinch it—or Vargan—or both. And then we'd be dished for ever. We've only got a chance for so long as Vargan is the one man in the wide world who carries that invention of the devil under his hat. And every hour we wait gives Tiny Tim a chance to get in before us!"

Conway frowned at a photograph of Patricia Holm on the mantelpiece. Then he nodded at it.

"Where is she?"

"Spending a couple of days in Devonshire with the Mannerings. The coast's dead clear. I'm glad to have her out of it. She's due back tomorrow evening, which is just right for us. We take Vargan to Maidenhead tonight, sleep off our honest weariness tomorrow, and toddle back in time to meet her. Then we all go down to the bungalow— and we're sitting pretty. How's that?"

Conway nodded again slowly. He was still frowning, as if there was something troubling the back of his mind.

Presently it came out.

"I never was the bright boy of the class," he said, "but I'd like one thing plain. We agree that Vargan, on behalf of certain financial interests, is out to start a war. If he brings it off we shall be in the thick of it. We always are. The poor blessed Britisher gets roped into everybody else's squabbles . . . Well, we certainly don't want Vargan's bit of frightfulness used against us, but mightn't it save a lot of trouble if we could use it ourselves?"

The Saint shook his head.

"If Marius doesn't get Vargan," he said, "I don't think the war will come off. At least, we'll have said check to it—and a whole heap may happen before he can get the show started again. And as for using it ourselves . . . No, Roger, I don't think so. We've argued that already. It wouldn't be kept to ourselves. And even if it could be—do you know, Roger?—I still think the world would be a little better and cleaner without it. There are foul things enough in the armoury without that. And I say that it shall not be . . ."

Conway looked at him steadily for some seconds.

Then he said, "So Vargan will take a trip to Maidenhead. You won't kill him tonight?"

"Not unless it's forced on me," said the Saint quietly. "I've thought it out. I don't know how much hope there is of appealing to his humanity, but as long as that hope exists, he's got a right to live. What the hope is, is what we've got to find out. But if I find that he won't listen—"

"Quite."

The Saint gave the same explanation to the third musketeer when Norman Kent arrived ten minutes later, and Norman's reply was only a little less terse than Roger Conway's had been.

"We may have to do it," he said.

His dark face was even graver than usual, and he spoke very quietly, for although Norman Kent had once sent a bad man to his death, he was the only one of the three who had never seen a man die.

4

HOW SIMON TEMPLAR LOST AN AUTOMOBILE, AND WON AN ARGUMENT

"The ancient art of generalship," said the Saint, "is to put yourself in the enemy's place. Now, how should I guard Vargan if I were as fat as Chief Inspector Teal?"

They stood in a little group on the Portsmouth Road about a mile from Esher, where they had stopped the cars in which they had driven down from London. They had been separated for the journey, because the Saint had insisted on taking his own Furillac as well as Norman Kent's Hirondel, in case of accidents. And he had refused to admit that there was time to make plans before they started. That, he had said, he would attend to on the way, and thereby save half an hour.

"There were five men when we came down yesterday," said Conway. "If Teal hasn't got many more than that on the night-shift, I should say they'd be arranged much as we saw them—outposts in the lane, the front garden, and the back garden, and a garrison in the greenhouse and the house itself. Numbers uncertain, but probably only couples."

The Saint's inevitable cigarette glowed like a fallen star in the darkness.

"That's the way I figured it out myself. I've roughed out a plan of attack on that basis."

He outlined it briefly. That was not difficult, for it was hardly a plan at all—it was little more than an idea for desperate and rapid action, a gamble on the element of surprise. The Saint had a pleasant habit of tackling some things in that mood, and getting away with it. And yet, on this occasion, as it happened, even that much planning was destined to be unnecessary.

A few minutes later they were on their way again.

The Saint led, with Conway beside him, in the Furillac. The Hirondel, with Norman Kent, followed about fifty yards behind. Norman, much to his disgust, was not considered as an active performer in the early stages of the enterprise. He was to stop his car a little way from the end of the lane, turn round, and wait with the engine ticking over until either Conway or the Saint arrived with Vargan. The simplicity of this arrangement was its great charm, but they were not able to make Norman see their point—which, they said, was the fault of his low and brawlsome mind.

And yet, if this reduction of their mobile forces had not been an incidental part of the Saint's sketchy plan of campaign, the outcome of the adventure might have been very different.

As Simon pulled up at the very mouth of the lane, he flung a lightning glance over his shoulder, and saw the Hirondel already swerving across the road for the turn.

Then he heard the shot.

"For the love of Pete!"

The invocation dropped from the Saint's lips in a breathless undertone. He was getting out of the car at that moment, and he completed the operation of placing his second foot on the road with a terrifically careful intentness. As he straightened up with the same frozen deliberation, he found Conway at his elbow.

"You heard it?"

Conway's curt, half-incredulous query.

"And how . . ."

"Angel Face—"

"Himself!"

Simon Templar was standing like a rock. He seemed, to Conway's impatience, to have been standing like that for an eternity, as though his mind had suddenly left him. And yet it had only been a matter of a few seconds, and in that time the Saint's brain had been whirling and wheeling with a wild precision into the necessary readjustments.

So Angel Face had beaten them to the jump—it could have been by no more than a fraction. And, as they had asked for trouble, they were well and truly in the thick of it. They had come prepared for the law; now they had to deal with both law and lawlessness, and both parties united in at least one common cause—to keep K. B. Vargan to themselves. Even if both parties were at war on every other issue . . .

"So we win this hands down," said the Saint softly, amazingly. "We're in luck!"

"If you call this luck!"

"But I do! Could we have arrived at a better time? When both gangs have rattled each other—and probably damaged each other—and Tiny Tim's boy friends have done the dirty work for us—"

He was cut short by another shot . . . then another . . . then a muddled splutter of three or four . . .

"Our cue!" snapped the Saint, and Roger Conway was at his side as he leapt down the lane.

There was no sign of the sentries, but a man came rushing towards them out of the gloom, heavy footed and panting. The Saint pushed Conway aside and flung out a well-timed foot. As the man sprawled headlong, Simon pounced on him and banged his head with stunning force against the road. Then he yanked the dazed man to his feet and looked closely at him.

"If he's not a policeman, I'm a Patagonian Indian," said the Saint. "A slight error, Roger."

The man answered with a wildly swinging fist, and the Saint hit him regretfully on the point of the jaw and saw him go down in a limp heap.

"What next?" asked Conway, and a second fusillade clattered out of the night to answer him.

"This is a very rowdy party," said the Saint mournfully. "Let's make it worse, shall we?"

He jerked an automatic from his pocket and fired a couple of shots into the air. The response was far more prompt than he had expected— two little tongues of flame that spat at them out of the farther blackness, and two bullets that sang past their heads.

"Somebody loves us," remarked Simon calmly. "This way—"

He started to lead down the lane.

And then, out of the darkness, the headlights of a car came to life dazzlingly, like two monstrous eyes. For a second Conway and the Saint stood struck to stillness in the glare that had carved a great trough of luminance out of the obscurity as if by the scoop of some gigantic dredge. So sudden and blinding was that unexpected light that an instant of time was almost fatally lost before either of them could see that it was not standing still but moving towards them and picking up speed like an express train.

"Glory!" spoke the Saint, and his voice overlapped the venomous rat-rat-tat of another unseen automatic.

In the same instant he was whirling and stooping with the pace of a striking snake. He collared Conway at the knees and literally hurled him bodily over the low hedge at the side of the lane with an accuracy and expedition that the toughest and most seasoned footballer could hardly have bettered.

The startled Conway, getting shakily to his feet, found the Saint landing from a leap beside him, and was in time to see the dark shape of a closed car flash past in the wake of that eye-searing blaze of headlights—so close that its wings and running-board tore a flurry of crackling twigs from the hedge. And he realised that, but for the Saint's speed of action, they would have stood no chance at all in that narrow space.

He might have said something about it. By ordinary procedure he should have given thanks to his saviour in a breaking voice; they should have wrung each other's hands and wept gently on each other's shoulders for a while, but something told Conway that it was no time for such trimmings. Besides, the Saint had taken the incident in his stride: by that time it had probably slithered through his memory into the dim limbo of distant reminiscence, and he would probably have been quite astonished to be reminded of it at that juncture. By some peaceful and lazy fireside, in his doddering old age, possibly . . . But in the immediate present he was concerned only with the immediate future.

He was looking back towards the house. There were lights showing still in some of the windows—it might altogether have been a most serene and tranquil scene, but for the jarring background of intermittent firing, which might have been nothing worse than a childish celebration of Guy Fawkes' day if it had been Guy Fawkes' day. But the Saint wasn't concerned with those reflections either. He was searching the shadows by the gate, and presently he made out a deeper and more solid-looking shadow among the other shadows, a bulky shadow . . .

Crack!

A tiny jet of flame licked out of the bulky shadow, and they heard the tinkle of shattered glass, but the escaping car was now only a few yards from the main road.

Conway was shaking Simon by the shoulder, babbling, "They're getting away! Saint, why don't you shoot?"

Mechanically the Saint raised his automatic, though he knew that the chance of putting in an effective shot, in that light, was about a hundred to one against anybody—and the Saint, as a pistol shot, had never been in the championship class.

Then he lowered the gun again, with something like a gasp, and his left hand closed on Conway's arm in a vice-like grip.

"They'll never do it!" he cried. "I left the car slap opposite the lane, and they haven't got room to turn!"

And Roger Conway, watching fascinated, saw the lean blue shape of the Furillac revealed in the blaze of the flying head-lights, and heard, before the crash, the scream of tortured tyres tearing ineffectually at the road.

Then the lights vanished in a splintering smash, and there was darkness and a moment's silence.

"We've got 'em!" rapped the Saint exultantly.

The bulky shadow had left the gate and was lumbering towards them up the lane. The Saint was over the hedge like a cat, landing lightly on his toes directly in Teal's path, and the detective saw him too late.

"Sorry!" murmured the Saint and really meant it, but he crowded every ounce of his one hundred and sixty pounds of dynamic fighting weight into the blow he jerked at the pit of Teal's stomach.

Ordinarily, the Saint entertained a sincere regard for the police force in general and Chief Inspector Teal in particular, but he had no time that night for more than the most laconic courtesies. Moreover, Inspector Teal had a gun, and, in the circumstances, would be liable to shoot first and ask questions afterwards. Finally, the Saint had his own ideas and plans on the subject of the rescue of Vargan from the raiding party, and they did not include either the co-operation or interference of the law. These three cogent arguments he summed up in that one pile-driving jolt to Teal's third waistcoat button, and the detective dropped with a grunt of agony.

Then the Saint turned and went flying up the lane after Roger Conway.

He heard a shout behind him, and again a gun barked savagely in the night. The Saint felt the wind of the bullet actually stroke his cheek. Clearly, then, there was at least one more police survivor of Marius's raid, but Simon judged that further disputes with the law could be momentarily postponed. He swerved like a hare and raced on, knowing that only the luckiest—or unluckiest—of blind shots could have come so near him in such a light, and having no fear that a second would have the same fortune.

As it happened, the detective who had come out of the garden behind Teal must have realised the same thing, for he held his fire. But as the Saint stopped by the yellow sedan, now locked inextricably with the wreckage of the battered Furillac, he heard the man pounding on through the darkness towards him.

Conway was opening the near-side door, and it was a miracle that his career was not cut short then and there by the shot from the interior of the car that went snarling past his ear. But there was no report—just the throaty plop! of an efficient silencer—and he understood that the only shooting they had heard had been done by the police guards. The raiders had not been so rowdy as the Saint had accused them of being.

The next moment Simon Templar had opened a door on the other side of the sedan.

"Naughty boy!" said Simon Templar reproachfully.

His long arm shot over the gun artist's shoulder, and his sinewy hand closed and twisted on the automatic in time to send the next shot through the roof of the car instead of through Conway's brain.

Then the Saint had the gun screwed round till it rammed into the man's own ribs.

"Now shoot, honeybunch," encouraged the Saint, but the man sat quite still.

He was in the back of the car, beside Vargan. There was no one in the driver's seat, and the door on that side was open. The Saint wondered who the chauffeur had been, and where he had got to, and whether it had been Angel Face himself, but he had little time to give to that speculation, and any possibility of danger from the missing driver's quarter would have to be faced if and when it materialised.

Conway yanked Vargan out into the road on one side, and the Saint, taking a grip on the gun artist's neck with his free hand, yanked him out into the road on the other side. One wrench disarmed the man, and then the Saint spun him smartly round by the neck.

"Sleep, my pretty one," said the Saint, and uppercut him with a masterly blend of science and brute strength.

He turned, to look down the muzzle of an automatic, and put up his hands at once. He had slipped his own gun into his pocket in order to deal more comfortably with the man from the car, and he knew it would be dangerous to try to reach it.

"Lovely weather we've been having, haven't we?" drawled the Saint genially.

This, he decided, must be the guard who had fired at him down the lane; the build, though hefty, was nothing like Angel Face's gigantic proportions. Besides, Angel Face, or any of his men, would have touched off the trigger ten seconds ago.

The automatic nosed into the Saint's chest, and he felt his pocket deftly lightened of its gun. The man exhaled his satisfaction in a long breath.

"That's one of you, anyway," he remarked grimly.

"Pleased to meet you," said the Saint.

And there it was.

The Saint's voice was as unperturbed as if he had been conducting some trivial conversation in a smoke-room, instead of talking with his hands in the air and an unfriendly detective focusing a Smith-Wesson on his diaphragm. And the corner was undoubtedly tight. If the circumstances had been slightly different, the Saint might have dealt with this obstacle in the same way as he had dealt with Marius on their first encounter. Marius had had the drop on him just as effectively as this. But Marius had been expecting a walk-over, and had therefore been just the necessary fraction below concert pitch; whereas this man was obviously expecting trouble. In view of what he must have been through already that night, he would have been a born fool if he hadn't. And something told Simon that the man wasn't quite a born fool. Something in the businesslike steadiness of that automatic . . .

But the obstacle had to be surmounted, all the same.

"Get Vargan away, Roger," sang out the Saint cheerfully, coolly. "See you again some time . . ."

He took two paces sideways, keeping his hands well up.

"Stop that!" cracked the detective, and the Saint promptly stopped it, but now he was in a position to see round the back of the sedan.

The red tail-light of the Hirondel was moving—Norman Kent was backing the car up closer to save time.

Conway bent and heaved the professor up on to his shoulder like a bag of potatoes; then he looked back hesitantly at Simon.

"Get him away while you've got the chance, you fool!" called the Saint impatiently.

And even then he really believed that he was destined to sacrifice himself to cover the retreat. Not that he was going quietly. But . . .

He saw Conway turn and break into a trot, and sighed his relief.

Then, in a flash, he saw how a chance might be given, and tensed his muscles warily. And the chance was given to him.

It wasn't the detective's fault. He merely attempted the impossible. He was torn between the desire to retain his prisoner and the impulse to find out what was happening to the man it was his duty to guard. He knew that that man was being taken away, and he knew that he ought to be trying to do something to prevent it, and yet his respect for the desperation of his captive stuck him up as effectively as if it had been the captive who held the gun. And, of course, the detective ought to have shot the captive and gone on with the rest of the job, but he tried, in a kind of panic, to find a less bloodthirsty solution, and the solution he found wasn't a solution at all. He tried to divide his mind and apply it to two things at once, and that, he ought to have known, was a fatal thing to do with a man like the Saint. But at that moment he didn't know the Saint very well.

Simon Templar, in those two sideways steps that the detective had allowed him to take, had shifted into such a position that the detective's lines of vision, if he had been able to look two ways at once, at Conway with one eye and at the Saint with the other, would have formed an obtuse angle. Therefore, since the detective's optic orbits were not capable of this feat, he could not see what Conway was doing without taking his eyes off Simon Templar.

And the detective was foolish.

For an instant his gaze left the Saint. How he imagined he would get away with it will remain a mystery. Certainly Simon did not inquire the answer then, nor discover it afterwards. For in that instant's grace, ignoring the menace of the automatic, the Saint shot out a long, raking left that gathered strength from every muscle in his body from the toes to the wrist.

And the Saint was on his way to the Hirondel before the man reached the ground.

Conway had only just dumped his struggling burden into the back seat when the Saint sprang to the running-board and clapped Norman Kent on the shoulder.

"Right away, sonny boy!" cried the Saint, and the Hirondel was sliding away as he and Conway climbed into the back.

He collected Vargan's flailing legs in an octopus embrace, and held the writhing scientist while Conway pinioned his ankles with the rope they had brought for the purpose. The expert hands of the first set of kidnappers had already dealt with the rest of him—his wrists were lashed together with a length of stout cord, and a professional gag stifled the screams which otherwise he would undoubtedly have been loosing.

"What happened?" asked Norman Kent, over his shoulder, and the Saint leaned over the front seat and explained.

"In fact," he said, "we couldn't have done better if we'd thought it out. Angel Face certainly brought off that raid like no amateur. But can you beat it? No stealth or subtlety, as far as we know. Just banging in like a Chicago bandit, and hell to the consequences. That shows how much he means business."

"How many men on the job?"

"Don't know. We only met one, and that wasn't Angel Face. Angel Face himself may have been in the car with Vargan, but he'd certainly taken to the tall timber when Roger and I arrived. A man like that wouldn't tackle the job with one solitary car and a couple of pals. There must have been a spare bus, with load, somewhere—probably up the lane. There should be another way in, though I don't know where it is . . . You'd better switch on the lights—we're out of sight now."

He settled back and lighted a cigarette.

In its way, it had been a most satisfactory effort, even if its success had been largely accidental, but the Saint was frowning rather thoughtfully. He wasn't worrying about the loss of his car—that was a minor detail. But that night he had lost something far more important.

"This looks like my good-bye to England," he said, and Conway, whose brain moved a little less quickly, was surprised.

"Why—are you going abroad after this?"

The Saint laughed rather sadly.

"Shall I have any choice?" he answered. "We couldn't have got the Furillac away, and Teal will trace me through that. He doesn't know I'm the Saint, but I guess they could make the Official Secrets Act heavy enough on me without that. Not to mention that any damage Angel Face's gang may have done to the police will be blamed on us as well. There's nothing in the world to show that we weren't part of the original raid, except the evidence of the gang themselves—and I shouldn't bet on their telling . . . No, my Roger. We are indubitably swimming in a large pail of soup. By morning every policeman in London will be looking for me, and by tomorrow night my photograph will be hanging up in every police station in England. Isn't it going to be fun?—as the bishop said to the actress."

But the Saint wasn't thinking it as funny as it might have been.

"Is it safe to go to Maidenhead?" asked Conway.

"That's our consolation. The deeds of the bungalow are in the name of Mrs Patricia Windermere, who spends her spare time being Miss Patricia Holm. I've had that joke up my sleeve for the past year in case of accidents."

"And Brook Street?"

The Saint chuckled.

"Brook Street," he said, "is held in your name, my sweet and respectable Roger. I thought that'd be safer. I merely installed myself as your tenant. No—we're temporarily covered there, though I don't expect that to last long. A few days, perhaps . . . And the address registered with my car is one I invented for the purpose . . . But there's a snag . . . Finding it's a dud address, they'll get on to the agents I bought it from. And I sent it back to them for decarbonising only a month ago, and gave Brook Street as my address. That was careless! . . . What's today?"

"It's now Sunday morning."

Simon sat up.

"Saved again! They won't be able to find out much before Monday. That's all the time we want. I must get hold of Pat . . ."

He sank back again in the seat and fell silent, and remained very quiet for the rest of the journey, but there was little quietude in his mind. He was planning vaguely, scheming wildly, daydreaming, letting his imagination play as it would with this new state of affairs, hoping that something would emerge from the chaos, but all he found was a certain rueful resignation.

"At least, one could do worse for a last adventure," he said.

It was four o'clock when they drew up outside the bungalow, and found a tireless Orace opening the front door before the car had stopped. The Saint saw Vargan carried into the house, and found beer and sandwiches set out in the dining-room against their arrival.

"So far, so good," said Roger Conway, when the three of them reassembled over the refreshment.

"So far," agreed the Saint—so significantly that the other two both looked sharply at him.

"Do you mean more than that?" asked Norman Kent.

Simon smiled.

"I mean—what I mean. I've a feeling that something's hanging over us. It's not the police—as far as they're concerned I should say the odds are two to one on us. I don't know if it's Angel Face. I just don't know at all. It's a premonition, my cherubs."

"Forget it," advised Roger Conway sanely.

But the Saint looked out of the window at the bleak pallor that had bleached the eastern rim of the sky, and wondered.

5

HOW SIMON TEMPLAR WENT BACK TO BROOK STREET, AND WHAT HAPPENED THERE

Breakfast was served in the bungalow at an hour when all ordinary people, even on a Sunday, are finishing their midday meal. Conway and Kent sat down to it in their shirtsleeves and a stubby tousledness, but the Saint had been for a swim in the river, shaved with Orace's razor, and dressed himself with as much care as if he had been preparing to pose for a magazine cover, and the proverbial morning daisy would have looked positively haggard beside him.

"No man," complained Roger, after inspecting the apparition, "has a right to look like this at this hour of the morning."

The Saint helped himself to three fried eggs and bacon to match, and sat down in his place.

"If," he said, "you could open your bleary eyes enough to see the face of that clock, you'd see that it's after half past two in the afternoon."

"It's the principle of the thing," protested Conway feebly. "We didn't get to bed till nearly six. And three eggs . . ."

The Saint grinned.

"Appetite of the healthy open-air man. I was splashing merrily down the Thames while you two were snoring."

Norman opened a newspaper.

"Roger was snoring," he corrected. "His mouth stays open twenty-four hours a day. And now he's talking with his mouth full," he added offensively.

"I wasn't eating," objected Conway.

"You were," said the Saint crushingly. "I heard you."

He reached for the coffee-pot and filled a cup for himself with a flourish.

The premonition of danger that he had had earlier that morning was forgotten—so completely that it was as if a part of his memory had been blacked out. Indeed, he had rarely felt fitter and better primed to take on any amount of odds.

Outside, over the garden and the lawn running down to the river, the sun was shining, and through the open French windows of the morning-room came a breath of sweet, cool air fragrant with the scent of flowers.

The fevered violence of the night before had vanished as utterly as its darkness, and with the vanishing of darkness and violence vanished also all moods of dark foreboding. Those things belonged to the night; in the clear daylight they seemed unreal, fantastic, incredible. There had been a battle—that was all. There would be more battles. And it was very good that it should be so—that a man should have such a cause to fight for and such a heart and body with which to fight it . . . As he walked back from his bathe an hour ago, the Saint had seemed to hear again the sound of the trumpet . . .

At the end of the meal he pushed back his chair and lighted a cigarette, and Conway looked at him expectantly.

"When do we go?"

"We?"

"I'll come with you."

"O.K.," said the Saint "We'll leave when you're ready. We've got a lot to do. On Monday, Brook Street and all it contains will probably be in the hands of the police, but that can't be helped. I'd like to salvage my clothes, and one or two other trifles. The rest will have to go. Then there'll be bags to pack for you two, to last you out our stay here, and there'll be Pat's stuff as well. Finally, I must get some money. I think that's everything and it'll keep us busy."

"What train is Pat travelling on?" asked Norman.

"That might be worth knowing," conceded the Saint. "I'll get through on the phone and find out while Roger's dressing."

He got his connection in ten minutes, and then he was speaking to her.

"Hullo, Pat, old darling. How's life?"

She did not have to ask who was the owner of that lazy, laughing voice.

"Hullo, Simon, boy!"

"I rang up," said the Saint, "because it's two days since I told you that you're the loveliest and most adorable thing that ever happened, and I love you. And further to ours of even date, old girl, when are you coming home? . . . No, no particular engagement . . . Well, that doesn't matter. To tell you the truth, we don't want you back too late, but also, to tell you the truth, we don't want you back too early, either . . . I'll tell you when I see you. Telephones have been known to have ears . . . Well, if you insist, the fact is that Roger and I are entertaining a brace of Birds, and if you came back too early you might find out . . . Yes, they are very Game . . . That's easily settled—I'll look you out a train now if you like. Hold on."

He turned.

"Heave over the time-table, Norman—it's in that corner, under the back numbers of *La Vie Parisienne* . . ."

He caught the volume dexterously.

"What time can you get away from this fête effect? . . . Sevenish? . . . No, that'll do fine. Terry can drive you over to Exeter, and if you get there alive you'll have heaps of time to catch a very jolly looking train at—Damn! I'm looking at the week-day trains . . . And the Sunday trains are as slow as a Scotchman saying good-bye to a bawbee . . . Look here, the only one you'll have time to catch now is the 4:58. Gets in at 9:20. The only one after that doesn't get to London till nearly four o'clock tomorrow morning. I suppose you were thinking of staying over till tomorrow . . . I'm afraid you mustn't, really. That is important . . . Good enough, darling. Expect you at Brook Street about half past nine . . . So long, lass. God bless . . ."

He hung up the receiver with a smile as Roger Conway returned after a commendably quick toilet.

"And now, Roger, me bhoy, we make our dash!"

"All set, skipper."

"Then let's go."

And the Saint laughed softly, hands on hips. His dark hair was at its sleekest perfection, his blue eyes danced, his brown face was alight with an absurdly boyish enthusiasm. He slipped an arm through Conway's, and they went out together.

Roger approached the car with slower and slower steps. An idea seemed to have struck him.

"Are you going to drive?" he asked suspiciously.

"I am," said the Saint.

Conway climbed in with an unhappy sigh. He knew, from bitter past experience, that the Saint had original and hair-raising notions of his own about the handling of high-powered automobiles.

They reached Brook Street at half past four.

"Are you going to drive back as well?" asked Roger.

"I am," said the Saint.

Mr Conway covered his eyes.

"Put me on a nice slow train first, will you?" he said. "Oh, and make a will leaving everything to me. Then you can die with my blessing."

Simon laughed, and took him by the arm.

"Upstairs," he said, "there is beer. And then—work. Come on, sonny boy!"

For three hours they worked. Part of that time Conway gave to helping the Saint; then he went on to attend to his own packing and Norman Kent's. He returned towards eight o'clock, and dumped the luggage he brought with him directly out of his taxi into the Hirondel. The Saint's completed contribution—two steamer trunks on the carrier and a heavy valise inside—was already there. The Hirondel certainly had the air of assisting in a wholesale removal.

Conway found the Saint sinking a tankard of ale with phenomenal rapidity.

"Oi!" said Conway in alarm.

"Get yours down quickly," advised the Saint, indicating a second mug, which stood, full and ready, on the table. "We're off."

"Off?" repeated Roger puzzledly.

Simon jerked his empty can in the direction of the window.

"Outside," he said, "are a pair of prize beauties energetically doing nothing. I don't suppose you noticed them as you came in. I didn't myself, until a moment ago. I'll swear they've only just come on duty—I couldn't have missed them when I was loading up the car. But they've seen too much. Much too much."

Conway went to the window and looked out.

Presently:

"I don't see anyone suspicious."

"That's your innocent and guileless mind, my pet," said the Saint, coming over to join him. "If you were as old in sin as I am, you'd . . . Well, I'll be b-b-blowed!"

Conway regarded him gravely.

"It's the beer," he said. "Never mind. You'll feel better in a minute."

"Damned if I will!" crisped the Saint.

He slammed his tankard down on the window-sill and caught Roger by both shoulders.

"Don't be an old idiot, Roger!" he cried. "You know me. I tell you this place was being watched. Police or Angel Face. We can't say which, but almost certainly Angel Face. Teal couldn't possibly have got as far as this in the time, I'll bet anything you like. But Angel Face could. And the two sleuths have beetled off with the news about us. So, to save trouble, we'll beetle off ourselves. Because, if I know anything about Angel Face yet, Brook Street is going to be rather less healthy than a hot spot in hell—inside an hour!"

"But Pat . . ."

The Saint looked at his watch.

"We've got two hours to fill up somehow. The Hirondel'll do it easy. Down to Maidenhead, park the luggage, and back to Paddington Station in time to meet the train."

"And suppose we have a breakdown?"

"Breakdown hell! . . . But you're right . . . Correction, then:

"I'll drop you at the station, and make the return trip to Maidenhead alone. You can amuse yourself in the bar, and I'll meet you there . . . It's a good idea to get rid of the luggage, too. We don't know that the world won't have become rather sticky by half past nine and it'd be on the safe side to make the heavy journey while the going's good. If I leave now they won't have had time to make any preparations to follow me, and later we'd be able to slip them much more easily, if they happened to get after us, without all the impedimenta to pull our speed down."

Conway found himself being rushed down the stairs as he listened to the Saint's last speech. The speech seemed to begin in Brook Street and finish at Paddington. Much of this impression, of course, was solely the product of Conway's overwrought imagination: but there was a certain foundation of fact in it, and the impression built thereon was truly symptomatic of Simon Templar's appalling velocity of transforming decision into action.

Roger Conway recovered coherent consciousness in the station buffet and a kind of daze, and by that time Simon Templar was hustling the Hirondel westwards.

The Saint's brain was in a ferment of questions. Would Marius arrange a raid on the flat in Brook Street? Or would he, finding that the loaded car which his spies had reported had gone, assume that the birds had flown? Either way, that didn't seem to matter, but the point it raised was what Marius would do next, after he had either discovered or decided that his birds had flown . . . And, anyway, since Marius must have known that the Saint had attended the rough party at Esher, why hadn't Brook Street been raided before? . . . Answer: Because (a) a show like that must take a bit of organising, and (b) it would be easier, anyhow, to wait until dark. Which, at that time of year, was fairly late at night. Thereby making it possible to do the return journey to and from Maidenhead in good time . . . But Marius would certainly be doing something. Put yourself in the enemy's place . . .

So the Saint reached Maidenhead in under an hour, and was on the road again five minutes later.

It was not his fault that he was stopped half-way back by a choked carburettor jet which it took him fifteen minutes to locate and remedy.

Even so, the time he made on the rest of the trip amazed even himself.

In the station entrance he actually cannoned into Roger Conway.

"Hullo," said the Saint. "Where are you off to? The train's just about due in."

Conway stared at him.

Then he pointed dumbly at the clock in the booking-hall.

Simon looked at it and went white.

"But my watch," he began stupidly, "my watch . . ."

"You must have forgotten to wind it up last night."

"You met the train?"

Conway nodded.

"It's just possible that I may have missed her, but I'd swear she wasn't on it. Probably she didn't catch it . . ."

"Then there's a telegram at Brook Street to say so. We'll go there—if all the armies of Europe are in the way!"

They went. Conway, afterwards, preferred not to remember that drive.

And yet peace seemed to reign in Brook Street. The lamps were alight, and it was getting dark rapidly, for the sky had clouded over in the evening. As was to be expected on a Sunday, there were few people about and hardly any traffic. There was nothing at all like a crowd—no sign that there had been any disturbance at all. There was a man leaning negligently against a lamp-post, smoking a pipe as though he had nothing else to do in the world. It happened that, as the Hirondel stopped, another man came up and spoke to him. The Saint saw the incident, and ignored it.

He went through the front door and up the stairs like a whirlwind. Conway followed him.

Conway really believed that the Saint would have gone through a police garrison or a whole battalion of Angel Faces, but there were none there to go through. Nor had the flat been entered, as far as they could see. It was exactly as they left it.

But there was no telegram.

"I might have missed her," said Conway helplessly. "She may be on her way now. The taxi may have broken down—or had a slight accident . . ."

He stopped abruptly at the blaze in the Saint's eyes.

"Look at the clock," said the Saint, with a kind of curbed savagery.

Roger looked at the clock. The clock said that it was a quarter to ten.

And he saw the terrible look on the Saint's face, and it hypnotised him. The whole thing had come more suddenly than anything that had ever happened to Roger Conway before, and it had swirled him to the loss of his bearings in the same way that a man in a small boat in tropical seas may be lost in a squall. The blow had fallen too fiercely for him. He could feel the shock, and yet he was unable to determine what manner of blow had been struck, or even if a blow had been struck at all, in any comprehensible sense.

He could only look at the clock and say helplessly, "It's a quarter to ten."

The Saint was saying, "She'd have let me know if she'd missed the train . . ."

"Or waited for the next one."

"Oh, for the love of Mike!" snarled the Saint. "Didn't you hear me ring her up from Maidenhead? I looked out all the trains then, and the only next one gets in at three fifty-one tomorrow morning. D'you think she'd have waited for that one without sending me a wire?"

"But if I didn't see her at Paddington, and anything had happened to her taxi . . ."

But the Saint had taken a cigarette, and was lighting it with a hand that could never have been steadier, and the Saint's face was a frozen mask.

"More beer," said the Saint.

Roger moved to obey.

"And talk to me," said the Saint, "talk to me quietly and sanely, will you? Because fool suggestions won't help me. I don't have to ring up Terry and ask if Pat caught that train, because I know she did. I don't have to ask if you're quite sure you couldn't have missed her at the station, because I know you didn't . . ."

The Saint was deliberately breaking a matchstick into tiny fragments and dropping them one by one into the ash-tray.

"And don't tell me I'm getting excited about nothing," said the Saint, "because I tell you I know. I know that Pat was coming on a slow train, which stops at other places before it gets to London. I know that Marius has got Pat, and I know that he's going to try to use her to force me to give up Vargan, and I know that I'm going to find Dr Rayt Marius and kill him. So talk to me very quietly and sanely, Roger, because if you don't I think I shall go quite mad."

6

HOW ROGER CONWAY DROVE THE HIRONDEL, AND THE SAINT TOOK A KNIFE IN HIS HAND

Conway had a full tankard of beer in each hand. He looked at the tankards as a man might look at a couple of dragons that have strayed into his drawing-room. It seemed to Roger, for some reason, that it was unaccountably ridiculous for him to be standing in the middle of the Saint's room with a tankard of beer in each hand. He cleared his throat.

He said, "Are you sure you aren't—making too much of it?"

And he knew, as he said it, that it was the fatuously useless kind of remark for which he would cheerfully have ordered anyone else's execution. He put down the tankards on the table and lighted a cigarette as if he hated it.

"That's not quiet and sane," said the Saint. "That's wasting time. Damn it, old boy, you know how it was between Pat and me! I always knew that if anything happened to her I'd know it at once—if she were a thousand miles away. I know."

The Saint's icy control broke for a moment. Only for a moment. Roger's arm was taken in a crushing grip. The Saint didn't know his strength. Roger could have cried out with pain, but he said nothing at all. He was in the presence of something that he could only understand dimly.

"I've seen the whole thing," said the Saint, with a cold devil in his voice. "I saw it while you were gaping at that clock. You'll see it, too, when you've got your brain on to it. But I don't have to think."

"But how could Marius . . ."

"Easy! He'd already tracked us here. He'd been watching the place. The man's thorough. He'd naturally have put other agents on to the people he saw visiting me. And how could he have missed Pat? . . . One of his men probably followed her down to Devonshire. Then, after the Esher show, Marius got in touch with that man. She could easily be got at on the train. They could take her off, say, at Reading—doped . . . She wasn't on her guard. She didn't know there was any danger. That one man could have done it . . . With a car to meet him at Reading . . . And Marius is going to hold Pat in the scales against me—against everything we've set out to do. Binding me hand and foot. Putting my dear one in the forefront of the battle, and daring me to fire. And laying the powder trail for his foul slaughter under the shield of her blessed body. And laughing at us . . ."

Then Roger began to understand less dimly, and he stared at the Saint as he would have stared at a ghost.

He said, like a man waking from a dream, "If you're right, our show's finished."

"I am right," said the Saint. "Ask yourself the question."

He released Roger's arm as if he had only just become aware that he was holding it.

Then, in three strides, the Saint was at the window, and Conway had just started to realise his intention when the Saint justified, and at the same time smithereened, that realisation with one single word.

"Gone."

"You mean the . . ."

"Both of 'em. Of course, Marius kept up the watch on the house in case we were being tricky. The man who arrived at the same time as we did was the relief. Or a messenger to say that Marius had lifted the trump card, and the watch could pack up. Then they saw us arrive."

"But they can't have been gone a moment . . ."

The Saint was back by the table.

"Just that," snapped the Saint. "They've gone—but they can't have been gone a moment. The car's outside. Could you recognise either of them again?"

"I could recognise one."

"I could recognise the other. Foreign-looking birds, with ugly mugs. Easy again. Let's go!"

It was more than Roger could cope with. His brain hadn't settled down yet. He couldn't get away from a sane, reasonable, conventional conviction that the Saint was hurling up a solid mountain from the ghost of a molehill. He couldn't quite get away from it even while the clock on the mantelpiece was giving him the lie with every tick. But he got between the Saint and the door, somehow—but he wasn't sure how.

"Hadn't you better sit down and think it out before you do anything rash?"

"Hadn't you better go and hang yourself?" rapped the Saint impatiently.

Then his bitterness softened. His hands fell on Roger's shoulders.

"Don't you remember another time when we were in this room, you and I?" he said. "We were trying to get hold of Marius then—

for other reasons. We could only find out his telephone number. And that's all we know to this day—unless we can make one of those birds who were outside tell us more than the man who gave us the telephone number. They're likely to know more than that—we're big enough now to have the bigger men after us. They're the one chance of a clue we've got, and I'm taking it. This way!"

He swept Conway aside, and burst out of the flat. Conway followed. When the Saint stopped in Brook Street, and turned to look, Roger was beside him.

"You drive."

He was opening the door of the car as he cracked the order. As Roger touched the self-starter, the Saint climbed in beside him.

Roger said helplessly. "We've no idea which way they've gone."

"Get going! There aren't so many streets round here. Make this the centre of a circle. First into Regent Street, cut back through Conduit Street to New Bond Street—Oxford Street—back through Hanover Square. Burn it, son, haven't you any imagination?"

Now, in that district the inhabited streets are slashed across the map in a crazy tangle, and the two men might have taken almost any of them, according to the unknown destination for which they were making. The task of combing through that tangle, with so little qualification, struck Roger as being rather more hopeless than looking for one particular grain of sand in the shape of a taxi. But Conway could not suggest that to the Saint; he wouldn't have admitted it, anyway, and Roger wouldn't have had the heart to try to convince him.

And yet Roger was wrong, for the Saint sat beside him and drove with Roger's hands. And the Saint knew that people in cities tend to move in the best-beaten tracks, particularly in a strange city, for fear of losing their way—exactly as a man lost in the bush will follow a tortuous trail rather than strike across open country in the direction which he feels he should take. And the men looked foreign and probably were foreign, and the foreigner is afraid of losing himself in any but the long, straight, bright roads, though they may take him to his objective by the most roundabout route.

Unless, of course, the foreigners had taken a native guide in the shape of a taxi. But Conway could not suggest that to the Saint, either.

"Keep on down here," Simon Templar was saying. "Never mind what I told you before. Now I should cut away to the right—down Vigo Street."

Roger spun the wheel, and the Hirondel skidded and swooped across the very nose of an omnibus. For one fleeting second, in the bottleneck of Vigo Street, a taxi-driver appeared to meditate disputing their right of way; fortunately for all concerned, he abandoned that idea hurriedly.

Then Simon was speaking again.

"Right up Bond Street. That's the spirit."

Roger said, "You'll collect half a dozen summonses before you've finished with this . . ."

"Damn that," said the Saint, and they swept recklessly past a constable who had endeavoured to hold them up and drowned his outraged shout in the stutter of their departing exhaust.

By Roger Conway that day's driving was afterwards to be remembered in nightmares, and that last drive more than any other journey.

He obeyed the Saint blindly. It wasn't Roger's car, anyway. But he would never have believed that such feats of murderous road-hogging could have been performed in a London street—if he had not been made to perform them himself.

And yet it seemed to be to no purpose, for although he was scanning, in every second of that drive in which he was able to take his eyes off the road, the faces of the pedestrians as they passed, he did not see the face he sought. And suppose, after all, they did find the men they were after? What could be done about it in an open London street—except call for the police, whom they dared not appeal to?

But Roger Conway was alone in discouragement.

"We'll try some side streets now," said the Saint steadily. "Down there . . ."

And Roger, an automaton, lashed round the corner on two wheels.

And then, towards the bottom of George Street, Roger pointed, and the Saint saw two men walking side by side.

"Those two!"

"For Heaven's sake!" said the Saint softly, meaninglessly, desperately, and the car sprang forward like a spurred horse as Roger opened the throttle wide.

The Saint was looking about him and rising from his seat at the same moment. In Conduit Street there had been traffic, but in George Street, at that moment, there was nothing but a stray car parked empty by the kerb and three pedestrians going the other way, and—the two.

Said the Saint, "I think so . . ."

"I'm sure," said Roger, and, indeed, he was quite sure, because they had passed the two men by that time, and the Hirondel was swinging in to the kerb with a scream of brakes a dozen feet in front of them.

"Watch me!" said the Saint, and was out of the car before it had rocked to a standstill.

He walked straight into the path of the two men, and they glanced at him with curious but unsuspecting eyes.

He took the nearest man by the lapels of his coat with one hand, and the man was surprised. A moment later the man was not feeling surprise or any other emotion, for the Saint looked one way and saw Roger Conway following him, and then he looked the other way and hit the man under the jaw.

The man's head whipped back as if it had been struck by a cannon-ball, and in fact, there was very little difference between the speed and force of the Saint's fist and the speed and force of a cannon-ball.

But the man never reached the ground. As his knees gave limply under him, and his companion sprang forward with a shout awakening on his lips, the Saint caught him about the waist and lifted him from his feet, and heaved him bodily across the pavement, so that he actually fell into Conway's arms.

"Home, James," said the Saint, and turned again on his heel.

On the lips of the second man there was that awakening of a shout, and in his eyes was the awakening of something that might have been taken for fear, or suspicion, or a kind of vague and startled perplexity, but these expressions were nebulous and half-formed, and they never came to maturity, for the Saint spun the man round by one shoulder and locked an arm about his neck in such a way that it was impossible for him to shout or register any other expression than that of a man about to suffocate.

And in the same hold the Saint lifted him off the ground, mostly by the neck, so that the man might well have thought that his neck was about to be broken, but the only thing that was broken was the spring of one of the cushions at the back of the car, when the Saint heaved him on to it.

The Saint followed him into the back seat, and, when the man seemed ready to try another shout, Simon seized his wrists in a grip that might have changed the shout to a scream if the Saint had not uttered a warning.

"Don't scream, sweetheart," said the Saint coldly. "I might break both your arms."

The man did not scream. Nor did he shout. And on the floor of the car, at the Saint's feet, his companion lay like one dead.

In the cold light of sanity that came long afterwards, Simon Templar was to wonder how on earth they got away with it.

Roger Conway, who was even then far too coldly sane for his own comfort, was wondering all the time how on earth they were getting away with it. But for the moment Simon Templar was mad—and the fact remained that they had got away with it.

The Saint's resourceful speed, and the entirely fortuitous desertedness of the street, had made it possible to carry out the abduction without a sound being made that might have attracted attention. And the few people there were whose attention might have been attracted had passed on, undisturbed, unconscious of the swift seconds of hectic melodrama that had whirled through George Street, Hanover Square, behind their peaceful backs.

That the Saint would have acted in exactly the same way if the street had been crowded with an equal mixture of panicky population, plain-clothes men, and uniformed police men, was nothing whatever to do with anything at all. Once again the Saint had proved, to his own sufficient satisfaction, as he had proved many times in his life before, that desperate dilemmas are usually best solved by desperate measures and that intelligent foolhardiness will often get by where too much discretion betrays valour into the mulligatawny. And the thought of the notice that must have been taken of the Hirondel during the first part of that wild chase (it was not an inconspicuous car at the best of times, even when sedately driven, that long, lean, silver-grey King of the Road) detracted nothing from the Saint's estimate of his success. One could not have one's cake and eat it. And certainly he had obtained the cake to eat. Two cakes. Ugly ones . . .

Even then there might have been trouble in Brook Street when they returned with the cargo, but the Saint did not allow any trouble.

There were two men to be taken across the strip of pavement to the door of the flat. One man was long and lean, the other man short and fat, and the lean man slept. The Saint kept his grip on one wrist of the fat man, and half supported the lean man with his other arm. Roger placed himself on the other side of the lean man.

"Sing," commanded the Saint, and they crossed the pavement discordantly and drunkenly.

A man in evening dress passed them with a supercilious nose. A man in rags passed them with an envious nose. A patrolling policeman peered at them with an officious nose, but the Saint had opened the door, and they were reeling cacophonously into the house. So the officious nose went stolidly upon its way, after taking the number of the car from which they had disembarked, for the law has as yet no power to prevent men being as drunk and disorderly as they choose in their own homes. And, certainly, the performance, extempore as it was, had been most convincing. The lean man had clearly failed to last the course; the two tall and well-dressed young men who supported him between them were giving most circumstantial evidence of the thoroughness with which they had lubricated their withins, and if the sounds emitted by the fat man were too wild and shrill to be easily classified as song, and if he seemed somewhat unwilling to proceed with his companions into further dissipations, and if there was a strange, strained look in his eye—well, the state which he had apparently reached was regrettable, but nobody's business . . .

And before the suspicious nose had reached the next corner, the men who had passed beneath it were in the first-floor apartment above it, and the lean one was being carelessly dropped spread-eagle on the sitting-room carpet.

"Fasten the door, Roger," said the Saint shortly.

Then he released his agonising hold on the fat man's wrist, and the fat man stopped yelping and began to talk.

"Son of a pig," began the fat man, rubbing his wrist tenderly, and then he stopped, appalled at what he saw.

There was a little knife in the Saint's hand—a toy with a six-inch leaf-shaped blade and a delicately chased ivory hilt. It appeared to have come from nowhere, but actually it had come from the neat leather sheath strapped to the Saint's forearm under the sleeve, where it always lived, and the name of the knife was Anna. There was a story to Anna, a savage and flamboyant story of the godless lands, which may be told one day: she had taken many lives. To the Saint she was almost human, that beautifully fashioned, beautifully balanced little creature of death; he could do tricks with her that would have made most circus knife-throwers look like amateurs. But at that moment he was not thinking of tricks.

As Roger switched on the light, the light glinted on the blade, but the light in the Saint's eyes was no less cold and inclement than the light on the steel.

7

HOW SIMON TEMPLAR WAS SAINTLY, AND RECEIVED ANOTHER VISITOR

Simon Templar, in all his years of wandering and adventure, had only fallen for one woman, and that was Patricia Holm. Therefore, as might have been expected, he fell heavily. And yet—he was realising it dimly, as one might realise an unthinkable heresy—in the eighteen months that they had been together he had started to get used to her. He had, he realised, been growing out of the first ecstatic wonder, and the thing that had taken its place had been so quiet and insidious that it had enchanted him while he was still unaware of it. It had had to await this shock to be revealed.

And the revelation, when it came, carried with it a wonder that infinitely eclipsed the more blatant brilliance of the wonder that had slipped away. This was the kind of wild and awful wonder that might overtake a man who, having walked in the sunshine all the days of his life, sees the sun itself for the first time, with a dreadful and tremendous understanding, and sees at once a vision of the darkness that would lie over the world if the sun ceased from shining.

The Saint said, very softly, to the fat man, "Son of a pig to you, sweetheart. And now listen. I'm going to ask you some questions. You can either answer them, or die slowly and painfully, just as you like— but you'll do one or the other before you leave this room."

The fat man was in a different class from that of the wretched little weed in the pot hat from whom Simon Templar had extracted information before. There was a certain brute resolution in the fat man's beady eyes, a certain snarling defiance in the twist of the thin lips, like the desperate determination of a beast at bay. Simon took no count of that.

"Do you understand, you septic excrescence?" said the Saint gently.

And there was hatred in the Saint's heart, a hatred that was his very own, that no one else could have understood, but there was another kind of devilry in the Saint's eyes and in the purring gentleness of his voice, a kind of devilry that no one could have helped understanding, that the man in front of him understood with terror, an outward and visible and malignant hatred, and it was plainly centred upon the fat man, and the fat man recoiled slowly, step by step, as the Saint advanced, until he came up against the table and could not move backwards any farther.

"I hope you don't think I'm bluffing, dear little fat one," the Saint went on, in the same velvety voice. "Because that would be foolish of you. You've done, or had a hand in doing, something which I object to very much, I object to it in a general way, and always have, but this time I object to it even more, in a personal way, because this time it involves someone who means more to me than your gross mind will ever understand. Do you follow the argument, you miserable wart?"

The man was trying to edge away backwards round the table, but he could not break away, for the Saint moved sideways simultaneously.

And he could not break away from the Saint's eyes—those clear blue eyes that were ordinarily so full of laughter and bubbling mischief that were then so bleak and pitiless.

And the Saint went on speaking.

"I'm not concerned with the fact that you're merely the agent of Dr Rayt Marius—ah, that makes you jump! I know a little more than you thought I did, don't I? . . . But we're not concerned with that either . . . If you insist on mixing with people like that, you must be prepared to take the consequences. And if you think the game's worth the candle, you must also be prepared for an accident with the candle. That's fair, isn't it? . . . So that the point we're going to disagree about is that you've had a share in annoying me—and I object very much to being annoyed . . . No you don't, sonny boy!"

There was a gun in the fat man's hand, and then there was not a gun in the fat man's hand, for the Saint moved forward and to one side with a swift, stealthy, cat-like movement, and this time the fat man could not help screaming as he dropped the gun.

"Ach! You would my wrist break . . ."

"Cheerfully, beloved," said Simon. "And your neck later on. But first . . ."

Tightening instead of slackening that grip on the fat man's wrist, the Saint bent him backwards over the table, holding him easily with fingers of incredible strength, and the man saw the blade of the knife flash before his eyes.

"Once upon a time, when I was in Papua," said the Saint, in that dispassionately conversational way which was indescribably more terrifying than any loud-voiced anger, "a man came out of the jungle into the town where I was. He was a prospector, and a pig-headed prospector, and he had insisted on prospecting a piece of country that all the old hands had warned him against. And the natives had caught him at the time of the full moon. They're always very pleased to catch white men at that time, because they can be used in the scheme of festivities and entertainment. They have primitive forms of amusement—very. And one of their ways of amusing themselves with this man had been to cut off his eyelids. Before I start doing the same thing to you, will you consider for a moment the effect that that operation will probably have on your beauty sleep?"

"God!" babbled the man shrilly. "You cannot . . ."

The man tried to struggle, but he was held with a hand of iron. For a little while he could move his head, but then the Saint swung on to the table on top of him and clamped the head between his knees.

"Don't talk so loud," said the Saint, and his fingers left the wrist and sidled round the throat. "There are other people in this building, and I should hate you to alarm them. With regard to this other matter, now—did I hear you say I couldn't do it? I beg to differ. I could do it very well. I shall be very gentle, and you should not feel very much pain—just at the moment. It's the after-effects that will be so unpleasant. So think. If you talk, and generally behave like a good boy, I might be persuaded to let you off. I won't promise you anything, but it's possible."

"I will not . . ."

"Really not? . . . Are you going to be difficult, little one? Are you going to sacrifice your beautiful eyelids and go slowly blind? Are you going to force me to toast the soles of your feet at the gas-fire, and drive chips of wood under your finger-nails, and do other crude things like that—before you come to your senses? Really, you'll be giving yourself a lot of unnecessary pain—"

And the Saint held the knife quite close to the man's eyes and brought it downwards very slowly. The point gleamed like a lonely star, and the man stared at it, hypnotised, mute with terror. And Roger Conway was also hypnotised, and stood like a man carved in ice.

"Do you talk?" asked the Saint caressingly.

Again the man tried to scream, and again the Saint's fingers choked the scream back into his windpipe. The Saint brought the knife down farther, and the point of it actually pricked the skin.

Roger Conway felt cold beads of perspiration breaking out on his forehead, but he could not find his voice. He knew that the Saint would do exactly what he had threatened to do, if he were forced to it. He knew the Saint. He had seen the Saint in a hundred strange situations and a hundred moods, but he had never seen the Saint's face chiselled into such an inexorable grimness as it was then. It was like granite.

And Roger Conway knew then, in the blazing light of experience, what before then he had only understood mistily, in the twilight of theory—that the wrath of saints can be a far more dreadful thing than the wrath of sinners.

The man on the table must have understood it also—the fantastic fact that a man of Simon Templar's calibre in such an icy rage, even in civilised England, would stop at nothing. And the breath that the Saint let him take came in a kind of shuddering groan.

"Do you talk, beautiful?" asked the Saint again, ever so gently.

"I talk."

It was not a voice—it was a whimper.

"I talk," whimpered the man. "I will do anything. Only take away that knife . . ."

For a moment the Saint did not move.

Then, very slowly, like a man in a trance, he took the knife away and looked at it as if he had never seen it before. And a queer little laugh trickled through his lips.

"Very dramatic," he remarked. "And almost horrible. I didn't know I had it in me."

And he gazed at the man curiously, as he might have gazed at a fly on a window-pane in an idle moment and remembered stories of schoolboys who were amused to pull off their wings.

Then he climbed slowly down from the table and took out his cigarette-case.

The man he had left did not so much raise himself off the table as roll off it, and, when his feet touched the floor, it was seen that he could scarcely stand.

Roger pushed him roughly into a chair, from which, fingering his throat, he could see the man who still lay where he had fallen.

"Don't look so surprised," said Roger. "The last man the Saint hit like that was out for half an hour, and your pal's only been out twenty minutes."

Simon flicked a match into the fireplace and returned to face the prisoner.

"Let's hear your little song, honeybunch," he said briefly.

"What do you want to know?"

"First thing of all, I want to know what's been done with the girl who was taken tonight."

"That I do not know."

The Saint's cigarette tilted up to a dangerous angle between his lips and his hands went deep into his trousers pockets.

"You don't seem to have got the idea, beautiful," he remarked sweetly. "This isn't a game—as you'll find out if you don't wake yourself up in rather less time than it takes me to get my hands on you again. I'm quite ready to resume the surgical operation as soon as you like. So go on talking, because I just love your voice, and it helps me to forget all the unpleasant things I ought to be doing to your perfectly appalling face."

The man shuddered and cowered back into the depths of the chair. His hands flew to his eyes; it may have been to shut out a ghastly vision, or it may have been to try to escape from the Saint's merciless blue stare.

"I do not know!" he almost screamed. "I swear it . . ."

"Then tell me what you do know, you rat," said Simon, "and then I'll make you remember some more."

Words came to the fat man in an incoherent, pelting stream, lashed on by fear.

He was acting on the instructions of Dr Marius. That was true. The house in Brook Street had been closely watched for the last twenty-four hours, he himself being one of the watchers. He had seen the departure the previous night, but they had not had the means to follow a car. Two other men had been sent to inspect the premises that afternoon, had seen the loaded car outside, and had rushed away together to report.

"Both of them?" interrupted the Saint.

"Both of them. It was a criminal mistake. But they will be punished."

"How will you be rewarded, I wonder?" murmured Simon.

The fat man shivered, and went on.

"One was sent back immediately, but the car had gone. The Doctor then said that he had made other plans, and one man would be enough to keep watch, in case you returned. I was that man. Hermann"—he pointed to the inert figure on the floor—"had just come to relieve me when you came back. We were going to report it."

"Both of you?"

"Both of us."

"A criminal mistake," drawled the Saint sardonically. "But I expect you will be punished. Yes?"

The man winced.

Another of his comrades, he said, had been told off to follow the girl. It had been impressed upon the sleuths that no movement should be missed, and no habit overlooked, however trifling. Marius had not divulged the reason for this vigilance, but he had left them in no doubt of its importance. In that spirit Patricia had been followed to Devonshire.

"Your boss seems very unwilling to meet me again personally," observed the Saint grimly. "How wise of him!"

"We could afford to take no risks . . ."

"'We?'"

Simon swooped on the pronoun like a hawk.

"I mean . . ."

"I know what you mean, sweetness," said the Saint silkily. "You mean that you didn't mean to let on that you knew more about this than you said. You're not just a hired crook, like the last specimen of your kind I had to tread on. You're a secret agent. We understand that. We understand also that, however much respect you may have for the continued wholeness of your own verminous hide, a most commendable patriotism for your misbegotten country will make you keep on fighting and lying as long as you can. Very good. I applaud. But I'm afraid my appreciation of your one solitary virtue will have to stop there—at just that one theoretical pat on the back. After which, we go back to our own private, practical quarrel. And what you've got to get jammed well into the misshapen lump of bone that keeps your unwashed ears apart, is that I'm a bit of a fighter myself, and I think— somehow, somehow, I think, dear one—I think I'm a better fighter than you are."

"I did not mean . . ."

"Don't lie," said the Saint, in a tone of mock reproach that held behind its superficial flippancy a kind of glacial menace. "Don't lie to me. I don't like it."

Roger moved off the wall which he had been propping up.

"Put him back on the table, old boy," he suggested.

"I'm going to," said the Saint, "unless he spills the beans in less than two flaps of a duck's rudder."

He came a little closer to the fat man.

"Now, you loathsome monstrosity—listen to me. The game's up. You've put both feet in it with that little word 'we.' And I'm curious. Very, very curious and inquisitive. I want to know everything about you—the story of your life, and your favourite movie star, and your golf handicap, and whether you sleep with your pyjama trousers inside or outside the jacket. I want you to tell me all about yourself. For instance, when Marius told you that you could let up on the watch here, as he'd made 'other plans'—didn't he say that there was a girl concerned in those plans?"

"No."

"That's two lies," said the Saint. "Next time you lie, you will be badly hurt. Second question: I know that Marius arranged for the girl to be drugged on the train, and taken off it before it reached London— but where was she to be taken to?"

"I do not . . . A-a-a-a-ah!"

"I warned you," said the Saint.

"Are you a devil?" sobbed the man, and the Saint showed his teeth.

"Not really. Just an ordinary man who objects to being molested. I thought I'd made that quite plain. Of course, I'm in a hurry this evening, so that may make me seem a little hasty. Now, are you going to remember things—truthful things—or shall we have some more unpleasantness?"

The man shrank back from him, quivering.

"I do not know any more," he blubbered. "I swear . . ."

"Where is Marius now?"

But the man did not answer immediately, for the sudden ringing of a bell sounded clearly through the apartment.

For a second the Saint was immobile.

Then he stepped round behind the prisoner's chair, and the little knife slid out of its sheath again. The prisoner saw the flash of it, and his eyes dilated with terror. A cry rose to his lips, and the Saint stifled it with a hand over his mouth. Then the point stung the man over the heart.

"Just one word," said the Saint, "just one word, and you'll say the rest of the sentence to the Recording Angel. Who d'you think it is, Roger?"

"Teal?"

"Having traced that motor agent to his Sunday lair, and got on our trail?"

"If we don't answer . . ."

"They'll break in. There's the car outside to tell them we're here. No, they'll have to come in . . ."

"Just when we're finding out things?"

Simon Templar's eyes glittered.

"Give me that gun!"

Conway picked up the automatic that the fat man had dropped, which had lain neglected on the floor ever since, and handed it over obediently.

"I'll tell you," said the Saint, "that no man born of woman is going to interfere with me. I'm going to finish getting everything I want out of this lump of refuse, and then I'm going on to act on it—to find Pat—and I'll shoot my way through the whole of Scotland Yard to do it, if I have to. Now go and open that door."

Conway nodded.

"I'm with you," he said, and went out.

The Saint waited calmly.

His left hand still held the slim blade of Anna over the fat man's heart, ready to drive it home, and his ears were alert for the faintest sound of a deeply drawn breath that might be the prelude to a shout. His right hand held the automatic, concealed behind the back of the chair.

But when Roger came back, and the Saint saw the man who came with him, he remained exactly as he was, and no one could have remarked the slightest change in the desolate impassivity of his face. Only his heart leapt sickeningly, and slithered back anyhow into its place, leaving a strange feeling of throbbing emptiness spreading across the track of that thudding somersault.

"Pleased to meet you again, Marius," said the Saint.

8

HOW SIMON TEMPLAR
ENTERTAINED HIS GUEST, AND
BROKE UP THE PARTY

Then, slowly, the Saint straightened up.

No one would ever know what an effort his calm and smiling
imperturbability cost him, and yet, as a matter of fact, it was easier than
the calm he had previously maintained before Roger Conway when
there was really nothing to be calm about.

For this was something that the Saint understood. He had not
the temperament to remain patient in periods of enforced inaction; he
could never bring his best to bear against an enemy whom he could
not see; subtleties were either above or beneath him, whichever way
you like to look at it.

In Simon Templar there was much of his celebrated namesake, the
Simple One. He himself was always ready to confess it, saying that, in
spite of his instinctive understanding of the criminal mind, he would
never have made a successful detective. His brain was capable of it, but

his character wasn't. He preferred the more gaudy colours, the broader and more clean-cut line, the simple and straightforward and startling things. He was a fighting man. His genius and inspiration led him into battles and showed him how to win them, but he rarely thought about them. He had ideals, and he rarely thought about those: they were laid down for him by an authority greater than himself, and remained apart and unquestionable. He disliked any sort of thought that was not as concrete as a weapon. To him, any other sort of thought was a heresy and a curse, an insidious sickness, sapping honesty and action. He asked for different things—the high heart of the happy warrior, the swagger and the flourish, the sound of the trumpet. He had said it himself, and it should go down as one of the few statements the Saint ever made about himself with no suggestion of pose. "Battle, murder, and sudden death," he had said.

And now, at last, he was on ground that he knew, desperate and dangerous as it might be.

"Take over the pop-gun, Roger."

Cool, smooth, mocking, with a hint of laughter—the voice of the old Saint. He turned again to Marius, smiling and debonair.

"It's nice of you," he said genially, "to give us a call. Have a drink, Tiny Tim?"

Marius advanced a little farther into the room.

He was robed in conventional morning coat and striped trousers. The stiff perfection of the garb contrasted grotesquely with his neolithic stature and the hideously ugly expressionlessness of a face that might have been fashioned after the model of some savage devil-god.

He glanced round without emotion at Roger Conway, who leaned against the door with his commandeered automatic comfortably concentrating on an easy target, and then he turned again to the Saint, who was swinging his little knife like a pendulum between his finger and thumb.

Thoughtful was the Saint, calm with a vivid and violent calm, like a leopard gathering for a spring, but Marius was as calm as a gigantic Buddha.

"I see you have some servants of mine here," said Marius.

His voice, for such a man, was extraordinarily soft and high-pitched; his English would have been perfect but for its exaggerated precision.

"I have," said the Saint blandly. "You may think it odd of me, but I've given up standing on my dignity, and I'm now a practising Socialist. I go out into the highways and byways every Sunday evening and collect bits and pieces. These are tonight's bag. How did you know?"

"I did not know. One of them should have reported to me a long time ago, and my servants know better than to be late. I came to see what had happened to him. You will please let him go—and his friend."

The Saint raised one eyebrow.

"I'm not sure that they want to," he remarked. "One of them, at least, is temporarily incapable of expressing his views on the subject. As for the other—well, we were just starting to get on so nicely together. I'm sure he'd hate to have to leave me."

The man thus indirectly appealed to spat out some words in a language which the Saint did not understand. Simon smothered him with a cushion.

"Don't interrupt," he drawled. "It's rude. First I have my say, then you have yours. That's fair. And I'm sure Dr Marius would like to share our little joke, particularly as it's about himself."

The giant's mouth fanned into something like a ghastly smile.

"Hadn't you better hear my joke first?" he suggested.

"Second," said the Saint. "Quite definitely second. Because your joke is sure to be so much funnier than mine, and I'd hate mine to fall flat after it. This joke is in the form of a little song, and it's about a man

THE SAINT CLOSES THE CASE

whom we call Tiny Tim, whom I once had to kick with some vim. He recovered, I fear, but fox-hunting this year will have little attraction for him. You haven't given us time to rehearse it, or I'd ask the boys to sing it for you. Never mind. Sit right down and tell me the story of your life."

The giant was not impressed.

"You appear to know my name," he said.

"Very well," beamed the Saint. "Any relation to the celebrated Dr Marius?"

"I am not unknown."

"I mean," said the Saint, "the celebrated Dr Marius whose living was somewhat precarious, for his bedside technique was decidedly weak, though his ideas were many and various. Does that ring the bell and return the penny?"

Marius moved his huge right hand in an impatient gesture.

"I am not here to listen to your humour, Mr . . ."

"Templar," supplied the Saint. "So pleased to be met."

"I do not wish to waste any time . . ."

Simon lowered his eyes, which had been fixed on the ceiling during the labour of poetical composition, and allowed them to rest upon Marius. There was something very steely and savage about those eyes. The laughter had gone out of them utterly. Roger had seen it go.

"Naturally, we don't want to waste any time," said the Saint quietly. "Thank you for reminding me. It's a thing I should hate very much to forget while you're here. I may tell you that I'm going to murder you, Marius. But before we talk any more about that, let me save you the trouble of saying what you were going to say."

Marius shrugged.

"You appear to be an intelligent man, Mr Templar."

"Thanks very much. But let's keep the bouquets on ice till we want them, will you? Then they might come in handy for the wreath . . . The business of the moment interests me more. One: you're going to tell me that a certain lady named Patricia Holm is now your prisoner."

The giant bowed.

"I'm sorry to have had to make such a conventional move," he said. "On the other hand, it is often said that the most conventional principles have the deepest foundations. I have always found that saying to be true when applied to the time-honoured expedient of taking a woman whom a man loves as a hostage for his good behaviour—particularly with a man of what I judge to be your type, Mr Templar."

"Very interesting," said the Saint shortly. "And I suppose Miss Holm's safety is to be the price of the safety of your—er—servants? I believe that's also in the convention."

Marius spread out his enormous hands.

"Oh, no," he said, in that thin, soft voice. "Oh, dear me, no! The convention is not by any means as trivial as that. Is not the fair lady's safety always the price of something more than mere pawns in the game?"

"Meaning?" inquired the Saint innocently.

"Meaning a certain gentleman in whom I am interested whom you were successful in removing from the protection of my servants last night."

"Was I?"

"I have reason to believe that you were. Much as I respect your integrity, Mr Templar, I fear that in this case your contradiction will not be sufficient to convince me against the evidence of my own eyes."

The Saint swayed gently on his heels.

"Let me suggest," he said, "that you're very sure I got him."

"Let me suggest," said Marius suavely, "that you're very sure I've got Miss Holm."

"I haven't got him."

"Then I have not got Miss Holm."

Simon nodded.

"Very ingenious," he murmured. "Very ingenious. Not quite the way I expected it—but very ingenious, all the same. And quite unanswerable. Therefore . . ."

"Therefore, Mr Templar, why not put the cards on the table? We have agreed not to waste time. I frankly admit that Miss Holm is my prisoner. Why don't you admit that Professor Vargan is yours?"

"Not so fast," said the Saint. "You've just admitted, before witnesses, that you are a party to an abduction. Now, suppose that became known to the police? Wouldn't that be awkward?"

Marius shook his head.

"Not particularly," he said. "I have a very good witness to deny any such admission . . ."

"A crook?"

"Oh, no. A most respectable countryman of mine. I assure you, it would be quite impossible to discredit him."

Simon lounged back against the table.

"I see," he drawled. "And that's your complete song-and-dance act, is it?"

"I believe I have stated all the important points."

"Then," said the Saint, "I will now state mine."

Carefully he replaced the little knife in its sheath and adjusted his sleeve. A glance at the man on the floor told him that unlucky servant of the Cause was recovering, but Simon was not interested. He addressed himself to the man in the chair.

"Tell your master about the game we were playing," he invited. "Confess everything, loveliness. He has a nice kind face, and perhaps he won't be too hard on you."

The man spoke again in his own language. Marius listened woodenly. The Saint could not understand a word of what was being said, but he knew, when the giant interrupted the discourse with a movement of his hand and a sharp, harsh syllable of impatience, that the recital had passed through the stage of being a useful statement of facts, and had degenerated into a string of excuses.

Then Marius was looking curiously at Simon Templar. There seemed to be a kind of grim humour in that gaze.

"And yet you do not look a ferocious man, Mr Templar."

"I shouldn't rely too much on that."

Again that jerky gesture of impatience.

"I am not relying on it. With a perspicacity which I should have expected, and which I can only commend, you have saved me many words, many tedious explanations. You have summed up the situation with admirable briefness. May I ask you to be as brief with your decision? I may say that the fortunate accident of finding you at home, which I did not expect, has saved me the considerable trouble of getting in touch with you through the agony columns of the daily papers, and has enabled me to put my proposition before you with the minimum of delay. Would it not be a pity, now, to mar such an excellent start with unnecessary paltering?"

"It would," said the Saint.

And he knew at once what he was going to do. It had come to him in a flash—an inspiration, a summarising and deduction and realisation that were instantaneous, and more clear and sure than anything of their kind which could have been produced by any mental effort.

That he was on toast, and that there was no ordinary way off the toast. That the situation was locked and double-locked into exactly the tangle of dithering subtleties and cross-causes and cross-menaces that he hated more than anything else in the world, as has been explained—the kind of chess-problem tangle that was probably the one thing in the world capable of reeling him off his active mental balance and sending him raving mad . . . That to think about it and try to scheme about it would be the one certain way of losing the game. That, obviously, he could never hope to stand up in the same class as Rayt Marius in a complicated intrigue—to try to enter into an even contest with such a past professional master of the art would be the act of a suicidal fool. That, therefore, his only chance to win out was to break the very rules of the game that Marius would least expect an opponent to break. That it was the moment when all the prejudices and convictions that made the Saint what he was must be put to the test. That all his fundamental faith in the superiority of reckless action over laborious ratiocination must now justify itself, or topple down to destruction and take him with it into hell . . . That, in fact, when all the pieces on the chessboard were so in-weaved and dovetailed and counter-blockaded, his only chance was to smash up the whole stagnant structure and sweep the board clean—with the slash of a sword . . .

"Certainly," said the Saint, "I'll give you my decision at once. Roger, give me back that gun, and go and fetch some rope. You'll find some in the kitchen."

As Conway went out, the Saint turned again to Marius.

"You have already observed, dear one," he remarked gently, "that I have a genius for summarising situations. But this one can be stated quite simply. The fact is, Angel Face, I propose to apply to you exactly the same methods of persuasion that I was about to employ on your servant. You observe that I have a gun. I can't shoot pips out of a playing-card at thirty paces, or do any other Wild West stuff like that, but still, I don't think I'm such a bad shot that I could miss anything your size at this range. Therefore, you can either submit quietly to being tied up by my friend, or you can be killed at once. Have it whichever way you like."

A flicker of something showed in the giant's eyes, and was gone as soon as it had come.

"You seem to have lost your grip on the situation, Mr Templar," he said urbanely. "To anyone as expert in these matters as you appear to be, it should be unnecessary to explain that I did not come here unprepared for such an obvious riposte. Must I bore you with the details of what will happen to Miss Holm if I fail to return to the place where she is being kept? Must I be compelled to make my conventional move still more conventional with a melodramatic exposition of her peril?"

"It's an odd thing," said the Saint, in mild reminiscence, "that more than half the crooks I've dealt with have been frantically anxious to avoid melodrama. Now, personally, I just love it. And we're going to have lots of it now—lots and lots, Marius, my little ray of sunshine . . ."

Marius shrugged.

"I thought better of your intelligence, Mr Templar."

The Saint smiled, a very Saintly smile.

His hands on his hips, teetering gently on his toes, he answered with the most reckless defiance of his life.

"You're wrong," he said. "You didn't think well enough of my intelligence. You thought it'd be feeble enough to let me be bluffed into meeting you on your own ground. And that's just what it isn't quite feeble enough to do."

"I do not follow you," said Marius.

"Then I'm not the one with softening of the brain," said Simon sweetly, "but you are. I invite you to apply your own admirable system of logic to the situation. I could tell the police things about you, but you could tell the police things about me. Deadlock. You could harm Miss Holm, but I could deprive you of Vargan. Deadlock again—with a shade of odds in your favour on each count."

"We can rule out the police for the present. If we did so, an exchange of prisoners . . ."

"But you don't get the point," said Simon, with a terrible simplicity. "That would be a surrender on my part. And I never surrender."

Marius moved his hands.

"I also surrender Miss Holm."

"And there's still a difference, loveliness," said the Saint. "You see, you don't really want Miss Holm, except as a hostage. And I do want Vargan very much indeed. I want to wash him and comb him and buy him a little velvet suit and adopt him. I want him to yadder childishly to me about the binomial theorem after breakfast. I want to be able to bring him into the drawing-room after dinner to amuse my guests with recitations from the differential calculus. But most of all I want one of his little toys . . . And so, you see, if I let you go, Miss Holm would be in exactly the same danger as if I kept you here, since I couldn't agree to your terms of ransom. But the difference is that if I let you go I lose my one chance of finding her, and I should have to trust to luck to come on the scent again. While I keep you here, though, I hold a very good card—and I'm not letting it go."

"You gain nothing . . ."

"On the contrary, I gain everything," said the Saint, in that dreamy sing-song. "I gain everything, or lose more than everything. But I'm tired of haggling. I'm tired of playing your safety game. You're going to play my game now, Marius, my cherub. "Wait a second while I rearrange the scene . . ."

As Conway came back with a length of cord, the Saint took from his pocket a little shining cylinder and screwed it swiftly on to the muzzle of the gun he held.

"This will now make no noise worth mentioning," he said, "You know the gadget, don't you? So let me have your decision quickly, Marius, before I remember what I want to do more than anything else in the world."

"It will not help you to kill me."

"It will not help me to let you go. But we've had all that before. Besides, I mightn't kill you. I might just shoot you through the kidneys, and long before you died of the wound you'd be ready to give me anything to put you out of your agony. I grant you it wouldn't improve my chance of finding Miss Holm, but, on the other hand, it wouldn't make it any worse—and you'd be so dead that it wouldn't worry you, anyway. Think it over. I give you two minutes. Roger, time him by that clock!"

Marius put his hands behind him at once.

"Suppose I save you the time. I will be tied now—if you think that will help you."

"Carry on, Roger," said the Saint.

He knew that Marius still did not believe him—that the fat man's description of his ordeal had not made the impression it should have made. He knew that Marius's acquiescence was nothing but a bland calling of what the giant estimated to be a hopeless bluff. And he stood by, watching with a face of stone, while Conway tied the man's hands behind his back and thrust him into a chair.

"Take over the peashooter again, Roger."

Then an idea struck the Saint.

He said, "Before we begin, Roger, you might search him."

A glimmer of fear, which nothing else in that interview had aroused, contorted the giant's face like a spasm, and the Saint could have shouted for joy. Marius struggled like a fiend, but he had been well bound, and his effort was wasted.

The weak spot in the armour . . .

Simon waited, almost trembling. Torture he had been grimly prepared to apply, but he recognised at the same time how futile it was likely to prove against a man like Marius. He might have resumed the torture of the fat man, but that also would have been less efficacious now that the moral support—or threat—of Marius was there to counteract it. He would obtain some sort of information, certainly—the limits of human endurance would inevitably see to that—but he would have no means of proving its truth. Something in writing, though . . .

And the colossal facility of the success made the Saint's heart pound like a trip-hammer, in a devastating terror lest the success should turn out to be no success at all. For, if success it was, the rightness of his riposte could not have been more shatteringly demonstrated. If it were true—if Marius had plunged so heavily on the rules of the game as he knew them—if Marius had been so blindly certain that, under the menace which he knew he could hold over them, neither of the men in Brook Street would dare to lay a hand on him—if . . .

"English swine!"

"Naughty temper," said Roger equably.

"Thank you," said the Saint, taking the letter which Roger handed to him. "Careless of you, Marius, to come here with that on you. Personally, I never commit anything to writing. It's dangerous. But perhaps you meant to post it on your way, and forgot it."

He glanced at the address.

"Our old friend the Crown Prince," he murmured. "This should be interesting."

He slit open the envelope with one swift flick of his thumb, and drew out the typewritten sheet.

It was in Marius's own language, but that was a small difficulty. The Saint took it with him to the telephone, and in a few minutes he was through to a friend who held down a soft job at the Foreign Office by virtue of an almost incredible familiarity with every language on the map of Europe.

"Glad to find you in," said the Saint rapidly. "Listen—I've got a letter here which I want translated. I don't know how to pronounce any of it, but I'll spell it out word by word. Ready?"

It took time, but the Saint had found an unwonted patience. He wrote between the lines as the receiver dictated, and presently it was finished.

He came back smiling.

Roger prompted him. "Which, being interpreted, means . . ."

"I'm leaving now."

"Where for?"

"The house on the hill, Bures, Suffolk."

"She's there?"

"According to the letter."

The Saint passed it over, and Conway read the scribbled notes between the lines: ". . . the girl, and she is being taken to a quiet part of Suffolk . . . Bures . . . house on the hill, far enough from the village to be safe . . . cannot fail this time . . ."

Conway handed it back.

"I'll come with you."

The Saint shook his head.

"Sorry, son, but you've got to stay here and look after the menagerie. They're my hostages."

"But suppose anything goes wrong, Simon?"

The Saint consulted his watch. It was still stopped. He wound it up and set it by the mantelpiece clock.

"I'll be back," he said, "before four o'clock tomorrow morning. That allows for punctures, breakdowns, and everything else. If I'm not here on the stroke, shoot these birds and come after me."

Marius's voice rasped in on Conway's hesitation.

"You insist on being foolish, Templar? You realise that my men at Bures have orders to use Miss Holm as a hostage in an attack or any other emergency?"

Simon Templar went over and looked down at him.

"I could have guessed it," he said. "And it makes me weep for your bad generalship, Marius. I suppose you realise that if they sacrifice her, your first and last hold over me is gone? But that's only half the fundamental weakness in your bright scheme. The other half is that you've got to pray against yourself. Pray that I win tonight, Marius—

pray as you've never prayed before in your filthy life! Because, if I fail, I'm coming straight back here to kill you in the most hideous way I can invent. I mean that."

He swung round, cool, cold, deliberate, and went to the door as if he were merely going for a stroll round the block before turning in. But at the door he turned to cast a slow, straight glance at Marius, and then to smile at Roger.

"All the best, old boy," said Roger.

"'Battle, murder, and sudden death,'" quoted the Saint softly, with a gay, reckless gesture, and the Saintly smile could never have shone more superbly. "Watch me," said the Saint, and was gone.

9

HOW ROGER CONWAY WAS CARELESS, AND HERMANN ALSO MADE A MISTAKE

Roger Conway shifted vaguely across the room as the hum of Norman Kent's Hirondel faded and was lost in the noises of Regent Street. He came upon the side table where the decanter lived, helped himself to a drink, and remembered that last cavalier wave of the Saint's hand and the pitiful torment in the Saint's eyes. Then he put down the drink and took a cigarette instead, suddenly aware that he might have to remain wide awake and alert all night.

He looked at Marius. The giant had sunk into an inscrutable apathy, but he spoke.

"If you would allow it, I should like to smoke a cigar."

Roger deliberated.

"It might be arranged—if you don't need your hands free."

"I can try. The case is in my breast pocket."

Conway found it, bit the end, and put it in Marius's mouth and lighted it. Marius thanked him.

"Will you join me?"

Roger smiled.

"Try something newer," he advised. "I never take smokes from strangers these days, on principle. Oh, and by the way, if I catch you trying to burn through your ropes with the end, I shall have much pleasure in grinding it into your face till it goes out."

Marius shrugged and made no reply, and Roger resumed his cigarette.

Coming upon the telephone, he hesitated, and then called a number. He was through in a few minutes.

"Can I speak to Mr Kent, Orace?—Oh, hullo, Norman!"

"Who's that? Roger?"

"Yes. I rang up in case you were getting worried about us. Heaven knows what time we shall get down . . . No, the car's all right—as far as I know. Simon's gone off in it . . . Brook Street . . . Well—Marius has got Pat . . . Yes, I'm afraid so. Got her on the train. But we've got Marius . . . Yes, he's here. I'm standing guard. We've found out where Pat's been taken, and Simon's gone after her . . . Somewhere in Suffolk."

"Shall I come up?"

"How? It's too late for a train, and you won't be able to hire anything worth calling a car at this hour. I don't see what you could do, anyway . . . Look here, I can't talk any more now. I've got to keep both eyes on Marius and Co. . . . I'll leave it to you . . . Right. So long, old boy."

He hooked up the receiver.

It occurred to him afterwards that there was something that Norman could have done. He could have tied up the fat man and the lean man, both of whom were now conscious and free to move as much as they dared. That ought to have been done before Simon left. They ought to have thought of it—or Simon ought to have thought of it. But the Saint couldn't, reasonably, have been expected to think of it, or anything else like it, at such a time. Roger knew both the Saint and Pat too well to be able to blame Simon for the omission. Simon had been mad when he left. The madness had been there all the time, since half past nine, boiling up in fiercer and fiercer waves behind all the masks of calmness and flippancy and patience that the Saint had assumed at intervals, and it had been at its whitest heat behind that last gay smile and gesture from the door.

Half an hour passed.

Roger was beginning to feel hungry. He had had a snack in the station buffet while he was waiting, but the satisfaction of that was starting to wear off. If he had gone to the kitchen to forage, that would have meant compelling his three prisoners to precede him at the point of his gun. And the kitchen was small . . . Ruefully Roger resigned himself to a hungry vigil. He looked unhappily at the clock. Four and a half hours before he could shoot the prisoners and dash to the pantry, if he obeyed the Saint's orders. But it would have to be endured. The Saint might have managed the cure, and got away with it, but then, the Saint was a fully qualified adventurer, and what he didn't know about the game was not knowledge. Conway was infinitely less experienced, and knew it. In the cramped space of the kitchen, while he was trying to locate food with one eye and one hand, he might easily be taken off his guard and overpowered. And, in the circumstances, the risk was too great to take. If only Norman decided to come . . .

Roger Conway sat on the edge of the table, swinging the gun idly in his hand. Marius remained silent. His cigar had gone out, and he had not asked for it to be relighted. The fat man slouched in another chair, watching Roger with venomous eyes. The lean man stood awkwardly in one corner. He had not spoken since he recovered consciousness, but he also watched. The clock ticked monotonously.

Roger started to whistle to himself. It was extraordinary how quickly the strain began to tell. He wished he were like the Saint. The Saint wouldn't have gone hungry, for one thing. The Saint would have made the prisoners cook him a four-course dinner, lay the table, and wait on him. The Saint would have kept them busy putting on the gramophone and generally running his errands. The Saint would probably have written a letter and composed a few limericks into the bargain. He certainly couldn't have been oppressed by the silence and the concentrated malevolence of three pairs of eyes. He would have dismissed the silence and whiled away the time by indulging in airy persiflage at their expense.

But it was the silence and the watchfulness of the eyes. Roger began to understand why he had never felt an irresistible urge to become a lion-tamer. The feeling of being alone in a cage of wild beasts, he decided, must be very much like what he was experiencing at that moment. The same fragile dominance of the man, the same unresting watchfulness of the beasts, the same tension, the same snarling submission of the beasts, the same certainty that the beasts were only waiting, waiting, waiting. These human beasts were sizing him up, searching his soul, stripping him naked of all bluff, finding out all his weaknesses in silence, planning, scheming, considering, alert to pounce. It was getting on Roger's nerves. Presently, sooner or later, somehow, he knew, there would be a bid for liberty. But how would it happen?

And that uncertainty must go on for hours and hours, perhaps. Move and counter-move, threat and counter-threat, the snarl and the lash, the silence and the watchfulness and the eyes. How long? . . .

Then from the fat man's lips broke the first rattle of words, in his own language.

"Stop that!" rapped Conway, with his nerves all on edge. "If you've anything to say, say it in English. Any more of that, and you'll get a clip over the ear with the soft end of this gun."

And the man deliberately and defiantly spoke again, still in his own language.

Roger came off the table as though it had been red-hot. He stood over the man with his hand raised, and the man stared back with sullen insolence.

Then it happened.

The plan was beautifully simple.

Roger had forgotten for the moment that only Marius's hands were tied. The giant's feet were free. And, standing over the fat man's chair, where he had been so easily lured by the bait that was also an explanation of the trap to the others, Roger's back was half turned to Marius.

Conway heard the movement behind him, but he had no time to spin round to meet it. The giant's foot crashed into the small of his back with a savage force that might well have broken the spine—if it had struck the spine. But it struck to one side of the spine, in a place almost as vulnerable, and Roger went to the floor with a gasp of agony.

Then both the fat man and the lean man leapt on him together.

The gun was wrenched out of Roger's hand. He could not have seen to shoot, anyway, for the pain had blinded him. He could not cry out—his throat was constricted with a horrible numbing nausea, and his lungs seemed to be paralysed. The lean man's fist smacked again and again into his defenceless jaw.

"Untie me quickly, fool!" hissed Marius, and the fat man obeyed, to the accompaniment of a babbling flood of excuses.

Marius cut him short.

"I will consider your punishment later, Otto. Perhaps this will atone for a little of your imbecility. Tie him up now with this rope . . ."

Roger lay still. Somehow—he did not know how—he retained his consciousness. There was no strength in any of his limbs; he could see nothing; his battered head sang and ached and throbbed horribly; the whole of his body was in the grip of a crushing, cramping agony that centred on the point in his back where he had taken the kick, and from that point spread iron tentacles of helplessness into every muscle; yet his mind hung aloof, high and clear above the roaring blackness, and he heard and remembered every word that was said.

"Look for more rope, Hermann," Marius was ordering.

The lean man went out and returned. Roger's feet were bound as his wrists had been.

Then Marius was at the telephone.

"A trunk call . . . Bures . . ."

An impatient pause. Then Marius cursed gutturally.

"The line is out of order? Tell me when it will be working again. It is a matter of life and death . . . Tomorrow? . . . God in Heaven! A telegram—would a telegram be delivered in Bures tonight?"

"I'll put you through to . . ."

Pause again.

"Yes. I wish to ask if a telegram would be delivered in Bures tonight . . . Bures, Suffolk . . . You think not? . . . You are almost sure not? . . . Very well. Thank you. No, I will not send it now."

He replaced the receiver, and lifted it again immediately.

This time he spoke to Westminster 9999, and gave staccato instructions which Roger could not understand. They appeared to be detailed instructions, and they took some time. But at last Marius was satisfied.

He rang off, and turned and kicked Roger contemptuously.

"You stay here, pig. You are a security for your friend's behaviour."

Then again he spoke to the lean man in the language which was double-Dutch to Roger: "Hermann, you remain to guard him. I will leave you the gun. Wait—I find out the telephone number . . ." He read it off the instrument. "If I have orders to give, I will telephone. You will not leave here without my permission . . . Otto, you come with me. We go after Templar in my car. I have agents on the road, and I have ordered them to be instructed. If they are not all as incapable as you, he will never reach Bures alive. But we follow to make sure . . . Wait again! That pig on the floor spoke to a friend at Maidenhead who may be coming to join him. You will capture him and tie him up also. Let there be no mistake, Hermann."

"There shall be no mistake."

"Good! Come, Otto."

Roger heard them go, and then the roaring blackness that lay all about him welled up and engulfed that lonely glitter of clarity in his mind.

He might have been unconscious for five minutes or five days; he had lost all idea of time. But the first thing he saw when he opened his eyes was the clock, and he knew it must have been about twenty minutes.

The man Hermann sat in a chair opposite him, turning the pages of a magazine. Presently he looked up and saw that Roger was awake, and he put down the magazine and came over and spat in his face.

"Soon, English swine, you will be dead. And your country . . ."

Roger controlled his tongue with a tremendous effort.

He found that he could breathe. The iron bands about his chest had slackened, and the bodily anguish had lessened. There was still the throbbing pain in his back and the throbbing pain in his head, but he was better. And he wasn't asking for any unnecessary aggravation of his troubles—not just then, anyway.

The man went on: "The Doctor is a great man. He is the greatest man in the world. You should have seen how he arranged everything in two minutes. It was magnificent. He is Napoleon born again. He is going to make our country the greatest country in the world. And you fools try to fight him . . ."

The speech merged into an unintelligible outburst in the man's native tongue, but Roger understood enough. He understood that a man who could delude his servants into such a fanatical loyalty was no small man. And he wondered what chance the Saint would ever have had of convincing anyone that Marius was concerned with no patriotisms and no nationalities, but only with his own gods of money and power.

The first flush of futile anger ebbed from Conway's face, and he lay in stolid silence as he was tied, revolving plot and counter-plot in his mind. Hermann, failing to rouse him with taunts, struck him twice across the face. Roger never moved. And the man spat at him again.

"It is as I thought. You have no courage, you dogs of Englishmen. It is only when you are many against one little one—then you are brave."

"Oh, quite," said Roger wearily.

Hermann glowered at him.

"Now, if you had been the one who hit me . . ."

Zzzzzzzzzzzing!

The shrill scream of a bell wailed through the apartment with a suddenness that made the conventional sound electrifying. Hermann stopped, stiffening, in the middle of his sentence. And a sour leer came into his face.

"Now I welcome your friend, pig."

Roger drew a deep breath.

He must have been careless, obvious about it, for Roger Conway's was not a mind much given to cunning. Or possibly Hermann had been expecting some such move, subconsciously, and had his ears pricked for the sound. But he stopped on his way to the door and turned.

"You would try to give warning, Englishman?" he purred.

His gun was in his hand. He reached Roger in three strides.

Roger knew he was up against it. If he didn't shout, his one chance of rescue, so far as he could see, was dished—and Norman Kent with it. If he looked like shouting, he'd be laid out again. And, if it came to that, since his intention of shouting had already been divined, he'd probably be laid out anyway. Hermann wasn't the sort of man to waste time gagging his prisoners. So . . .

"Go to blazes," said Roger recklessly.

Then he yelled.

An instant later Hermann's gun-butt crashed into the side of his head.

Again he should have been stunned, but he wasn't. He decided afterwards that he must have a skull a couple of inches thick, and the constitution of an ox with it, to have stood up to as much as he had. But the fact remained that he was laid out without being stunned, and he lay still, trying to collect himself in time to loose a second yell as Hermann opened the door.

Hermann straightened up, turning his gun round again. He put it in his coat pocket, keeping his finger on the trigger, and then, with something like a panicking terror that the warning might have been heard and accepted by the person outside the front door, he scrambled rather than ran out of the room, cursing under his breath.

But the ring was repeated as he reached the front door, and the sound reassured him. He could not believe that anyone who had heard and understood that one yell would have rung again so promptly after it. Whereby Hermann showed himself a less ingenious psychologist than the man outside . . .

He opened the door, keeping himself hidden behind it.

No one entered.

He waited, with a kind of superstitious fear trickling down his back like a tiny cascade of ice-cold water. Nothing happened—and yet the second ring had sounded only a moment before he opened the door, and no one who had rung a second time would go away at once, without waiting to see if the renewed summons would be answered.

Then Conway yelled again, "Look out, Norman!"

Hermann swore in a whisper.

But now he had no choice. He had been given his orders. The man who came was to be taken. And certainly the man who had come, who must have heard Conway's second cry even if he had not heard the first, could not be allowed to escape and raise an alarm.

Incautiously Hermann stepped to the door.

His feet were scarcely clear of the threshold, outside on the landing, when a hand like a ham caught his throat from behind, over his shoulder, and another enormous hand gripped his gun-wrist like a vice. He was as helpless as a child.

The hand at his throat twisted his face round to the light. He saw a ponderous red face with sleepy eyes, connected by a pillar of neck with shoulders worthy of a buffalo.

"Come along," said Chief Inspector Claud Eustace Teal drowsily. "Come along back to where you sprang from, and open your heart to Uncle!"

10

HOW SIMON TEMPLAR DROVE TO BURES, AND TWO POLICEMEN JUMPED IN TIME

The road out of London on the north-east is one of the less pleasant ways of finding the open country. For one thing, it is infested with miles of tramway, crawling, interminable, blocking the traffic, maddening to the man at the wheel of a fast car—especially maddening to the man in a hurry at the wheel of a fast car.

Late as it was, there was enough traffic on the road to balk the Saint of clear runs of more than a few hundred yards at a time. And every time he was forced to apply the brakes, pause, and re-accelerate was pulling his average down.

There was a quicker route than the one he was taking, he knew. He had been taken over it once—a route that wound intricately through deserted side streets, occasionally crossing the more populous thoroughfares, and then hurriedly breaking away into the empty roads again. It was longer, but it was quicker to traverse. But the Saint had only been over it that once, and that by daylight; now, in the dark, he could not have trusted himself to find it again. The landmarks that a driver automatically picks out by day are of little use to him in the changed aspect of lamplight. And to get lost would be more maddening than the obstruction of traffic. To waste minutes, and perhaps miles, travelling in the wrong direction, to be muddled by the vague and contradictory directions of accosted pedestrians and police, to be plagued and pestered with the continual uncertainty—that would have driven him to the verge of delirium. The advantage that might be gained wasn't worth all that might be lost. He had decided as much when he swung into the car in Brook Street. And he kept to the main roads.

He smashed through the traffic grimly, seizing every opportunity that offered, creating other opportunities of his own in defiance of every law and principle and point of etiquette governing the use of His Majesty's highway, winning priceless seconds where and how he could.

Other drivers cursed him; two policemen called on him to stop, were ignored, and took his number; he scraped a wing in a desperate rush through a gap that no one else would ever have considered a gap at all; three times he missed death by a miracle while overtaking on a blind corner; and the pugnacious driver of a baby car who ventured to insist on his rightful share of the road went white as the Hirondel forced him on to the kerb to escape annihilation.

It was an incomparable exhibition of pure hogging, and it made everything of that kind that Roger Conway had been told to do earlier in the evening look like a child's game with a push-cart, but the Saint didn't care. He was on his way, and if the rest of the population objected to the manner of his going, they could do one of two things with their objections.

Some who saw the passage of the Saint that night will remember it to the end of their lives, for the Hirondel, as though recognising the hand of a master at its wheel, became almost a living thing. King of the Road its makers called it, but that night the Hirondel was more than a king: it was the incarnation and apotheosis of all cars. For the Saint drove with the devil at his shoulder, and the Hirondel took its mood from his. If this had been a superstitious age, those who saw it would have crossed themselves and sworn that it was no car at all they saw that night, but a snarling silver fiend that roared through London on the wings of an unearthly wind.

For half an hour . . . with the Saint's thumb restless on the button of the klaxon, and the strident voice of the silver fiend howling for avenue in a tone that brooked no contention . . . and then the houses thinned away and gave place to the first fields, and the Saint settled down to the job—coaxing, with hands as sure and gentle as any horseman's, the last possible ounce of effort out of the hundred horses under his control . . .

There was darkness on either side: the only light in the world lay along the tunnel which the powerful headlights slashed out of the stubborn blackness. From time to time, out of the dark, a great beast with eyes of fire leapt at him, clamouring, was slipped as a charging bull is slipped by a toreador, went by with a baffled grunt and a skimming slither of wind. And again and again, in the dark the Hirondel swooped up behind ridiculous, creeping glow-worms, sniffed at their red tails, snorted derisively, swept past with a deep-throated blare. No car in England could have held the lead of the Hirondel that night.

The drone of the great engine went on as a background of gigantic song; it sang in tune with the soft swish of the tyres and the rush of the cool night air, and the song it sang was: "Patricia Holm . . . Patricia . . . Patricia . . . Patricia Holm!"

And the Saint had no idea what he was going to do. Nor was he thinking about it. He knew nothing of the geography of the "house on the hill"—nothing of the lie of the surrounding land—nothing of the obstacles that might bar his way, nor of the resistance that would be offered to his attack. And so he was not jading himself with thinking of these things. They were beyond the reach of idle speculation. He had no clue: therefore it would have been a waste of time to speculate. He could only live for the moment, and the task of the moment—to hurl himself eastwards across England like a thunderbolt into the battle that lay ahead.

"Patricia! . . . Patricia! . . ."

Softly the Saint took up the song, but his own voice could not be heard for the voice of the Hirondel. The song of the car bayed over wide spaces of country, was bruised and battered between the walls of startled village streets, was flung back in rolling echoes from the walls of hills.

That he was going to an almost blindfold assault took nothing from his rapture. Rather, he savoured the adventure the more, for this was the fashion of forlorn sally that his heart cried for—the end of inaction, the end of perplexity and helplessness, the end of a damnation of doubt and dithering. And in the Saint's heart was a shout of rejoicing, because at last the God of all good battles and desperate endeavour had remembered him again.

No, it wasn't selfish. It wasn't a mere lust for adventure that cared nothing for the peril of those who made the adventure worth while. It was the irresistible resurgence of the most fundamental of all the inspirations of man. A wild stirring in its ancient sleep of the spirit that sent the knights of Arthur out upon their quests, of Tristan crying for Isolde, of the flame in a man's heart that brought fire and sword upon Troy, of Roland's shout and the singing blade of Durendal amid the carnage of Roncesvalles. "The sound of the trumpet . . ."

Thus the miles were eaten up, until more than half the journey must have been set behind him.

If only there was no engine failure . . . He had no fear for fuel and oil, for he had filled up on the way back from Maidenhead.

Simon touched a switch, and all the instruments on the dashboard before him were illuminated from behind with a queer ghostly luminance. His eye flickered from the road and found one of them.

Seventy-two.

Seventy-four.

Seventy-five . . . six . . .

"Patricia! . . ."

"Battle, murder, and sudden death . . ."

"You know, Pat, we don't have a chance these days. There's no chance for magnificent loving. A man ought to fight for his lady. Preferably with dragons . . ."

Seventy-eight.

Seventy-nine.

A corner loomed out of the dark, flung itself at him, menacing, murderous. The tyres, curbed with a cruel hand, tore at the road, shrieking. The car swung round the corner, on its haunches, as it were . . . gathered itself, and found its stride again . . .

Ping!

Something like the crisp twang of the snapping of an overstrained wire. The Saint, looking straight ahead, blinking, saw that the windscreen in front of him had given birth to a star—a star of long slender points radiating from a neat round hole drilled through the glass. And a half-smile came to his lips.

Ping!

Bang!

Bong!

The first sound repeated; then, in quick succession, two other sounds, sharp and high, like the smack of two pieces of metal. In front of him they were. In the gleaming aluminium bonnet.

"Smoke!" breathed the Saint. "This is a wild party!"

He hadn't time to adjust himself to the interruption, to parse and analyse it and extract its philosophy. How he came to be under fire at that stage of the journey—that could wait. Something had gone wrong. Someone had blundered. Roger must have been tricked, and Marius must have escaped—or something. But, meanwhile . . .

Fortunately the first shot had made him slow up. Otherwise he would have been killed.

The next sound he heard was neither the impact of a bullet nor the thin, distant rattle of the rifle that fired it. It was loud and close and explosive, under his feet it seemed, and the steering wheel was wrenched out of his hand—nearly.

He never knew how he kept his grip on it. An instinct swifter than thought must have made him tighten his hold at the sound of that explosion, and he was driving with both hands on the wheel. He tore the wheel round in the way it did not want to go, bracing his feet on clutch and brake pedals, calling up the last reserve of every sinew in his splendid body.

Death, sudden as anything he could have asked, stared him in the face. The strain was terrific. The Hirondel had ceased to be his creature. It was mad, runaway, the bit between its tremendous teeth, caracoling towards a demoniac plunge to destruction. No normal human power should have been able to hold it. The Saint, strong as he was, could never have done it—normally. He must have found some supernatural strength.

Somehow he kept the car out of the ditch for as long as it took to bring it to a standstill.

Then, almost without thinking, he switched out the lights.

Dimly he wondered why, under that fearful gruelling, the front axle hadn't snapped like a dry stick, or why the steering hadn't come to pieces under his hands.

"If I come out of this alive," thought the Saint, "the Hirondel Motor Company will get an unsolicited testimonial from me."

But that thought merely crossed his mind like a swallow skimming a quiet pool—and was lost. Then, in the same dim way, he was wondering why he hadn't brought a gun. Now he was likely to pay for the reckless haste with which he had set out. His little knife was all very well—he could use it as accurately as any man could use a gun, and as swiftly—but it was only good for one shot. He'd never been able to train it to function as a boomerang.

It was unlikely that he was being sniped by one man alone. And that one solitary knife, however expertly he used it, would be no use at all against a number of armed men besieging him in a lamed car.

"Obviously, therefore," thought Simon, "get out of the car."

And he was out of it instantly, crouching in the ditch beside it. In the open, and the darkness, he would have a better chance.

He wasn't thinking for a moment of a getaway. That would have been fairly easy. But the Hirondel was the only car he had on him, and it had to be saved—or else he had to throw in his hand. Joke. The obvious object of the ambuscade was to make him do just that—to stop him, anyhow—and he wasn't being stopped . . .

Now, with the switching off of the lights the darkness had become less dark, and the road ran through it, beside the black bulk of the flanking trees, like a ribbon of dull steel. And, looking back, the Saint could see shadows that moved. He counted four of them.

He went to meet them, creeping like a snake in the dry ditch. They were separated. Avoiding the dull gleam of that strip of road, as if afraid that a shot from the car in front might greet their approach, they slunk along in the gloom at the sides of the road, two on one side and two on the other.

It was no time for soft fighting. There was that punctured front wheel to be changed, and those four men in the way. So the four men

THE SAINT CLOSES THE CASE

had to be eliminated—as quickly and definitely as possible. The Saint was having no fooling about.

The leader of the two men on Simon's side of the road almost stepped on the dark figure that seemed to rise suddenly out of the ground in front of him. He stopped and tried to draw back so that he could use the rifle he carried, and his companion trod on his heels and cursed.

Then the first man screamed, and the scream died in a choking gurgle.

The man behind him saw his leader sink to the ground, but there was another man beyond his leader—a man who had not been there before, who laughed with a soft whisper of desperate merriment. The second man tried to raise the automatic he carried, but two steely hands grasped his wrists, and he felt himself flying helplessly through the air. He seemed to fly a long way—and then he slept.

The Saint crossed the road.

A gun spoke from the hand of one of the two men on the other side, who had paused, irresolute, at the sound of the first scream. But the Saint was lost again in the shadows.

They crouched down, waiting, watching, intent for his next move. But they were looking down along the ditch and the grass beside the road, where the Saint had vanished like a ghost, but the Saint was above them then, crouched like a leopard under the hedge at the top of the embankment beside them, gathering himself stealthily.

He dropped on them out of the sky, and the heels of both his shoes impacted upon the back of the neck of one of them with all the Saint's hurtling weight behind, so that the man lay very still where he was and did not stir again.

The other man, rising and bringing up his rifle, saw a spinning sliver of bright steel whisking towards him like a flying fish over a dark sea, and struck to guard. By a miracle he succeeded, and the knife glanced from his gun-barrel and tinkled away over the road.

Then he fought with the Saint for the rifle.

He was probably the strongest of the four, and he did not know fear, but there is a trick by which a man who knows it can always take a rifle or a stick from a man who does not know it, and the Saint had known that trick from his childhood. He made the man drop the rifle, but he had no chance to pick it up for himself, for the man was on him again in a moment. Simon could only kick the gun away into the ditch, where it was lost.

An even break, then.

They fought hand to hand, two men on that dark road, lion and leopard.

This man had the advantage of strength and weight, but the Saint had the speed and fighting savagery. No man who was not a Colossus, or mad, would have attempted to stand in the Saint's way that night: but this man, who may have been something of both, attempted it. He fought like a beast. But Simon Templar was berserk. The man was not only standing in the way: he was the servant and the symbol of all the powers that the Saint hated. He stood for Marius, and the men behind Marius, and all the conspiracy that the Saint had sworn to break, and that had caused it to come to pass that at that moment the Saint should have been riding recklessly to the rescue of his lady. Therefore the man had to go, as his three companions had already gone. And perhaps the man recognised his doom, for he let out one sobbing cry before the Saint's fingers found an unshakable grip on his throat.

It was to the death. Simon had no choice, even if he would have taken it, for the man fought to the end, and even when unconsciousness stilled his struggles Simon dared not let him go, for he might be only playing 'possum, and the Saint could not afford to take any chances. There was only one way to make sure . . .

So presently the Saint rose slowly to his feet, breathing deeply like a man who has been under water for a long time, and went to find Anna. And no one else moved on the road.

As an afterthought, he commandeered a loaded automatic from one of the men who had no further use for it.

Then he went to change the wheel.

It should only have taken him five minutes, but he could not have foreseen that the spare tyre would settle down to a futile flatness as he slipped the jack from under the dumb-iron and lowered the wheel to the road.

There was only the one spare.

It was a very slight consolation to remember that Norman Kent, the ever-thoughtful, always carried an outfit of tools about twice as efficient as anything the ordinary motorist thinks necessary. And the wherewithal to mend punctures was included.

Even so, with only the spotlight to work by, and no bucket of water with which to find the site of the puncture, it would not be an easy job.

Simon stripped off his coat with a groan.

It was more than half an hour before the Hirondel was ready to take the road again. Nearly three-quarters of an hour wasted altogether. Precious minutes squandered, that he had gambled life and limb to win . . .

But it seemed like forty-five years, instead of forty-five minutes, before he was able to light a cigarette and climb back into the driver's seat.

He started the engine and moved his hand to switch on the headlights, but even as his hand touched the switch the road about him was flooded by lights that were not his.

As he engaged the gears, he looked back over his shoulder, and saw that the car behind was not overtaking. It had stopped.

Breathless with the reaction from the first foretaste of battle, he was not expecting another attack so soon. As he moved off, he was for an instant more surprised than hurt by the feel of something stabbing through his left shoulder like a hot spear-point. Then he understood, and turned in his seat with the borrowed automatic in his hand.

He was not, as he had admitted, the greatest pistol shot in the world, but on that night some divine genius guided his hand. Coolly he sighted, as if he had been practising on a range, and shot out both the headlights of the car behind. Then, undazzled, he could see to puncture one of its front wheels before he swept round the next corner with a veritable storm of pursuing bullets humming about his ears and multiplying the stars in the windscreen.

He was not hit again. The same power must have guarded him as with a shield.

As he straightened the car up he felt his injured shoulder tenderly. As far as he could discover, no bone had been touched: it was simply a flesh wound through the trapezius muscle, not in itself fatally disabling, but liable to numb the arm and weaken him from loss of blood. He folded his handkerchief into a pad, and thrust it under his shirt to cover the wound.

It was all he could do whilst driving along, and he could not stop to examine the wound more carefully or improvise a better dressing. In ten minutes, at most, the chase would be resumed. Unless the pursuers were as unlucky with their spare as he had been. And that was too much to bank on.

But how had that car come upon the scene? Had it been waiting up a side turning in support of the four men, and had it started on the warning of the first man's scream or the fourth man's cry? Impossible. He had been delayed too long with the mending of the puncture. The car would have arrived long before he had finished. Or had it been on its way to lay another ambush farther along the road, in case the first one failed?

Simon turned the questions in his mind as a man might flick over the pages of a book he already knew by heart, and passed over them all, seeking another page more easily read.

None was right. He recognised each of them, grimly, as a subconscious attempt to evade the facing of the unpleasant truth, and grimly he choked them down. The solution he had found when that first shot pinged through the windscreen still fitted in. If Marius had somehow escaped, or been rescued, or contrived somehow to convey a warning to his gang, the obvious thing to do would be to get in touch with agents along the road. And warn the men in the house on the hill itself, at Bures. Then Marius would follow in person. Yes, it must have been Marius . . .

Then the Saint remembered that the fat man and the lean man had not been tied up when he left Roger. And Roger Conway, incomparable lieutenant as he was, was a mere tyro at this game without the hand of his chief to guide him.

"Poor old Roger," thought the Saint, and it was typical of him that he thought only of Roger in that spirit.

And he drove on.

He drove with death in his heart and murder in the clear, cold blue eyes that followed the road like twin hawks swerving in the wake of their prey. And a mere wraith of the Saintly smile rested unawares on his lips.

For, figured out that way, it meant that he was on a foredoomed errand.

The thought gave him no pause.

Rather, he drove on faster, with the throbbing of his wounded shoulder submerged and lost beneath the more savage and positive throbbing of every pulse in his body.

Under the relentless pressure of his foot on the accelerator, the figures on the speedometer cylinder, trembling past the hairline in the little window where they were visible, showed crazier and crazier speeds.

Seventy-eight.

Seventy-nine.

Eighty.

Eighty-one . . . two . . . three . . . four . . . Eighty-five.

"Not good enough for a race-track," thought the Saint, "but on an ordinary road—and at night . . ."

The wind of the Hirondel's torrential passage buffeted him with almost animal blows, bellowing in his ears above the thunderous fanfare of the exhaust.

For a nerve-shattering minute he held the car at ninety.

"Patricia! . . ."

And he seemed to hear her voice calling him: "Simon!"

"Oh, my darling, my darling, I'm on my way!" cried the Saint, as if she could have heard him.

As he clamoured through Braintree, with thirteen miles still to go by the last signpost, two policemen stepped out from the side of the road and barred his way.

Their intention was plain, though he had no idea why they should wish to stop him. Surely his mere defiance of a London constable's order to stop would not have merited such a drastic and far-flung effort to bring him promptly to book? Or had Marius, to make the assurance of his ambushes doubly sure, informed Scotland Yard against him with some ingenious and convincing story about his activities as the Saint? But how could Marius have known of those? And Teal, he was certain, couldn't . . . Or had Teal traced him from the Furillac more quickly than he had expected? And, if so, how could Teal have known that the Saint was on that road?

Whatever the answers to those questions might be, the Saint was not stopping for anyone on earth that night. He set his teeth, and kept his foot flat down on the accelerator.

The two policemen must have divined the ruthlessness of his defiance, for they jumped to safety in the nick of time.

And then the Saint was gone again, breaking out in the open country with a challenging blast of klaxon and a snarling stammer of unsilenced exhaust, blazing through the night like the shouting vanguard of a charge of forgotten valiants.

11

HOW ROGER CONWAY TOLD THE TRUTH, AND INSPECTOR TEAL BELIEVED A LIE

Inspector Teal set Hermann down in the sitting-room, and adroitly snapped a pair of handcuffs on his wrists. Then he turned his slumbrous eyes on Roger.

"Hullo, Unconscious!" he sighed.

"Not quite," retorted Roger shortly. "But darn near it. I got a good crack on the head giving you that shout."

Teal shook his head. He was perpetually tired, and even that slight movement seemed to cost him a gargantuan effort.

"Not me," he said heavily. "My name isn't Norman. What are you doing there?"

"Pretending to he a sea-lion," said Roger sarcastically. "It's a jolly game. Wouldn't you like to join in? Hermann will throw us the fish to catch in our mouths."

Mr Teal sighed again, slumbrously.

"What's your name?" he demanded.

Roger did not answer for a few seconds.

In that time he had to make a decision that might alter the course of the Saint's whole life, and Roger's own with it—if not the course of all European history. It was a tough decision to take.

Should he give his name as Simon Templar? That was the desperate question that leapt into his head immediately . . . It so happened that he never carried much in his pockets, and so far as he could remember there was nothing in his wallet that would give him away when he was searched. The fraud would certainly be discovered before very long, but he might be able to bluff it out for twenty-four hours. And in all that time the Saint would be free—free to save Pat, return to Maidenhead, deal with Vargan, complete the mission to which he had pledged himself.

To the possible, and even probable, consequences to himself of such a course, Roger never gave a thought. The sacrifice would be a small one compared with what it might achieve.

"I am Simon Templar," said Roger. "I believe you're looking for me."

Hermann's eyes widened.

"It is a lie!" he burst out. "He is not Templar!"

Teal turned his somnambulistic gaze upon the man.

"Who asked you to speak?" he demanded.

"Don't take any notice of him," said Roger. "He doesn't know anything about it. I'm Templar, all right. And I'll go quietly."

"But he is not Templar!" persisted Hermann excitedly. "Templar has been gone an hour! That man . . ."

"You shut your disgusting mouth!" snarled Roger. "And if you don't, I'll shut it for you. You . . ."

Teal blinked.

"Somebody's telling a naughty fib," he remarked sapiently. "Now will you both shut up a minute?"

He locomoted fatly across the room, and stooped over Roger. But he based his decision on the tailor's tab inside Roger's coat pocket, and Roger had not thought of that.

"I'm afraid you're the story-teller, whoever you are," he sighed.

"That's my real name," said Roger bitterly. "Conway—Roger Conway."

"It sounds more likely."

"Though what that fatherless streak of misery . . ."

"A squeal," explained Teal patiently. "A time-honoured device among crooks to get off lightly themselves by helping the police to jump more heavily on their pals. I suppose he is your pal?" added the detective sardonically. "You seem to know each other's names."

Roger was silent.

So that was that. Very quickly settled. And what next?

Hermann, then, had patently decided to squeal. Which seemed odd, considering the type of man he had made Hermann out to be. But . . .

Roger looked at the man, and suddenly saw the truth. It wasn't a squeal. The protest had been thoughtless, instinctive, made in a momentary access of panic lest his master should be proved to have made a mistake. Even at that moment Hermann was regretting it, and racking his brains for a lie to cover it up. Racking his brains, also, for his own defence . . .

The situation remained just about as complicated as it had been before the incident. Now Hermann would be racking his brains for lies, and Conway would be racking his brains for lies, and both of them would have the single purpose of covering their leaders at all costs, and they'd both inevitably be contradicting each other right and left, and both inevitably ploughing deeper and deeper into the mire. And neither of them could tell the truth.

But could neither of them tell the truth?

The idea shattered the groping darkness of Roger's dilemma like the sudden kindling of a battery of Klieg arcs. The boldness of it took his breath away.

Could neither of them tell the truth?

As Roger would have prayed for the guidance of his leader at that moment, his leader was there to help him.

Wasn't the dilemma the same in principle as the one which the Saint had solved an hour ago? The same deadlock, the same cross-purpose, the same cataleptic standstill? The same old story of the irresistible force and the immovable object? . . . And the Saint had solved it. By sweeping the board clear with the one wild move that wasn't allowed for in the rules.

Mightn't it work again—at least, to clear the air—and, in the resultant reshuffling, perhaps disclose a loophole that had not been there before—if Roger did much the same thing—did the one thing that he couldn't possibly do—and told the truth? The truth should convince Teal. Roger could tell the truth so much more convincingly and circumstantially than he could tell a lie, and it would be so easy to substantiate. Even Hermann would find it hard to discredit. And . . .

"Anyway," said Teal, "I'll be taking you boys along to the Yard, and we can talk there."

And the departure to the Yard might be postponed. The truth might be made sufficiently interesting to keep Teal in Brook Street. And then Norman Kent might arrive—and Norman was a much more accomplished conspirator than Roger . . .

"Before we go," said Roger, "there's something you might like to hear."

Teal raised his eyebrows one millimetre. "What is it?" he asked. "Going to tell me you're the King of the Cannibal Islands?"

Roger shook his head. How easy it was! Teal might have been the one man in the CID who would have fallen for it, but he at least was a certainty. Such a lethargic man could not by any stretch of imagination be in a hurry over anything—least of all over the prosaic task of taking his prisoners away to the station.

"I'll do a squeal of my own," said Roger. Teal nodded.

As if he had nothing to do for the rest of the night, he settled himself in a chair and took a packet of chewing-gum from his pocket.

With his jaws moving rhythmically, he prompted, "Well?"

"If it's all the same to you," said Roger, to waste time, "I'd like to sit in a chair. This floor isn't as soft as it might be. And if I could smoke a cigarette . . ."

Teal rose again and lifted him into an armchair; provided him also with a cigarette. Then the detective resumed his own seat with mountainous patience.

He made no objection to the delay on the grounds that there were men waiting for him outside the building. Which meant, almost certainly, that there weren't. Roger recalled that Teal had the reputation of playing a lone hand. It was a symptom of the man's languid confidence in his own experienced ability—a confidence, to give him his due, that had its justification in his record. But in this case . . .

"I'm telling you the truth this time," said Roger. "We're in the cart—Simon Templar included—thanks to some pals of Hermann there—only Templar doesn't know it. I don't want him to be pinched, but if you don't pinch him quickly something worse is going to happen to him. You see, we've got Vargan. But we weren't the first raiders. They were Hermann's pals . . ."

"Another lie!" interposed Hermann venomously. "Do you have to waste any more time with him, Inspector? You have already caught him in one lie . . ."

"And caught you sneaking about with a gun," snapped Roger. "What about that? And why the hell am I tied up here? Go on—tell him you're a private detective, and you were just going out to fetch a policeman and give me in charge!"

Teal closed his eyes.

"I can't listen to two people at once," he said. "Which of you is supposed to be telling this story?"

"I am," said Roger.

"You sound more interesting," admitted Teal, "even if Hermann does prove it to be a fairy-tale afterwards. Go on, Conway. Hermann—you wait for your turn, and don't butt in again."

Hermann relapsed into a sullen silence, and Roger inhaled deeply from his cigarette and blew out with the smoke a brief prayer of thanksgiving.

"We went down to Esher to take Vargan," he said. "But when we got there, we found Vargan was already being taken. He seemed very popular all round, that night. However, we were the party that won the raffle and got him away."

"Where did you take him?"

"You follow your own advice, and don't butt in," said Roger shortly. "I'll tell this story in my own way, or not at all."

"Go on, then."

"We took Vargan—somewhere out of London. Then Templar and I came back here to collect a few things . . . How did you find this place, by the way?"

"I went to Brighton, and found your motor agent," said Teal comfortably. "All motor agents spend Sunday in Brighton and the most expensive cars out of their showrooms. That was easy."

Roger nodded.

He went on, slowly, with one eye on the clock:

"Hermann's pals knew we were interested in Vargan before the fun started. Never mind how—that's another story . . . No, it isn't—now I come to think of it. You remember the first stunt at Esher?"

"I do."

"Two people escaped past Hume Smith's chauffeur—a man and a woman. They were Templar and a friend of his. They'd stumbled on the place by accident. They were driving past, and they saw a light and went to investigate. The alarm that scared them off was the second man—the giant whose footprints you found. I'll tell you his name, because he's the leader of Hermann's gang . . ."

Hermann cut in: "Inspector, this will be another lie!"

Teal lifted one eyelid.

"How do you know?" he inquired mildly.

"He knows I'm telling the truth!" cried Roger triumphantly. "He's given himself away. Now I'll tell you—the man's name was Dr Rayt Marius. And if you don't believe me, get hold of one of his shoes and see how it matches the plaster casts you've got of the footprints!"

Both Mr Teal's chins were sunk on his chest. He might have been asleep. His voice sounded as if he was.

"And these people traced you here?"

"They did," said Roger. "And on the way they got hold of the girl who was with Templar that first night—the girl he's in love with—and Marius came to say that he would exchange her with Templar for Vargan. But Templar wasn't swopping. He wanted 'em both. We were able to find out where the girl was being taken, and Templar went off to rescue her. I was left to guard the prisoners—Marius and Hermann and another man called Otto. They tricked me and got away—Marius and Otto—and Hermann was left to guard me. I was to be an additional hostage against Templar. Marius and Otto went off in pursuit—they'd already arranged for an ambush to stop Templar on the road. Marius did that by telephone from here—you can ring up the exchange and verify that, if you don't believe me. And Templar doesn't know what he's in for. He thinks he'll take the men in the house on the hill off their guard. And he's gone blinding off to certain death . . ."

"Half a minute," said Teal. "What house on the hill is this you're talking about?"

The tone of the question indicated that the authentic ring of truth in the story had not been lost on Teal's ears, and Roger drew a deep breath.

Now—what? He'd told as much as he meant to tell—and that was a long and interesting preface of no real importance. Now how much could he afford to add to it? How great was the Saint's danger?

Roger knew the Saint's fighting qualities. Would those qualities be great enough to pull off a victory against all the odds? And would the arrival of the police just after the victory serve for nothing but to give the Saint another battle to fight? . . . Or was the Saint likely to be really up against it? Might it be a kind of treachery to spill the rest of the beans—if only to save Pat? How could a man weigh a girl's safety against the peace of the world? For, even if the betrayal meant the sacrifice of the Saint and himself, it would leave Vargan with Norman Kent. And in case of accidents, Norman had definite instructions . . .

But where was Norman?

Roger looked into the small bright eyes of Chief Inspector Teal. Then he looked away, to meet the glittering, veiled eyes of Hermann. And, in the shifting of his gaze, he managed to steal another glimpse of the clock—without letting Teal see that he did so.

"What house on what hill?" demanded Teal again.

"Does that matter?" temporised Roger desperately.

"Just a little," said Teal, with frightful self-restraint. "If you don't tell me where Templar's gone, how am I going to rescue him from this trap you say he's going into?"

Roger bent his head.

Unless Norman Kent came quickly now, and outwitted Teal, so that Roger and Norman could go together to the relief of the Saint, there would be nothing for it but to tell some more of the truth. It would be the only way to save the Saint—whatever that salvation might cost. Roger saw that now.

"Get through on the phone to the police at Braintree first," he said. "Templar will pass through there. Driving an open Hirondel. I'll go on when you've done that. There's no time to lose . . ."

All at once, Teal's weary eyes had become very wide awake. He was studying Roger's face unblinkingly.

"That story's the truth?"

"On my word of honour!"

Teal nodded very deliberately.

"I believe you," he said, and went to the telephone with surprising speed.

Roger flicked his cigarette end into the fireplace, and sat with his eyes on the carpet and his brain reeling to encompass the tumult unleashed within it.

If Norman was coming, he should have arrived by then. So Norman had decided not to come. And that was that.

The detective's voice came to Roger through a dull haze of despair.

"An open Hirondel . . . probably driving hell-for-leather . . . Stop every car that comes through tonight, anyway . . . Yes, better be armed . . . When you've got him, put a guard in the car and send him back to London—New Scotland Yard—at once . . . Ring me up and tell me when he's on his way . . ."

Then the receiver went back on its hook.

"Well, Conway—what about this house?"

Something choked Roger's throat for a moment.

Then—

"We only know it as 'the house on the hill.' That was what it was called in the letter we found on Marius. But it's at . . ."

Zzzzzing . . . zzzzzing!

Teal looked at the door. Then he turned sharply.

"Do you know who that is?"

"I haven't the faintest idea."

Zzzzzzzzzing!

Again the strident summons, and Roger's heart leapt crazily. He never knew how he kept the mask of puzzlement on his face, but he knew that he did it: the fading suspicion in Teal's stare told him that. And he had put everything he knew into his lie. "I haven't the faintest idea . . ."

But he knew that it could only be one man out of all the world. Hermann also knew.

But Roger gave no sign, and never looked at the man. It remained a gamble. With Roger telling the truth—and intending, for all Hermann knew, to go on telling the truth—the man was in a quandary. The story that Roger was building up against himself was also giving Hermann a lot to answer . . . Would Hermann be wise and swift enough to see that he would have a better chance with his unofficial enemies than with the police? . . .

Hermann never spoke.

Then Teal went out into the hall, and Roger could have cried his relief aloud.

But he could not cry out—not even to warn Norman. That would be no use against Teal, as it would have been of use against Hermann. Norman had got to walk into the snare—and might all the

Saint's strange gods inspire him as they would have inspired the Saint himself . . .

Teal opened the front door. And he kept his right hand in his coat pocket.

Norman hesitated only the fraction of a second.

Afterwards, Norman said that the words came to his lips without any conscious thought, as if a guardian angel had put them unbidden into his mouth.

"Are you Mr Templar?" asked Norman Kent.

And, as he heard the words that he had not known he was going to speak, he stood appalled at the colossal simplicity and colossal daring of the ruse.

"No, I'm not," said Teal curtly.

"Is Mr Templar in?"

"Not at the moment."

"Well, is there anything you could do? I've never met Mr Templar, but I've just had an extraordinary message, and I thought, before I went to the police . . ."

The word pricked Teal's ears.

"Maybe I can do something for you," he said, more cordially. "Will you come in?"

"Certainly," said Norman.

Teal stood aside to let him pass, and turned to fasten the door again.

Hanging on the walls of the hall were a number of curious weapons, relics of the Saint's young lifetime of wandering in queer corners of the globe. There were Spanish knives and a matador's sword, muskets and old-fashioned pistols, South Sea Island spears, Malay krises and karambits and parangs, a scimitar, a boomerang from New Zealand, an Iroquois bow, an assegai, a bamboo blow-pipe from Papua, and other things of the same kind.

Norman Kent's eye fell on a knobkerrie. It hung very conveniently to his hand.

He took it down.

12

HOW SIMON TEMPLAR PARTED
WITH ANNA, AND TOOK PATRICIA
IN HIS ARMS

To attempt to locate, in a strange part of the country and on a dark night, a house distinguished by nothing but the fact of being situated on "the" hill—particularly in a district where hills are no more than slight undulations—might well have been considered a hopeless task even by the most optimistic man. As he began to judge himself near the village, the Saint realised that.

But even before he could feel despair, if he would have felt despair, his hurtling headlights picked up the figure of a belated rustic plodding down the road ahead. The Saint, no stranger to country life, and familiar with its habit of retiring to bed as soon as the village pub had ejected it at ten o'clock, knew that this gift could only have been an angel in corduroys, sent direct from Heaven. The Saint's gods were surely with him that night.

"Do you know the house on the hill?" demanded Simon brazenly.

"Ay, that Oi do!"

Then the Saint understood that in the English country districts all things are possible, and the natives may easily consider "the house on the hill" a full and sufficient address, just as a townsman may be satisfied with "the pub round the corner."

"Throo the village, tourrn round boi the church, an' keep straight as ever you can goo for 'arf a moile. You can't miss ut." So the hayseed declared, and the Saint sped on. But he ran the car into a side turning near the crest of the hill, parked it with lights out, and continued on foot. He might be expected, but he wasn't advertising his arrival unnecessarily.

He had been prepared to break into and shoot up every single house in the district to which the description "on the hill" might possibly have applied, until he came to the right one. But he had been saved that, and it remained to capitalise the godsend.

The gun in his pocket bumped his hip as he walked, and in the little sheath on his forearm he could feel the slight but reassuring weight of Anna, queen of knives, earned with blood and christened with blood. She was no halfling's toy. In blood she came, and in blood that night she was to go.

But this the Saint could not know, whatever presentiments he may have had, as he stealthily skirted the impenetrable blackthorn hedge that walled in the grounds of the house he had come to raid. The hedge came higher than his head, and impenetrable it was, except for the one gap where the gate was set, as he learned by making a complete circuit. But, standing back, he could see the upper part of the house looming over it, a black bulk against the dark sky, and in the upper story a single window was lighted up. He could see nothing of the ground floor from behind the hedge, so that he had no way of knowing what there might be on three sides of it, but in the front he could see at least one room alight. Standing still, listening with all the keyed acuteness of his ears, he could pick up no sound from the house.

Then that lighted upper window gave him an idea.

On the face of it, one single lighted upper window could only mean one thing—unless it were a trap. But if it were a trap, it was such a subtle one that the Saint couldn't see it.

What he did see, with a crushing force of logic, was that the garrison of a fortified house, expecting an attempt to rescue their prisoner, would be likely to put her as far away from the attacker's reach as possible. Prisoners are usually treated like that, almost instinctively, being ordinarily confined in attics or cellars even when no attempt at rescue is expected. And a country house of that type would be unlikely to have a cellar large enough to confine a prisoner, whose value would drop to zero if asphyxiated. Patricia could surely be in but one place— and that lighted window seemed to indicate it as plainly as if the fact had been labelled on the walls outside in two-foot Mazda letters.

The Saint could not know that this was the simple truth—that the same fortune that had watched over him all through the adventure had engineered that breakdown on the long-distance wire to prevent Marius communicating with the house on the hill. But he guessed and accepted it (except for the breakdown) with a force of conviction that nothing could have strengthened. And he knew, quite definitely, without any recourse to deduction or guesswork, that Marius by that time must be less than ten minutes behind him. His purpose must be achieved quickly if it were to be achieved at all.

For a moment the Saint hesitated, standing in a field on the wrong side of the blackthorn hedge. Then he bent and searched the ground for some small stones. He wanted very small stones, for they must not make too much noise. He found three that satisfied his requirements.

Then he wrote, by the light of a match cupped cautiously in one hand, on a scrap of paper he found in his pocket:

*I'm here, Pat darling. Throw Anna back over the hedge and
then start a disturbance to divide their attention. I'll be
right in.—Simon.*

He tied the scrap to the handle of Anna with a strip of silk ripped
from his shirt, and straightened up.

Gently and accurately he lobbed up two stones, and heard each of
them tap the lighted pane. Then he waited.

Now, if there were no response—suppose Pat had been tied up,
or was doped, or anything like that . . . The thought made his muscles
tighten up so that he felt them quivering all over his body like a mass
of braced steel hawsers . . . He'd have to wade in without the help of
the distracting disturbance, of course . . . But that wasn't the thought
that made his pulse beat quicker and his mouth narrow down into a
line that hardly smiled at all. It was the thought of Patricia herself—
the thought of all that might have happened to her, that might be
happening . . .

"By God!" thought the Saint, with an ache in his heart, "if any of
their filthy hands . . ."

But he wanted to see her once more before he went into the fight
that he was sure was jeopardised against him. In case of accidents. Just
to see her blessed face once more, to take the memory of it as a banner
with him into the battle . . .

Then he held his breath.

Slowly the sash of the window was being raised, with infinite
precautions against noise. And the Saint saw, at the same time, that
what he had taken, in silhouette, to be leaded panes, were, in fact, the
shadows of the network of closely set bars.

Then he saw her.

She looked out, down into the garden below, and along the side of the house, puzzledly. He saw the faltered parting of the red lips, the discorded gold of her hair, the brave light in the blue eyes . . .

Then he balanced Anna in his hand and sent her flickering through the dark. The knife fell point home, quivering in the wooden sill beside the girl's hand.

He saw Patricia start, and stare at it with wild surmise. Then she snatched it out of the wood and disappeared into the room.

Half a minute ticked away whilst the Saint waited with a tingling impatience, fearing at any moment to hear a car, which could only belong to one man, come purring up the hill. But, fearfully as he strained his ears, he found the stillness of the night unbroken.

And at last he saw the girl again. Saw her hand come through the bars, and watched Anna swooping back towards him like a scrap stripped from a moonbeam . . .

He found the little knife, after some difficulty, in a clump of long grass. His slip of paper was still tied to the handle, but when he unrolled it he found fresh words pencilled on the other side.

Eight men here. God bless you, darling.—Pat.

The Saint stuffed the paper into his pocket and slid Anna back into her sheath.

"God bless us both, Pat, you wonderful, wonderful child!" he whispered to the stillness of the night, and, looking up again, he saw her still at the window, straining her eyes to find him.

He waved his handkerchief for her to see, and she waved back. Then the window closed again. But she had smiled. He had seen her. And the ache in his heart became a song . . .

He was wasting no more time looking for a way through the hedge. His first survey had already shown that it was planted and trained as an effective palisade. But there was always the gate.

On the road. A perfectly ordinary gate.

That, of course, was the way they would expect him to come.

Pity to disappoint them!

He hardly spared the gate a glance. It was probably electrified. It was almost certainly wired with alarms. And it was covered by a rifleman somewhere, for a fiver. But it remained the only visible way in.

The Saint took a short run and leapt it cleanly.

Beyond was the gravel of the drive, but he only touched that with one foot. As he landed on that one foot, he squirmed aside and leapt again—to the silent footing of the lawn and the covering shadow of a convenient shrub. He stooped there, thumbing back the safety-catch of the automatic he had drawn, and wondering why no one had fired at him.

Then wondering went by the board, for he heard, through the silence, faintly, very far off, but unmistakable, the rising and falling drone of a powerful car. And he had barely attuned his bearing to that sound when another sound slashed through it like a sabre-cut—the scream of a girl in terror . . .

He knew it wasn't the real thing. Hadn't he directed it himself? Didn't he know that Patricia Holm wasn't the kind that screamed? Of course . . . But that made no difference to the effect that the sound had upon him. It struck deep-rooted chords of fierce protectiveness, violently reminding him that the cause for the scream might still be there, even if Pat would never have released it without his prompting. It froze something in him as a drench of icy water might have done, and, again as a drench of icy water might have done, it braced and stung and savaged something else into a fury of reaction, something primitive and homicidal and ruthless, something out of an age that had nothing to do with such clothes as he wore, or such weapons as he carried, or such a fortress as lay before his storming.

The Saint went mad.

There was neither sanity nor laughter in the way he covered the stretch of lawn that separated him from the house and the lighted ground-floor window which he had marked down as his objective directly he had cleared the gate. He was even unable to feel astonished that no shots spat at him out of the darkness, or to feel that the silence might forebode a trap. For Simon Templar had seen red.

Eight men, Patricia's note had told him, were waiting to oppose his entrance . . . Well, let 'em all come. The more the bloodier . . .

He who had always been the laughing cavalier, the man who would always exchange a joke as he exchanged a blow, who never fought but he smiled, nor greeted peril without a song in his heart, was certainly not laughing at all.

He went through that window as surely no man ever went through a window before, except in a film studio. He went through it in one flying leap, with his right shoulder braced to smash through the flimsy obstacle of the glass, and his left arm raised to shield his face from the splinters.

That mad rush took him into the room without a pause, to land on the floor inside with a jolt, stumbling for an instant, which gave the six men who were playing cards around the table time to scramble to their feet.

Six of them—meaning that the other two were probably dealing with the scream. It ought to have been possible to distract more of their attention than that, but since it had so fallen out . . .

And where, anyway, were the defences that he should have to break through? As far as that window, he had had an easy course to cover. And these men had none of the air of men prepared to be attacked.

These thoughts flashed through the Saint's mind in the split second it took him to recover his balance, and then he was concerned with further questions.

The gun was already in his hand, and two who were swift to draw against him were not swift enough and died in their tracks before the captured automatic jammed and gave the other four their chance.

Never before had the Saint attacked with such a fire of murderous hatred, for the cry from the upper room had not been repeated, and that could only mean that it had been forcibly stifled, somehow. And the thought of Patricia fighting her fight alone upstairs, as she would have to go on fighting alone unless Simon Templar won his own fight against all the odds . . . The first hint of a smile came to his lips when the first man fell, and when the gun froze useless in his hand, he looked at it and heard someone laugh, and recognised the voice as his own.

Then Anna flicked from her sheath and whistled across half the room like a streak of living light, to bite deep of the third man's throat.

If the Saint had thought, perhaps he would never have let Anna go, since she could only have been thrown once against the many times she could have stabbed. But he had not thought. He had only one idea, clear and bright above the swirl of red, murderous mist that rimmed his vision, and that was to work the most deadly havoc he could in the shortest possible space of time.

And the first man he met with his bare hands was catapulted back against the wall by a straight left that packed all the fiendish power of a sledge-hammer gone mad, a blow that shattered teeth in their sockets and smithereened a jawbone as if it had been made of glass.

And then the Saint laughed again—but this time he knew that he did it. The first outlet of his blind fury, the first taste of blood, that first primevally ferocious satisfaction in the battering contact of flesh and bone, had cleared his eyes and steadied down his nerves to their old fighting coolness.

"Come again, my beautiful," he drawled breathlessly, and, there was something more Saintly in the laugh in his voice, but his eyes were still as cold and bleak as two chips of blue ice . . . "Come again!"

The remaining two came at him together.

Simon Templar would not have cared if they had been twenty-two. He was warmed up now, and through the glacial implacability of his purpose was creeping back some of the heroic mirth and magnificence that rarely forsook him for long.

"Come again!"

They came abreast, but Simon, with one lightning spring sideways, made the formation tandem. The man who was left nearest swung round and lashed out a mule-kick of a punch at the Saint's mocking smile, but the Saint swerved a matter of a mere three inches, and the blow whipped harmlessly past his ear. Then, with another low laugh of triumph, Simon pivoted on his toes, his whole body seeming to uncoil in one smooth spasm of effort, and flashed in an uppercut that snapped the man's head back as if it had been struck by a pneumatic riveter, and dropped him like a poleaxed steer.

Then the Saint turned to meet the second man's attack, and at the same moment the door burst open and flopped the odds back again from evens to two to one against.

In theory. But actually this new arrival was fresh life to the Saint. For this man must have been one of those who had been busy suppressing the scream, who had laid his hands on Patricia . . . And against him and his fellow the Saint had a personal feud . . .

As Simon saw him come, the chips of blue ice under Simon's straight-lined brows glinted with an unholy light.

"Where have you been all my life, sonny boy?" breathed the Saint's caressing undertone. "Why haven't you come down before—so that I could knock your miscarriage of a face through the back of your monstrosity of a neck?"

He wove in towards the two in a slight crouch, on his toes, his fists stirring gently. And from the limit of his reach he snaked in a long, swerving left that only a champion could have guarded, and it split the man's nose neatly, for the Saint was only aiming to hurt—sufficiently—before he finished off the job.

And he should have won the fight on his head, according to plan, from the point onwards. Lithe, strong as a horse, swift as a rapier, schooled in the toughest schools of the fighting game ever since the day when he first learned to put up his hands, and always in perfect training, the Saint would never have hesitated to take on any two ordinary men. And in the mood in which they found him that night he was superman.

But he had forgotten his wound.

The nearest man was swinging a wild right at him—the kind of blow for which any trained, cool-headed boxer has a supreme contempt. And contemptuously, almost lazily, and certainly without thinking at all about a guard which approximated to a habit, Simon put up his shoulder.

The impact should have been nothing to a bunched pad of healthy muscle, but the Saint had forgotten. And it shot a tearing twinge of agony through him which seemed to find out every nerve in his system.

Suddenly he felt very sick, and for a second he could see nothing through the haze which whirled over his eyes.

In that second's blindness he took a high-explosive left cross to the side of the jaw from the man with the split nose.

Simon reeled, crumpling, against the wall.

For some reason, perhaps because they could not both conveniently reach him at once, the two men held back for a moment instead of charging in at once to finish him off. And for that moment's grace the Saint sagged where he leaned, titanically scourging numbed and tortured muscles to obey his will, wrestling with a brain that seemed to have gone to sleep.

And through the singing of a thousand thrumming dynamos in his head, he heard again the song of the Hirondel: "Patricia! . . . Patricia! . . ."

Suddenly he realised how much he had been exhausted by loss of blood. The first excitement, the first thrill and rapture of the fight, had masked his own weakness from him, but now he felt it all at once, in the dreadful slowness of his recovery from a punch on the jaw. And the blow he had taken on the shoulder had re-opened his wound. He could feel the blood coursing down his back in a warm stream. Only his will seemed left to him, bright and clear and aloof in the paralysing darkness, a thing with the terrible power of a cornered giant, fighting as it had never fought before.

And then, through the mists that doped his senses, he heard what all the time he had dreaded to hear—the sound of a car slowing up outside.

Marius.

Through the Saint's mind flashed again, like a long, shining spear, the brave reckless, vain-glorious words that he had spoken, oh, infinite ages ago: "Let 'em all come . . ."

And perhaps that recollection, perhaps anything else, perhaps the indomitable struggle of his fighting will snapped the slender fetters of weary dizziness that bound him, so that he felt a little life stealing back into his limbs.

As the two men stepped in to end it, the Saint held up one hand in a gesture that could not be denied.

"Your master is here," he said. "Perhaps you'd better wait till he's seen me."

They stopped, listening, for their hearing would have had to be keen indeed to match the Saint's, and for Simon that extra second's breather was the difference between life and death.

He gathered himself, with a silent prayer, for the mad gamble. Then he launched himself off the wall like a stone from a sling, and in one desperate rush he had passed between them.

They awoke too late, and he was at the door.

On the stairs he doubled his lead.

At the top of the stairs a corridor faced him, with doors on either side, but he would have had no excuse for hesitation, for, as he set foot in the corridor, the eighth man looked out of a door half-way along it.

The eighth man, seeing the Saint, tried to close the door again in his face, but he was too slow, or the Saint was too fast. The Saint fell on the door like a tiger, and it was the man inside who had it slammed in his face—literally slammed in his face, so that he was flung back across the room as helplessly as a scrap of thistledown might have been flung before a cyclone. And the Saint followed him in and turned the key in the lock.

One glance round the room the Saint took, and it showed him the eighth man coming off the floor with a mixture of rage and fear in his eyes, and Patricia bound to the bed by wrists and ankles.

Then, as the leader of the pursuit crashed against the door, the Saint whipped round again like a whirlwind, and, with one terrific heave, hurled a huge chest of drawers across the room from its place on the wall.

It stopped short of the door by a couple of feet, and, as Simon sprang to send it the rest of the way, the eighth man intercepted him with a knife.

The Saint caught his wrist, wrenched . . . and the man cried out with pain and dropped the knife.

He was strong above the average, but he could not stand for a moment against the Saint's desperation. Simon took him about the waist and threw him bodily against the door, knocking most of the breath out of him. And before the man could move again, the Saint had pinned him where he stood with the whole unwieldly bulk of the chest of drawers. A moment later the massive wardrobe followed, toppled over to reinforce the barricade, and the man was held there, fluttering feebly, like an insect nailed to a board.

The Saint heard the cursing and thundering beyond the door, and laughed softly, blessing the age of the house. That door was of solid oak, four inches thick, and set like a rock, and the furniture matched it. It would be a long time before the men outside would be able to force the barrier. Though that might only be postponing the inevitable end . . .

But the Saint wasn't thinking of that. He could still laugh, in that soft and Saintly way, for all his pain and weariness. For he was beside Patricia again, and no harm could come to her while he still lived with strength in his right arm. And he wanted her to hear him laugh.

With that laugh, and a flourish with it, he swept up the fallen knife from the floor. It was not Anna, but for one purpose, at least, it would serve him every whit as well. And with it, in swift, clean strokes, he slashed away the ropes that held Patricia.

"Oh, Simon, my darling . . ."

Her voice again, and the faith and unfaltering courage in it that he loved! . . . And the last rope fell away before the last slash of the knife, and she was free, and he gathered her up into his arms as if she had been a child.

"Oh, Pat, my sweet, they haven't hurt you, have they?"

She shook her head.

"But if you hadn't come . . ."

"If I'd come too late," he said, "there'd have been more dead men downstairs than there are even now. And they wouldn't have cleared a penny off the score. But I'm here!"

"But you're hurt, Simon!"

He knew it. He knew that in that hour of need he was a sorry champion. But she must not know it, not while there remained the least glimmer of hope—not while he could still keep on keeping on . . . And he laughed again, as gay and as devil-may-care a laugh as had ever passed his lips.

"It's nothing," he said cheerfully. "Considering the damage I've done to them, I should say it works out at about two thousand per cent clear profit. And it's going to be two hundred thousand per cent before I go to bed tonight!"

13

HOW SIMON TEMPLAR WAS BESIEGED, AND PATRICIA HOLM CRIED FOR HELP

Simon held her very close to him for a moment that was worth an eternity of battles, and then, very gently, he released her.

"Stand by for a sec., old dear," he murmured, "while I improve the fortifications."

The room was a narrow one, fortunately, and it held a large mass of furniture for its size. By dragging up the bed, the washstand, and another chest, it was just possible to extend the barricade in a tight jam across the room from the door to the opposite wall, so that nothing short of a battering-ram could ever force the door open. On the other hand, it was impossible to extend the barricade upwards in the same way to the height of the door. The Saint had been able to topple the wardrobe over, but even his strength, even if he had been fresh and uninjured, could not have shifted the thing to cover the doorway in an upright position. And if axes were brought . . .

But that again was a gloomy probability, which it wouldn't help anyone to worry about.

"They've got something to think about, anyway," said the Saint, standing back to view the result of his labours.

He had the air of listening while he talked, and when the sentence was finished he still listened.

The tumult outside had died down, and one voice rose clearly and stood alone out of the fading confusion.

Simon could not understand what it said, but he had no doubt who it was that spoke. No one could have mistaken that high-pitched, arrogant tone of command.

"Hullo, Marius, my little lamb!" he sang out breezily. "How's life?"

Then Marius spoke in English.

"I should stand well away from the door, Templar," he remarked suavely. "I am about to shoot out the lock."

The Saint chuckled.

"It's all the same to me, honeybunch," he answered, "but I think you ought to know that one of your bright boys is stuck against the door, right over the lock, and I'm afraid he can't move—and I can't get him away without busting the works."

"That will be unlucky for him," said Marius callously, and the man pinned against the door shrieked once horribly.

The Saint had Patricia away in a corner, covering her with his own body, when Marius fired. But, looking over his shoulder, he saw the man at the door bare his teeth dreadfully before he slopped limply forwards over the chest of drawers and lay still. The Saint's nerves were of pure tungsten, but the inhuman deliberateness of that murder made his blood run cold for an instant.

"Poor devil," he muttered.

But, outside, Marius had barked an order, and the assault was being renewed.

Simon went to the window, but one look at the bars told him that they had been too well laid for any unaided human effort to dislodge them. And, there was nothing in the room that might have been used as a lever, except, perhaps, one of the bedposts—to obtain which would have meant disorganising the whole of the barricade.

The trap was complete.

And no help could be expected from outside, unless Roger . . . But the mere fact that Marius was there ruled Roger Conway out.

"How did you get here?" the girl was asking.

Simon told her the whole story, with his mind on other things. Perhaps because his attention was so divided, he forgot that her quick intelligence would not take long to seize upon the salient deduction, and he was almost startled when she interrupted him.

"But if you left Roger with Marius . . ."

The Saint looked at her and nodded ruefully.

"Let's face it," he said. "Old Roger's dropped a stitch. But he may still be knitting away somewhere. Roger isn't our star pupil, but he has a useful knack of tumbling out of trouble. Unless Teal's chipped in . . ."

"Why Teal?"

Simon came back to earth. So much had happened since he last saw her that he had overlooked her ignorance of it.

He told her what she had missed of the story—the adventure to Esher and the flight to Maidenhead. For the first time she fully understood all that was involved, and understood also why she had been taken to the house on the hill.

Quietly and casually, with flippancy and jest, in his own vivid way, he told the story as if it were nothing but a trivial incident. And a trivial incident it had become for him, in fact: he could no longer see the trees for the wood.

"So," he said, "you'll see that Angel Face means business, and you'll see why there's so much excitement in Bures tonight."

And, as he spoke, he glanced voluntarily at the lifeless figure sprawled over the chest of drawers, a silent testimony to the truth of his words, and the girl followed his gaze.

Then Simon met her eyes, and shrugged.

He made her sit down on the bed, and sat down himself beside her; he took a cigarette from his case and made her take one also.

"It won't help us to get worked up about it," he said lightly. "It's unfortunate about Sam Stick-my-gizzard over there, but the cheerful way to look at it is to think that he makes one less of the ungodly. Let's be cheerful . . . And while we're being cheerful, tell me how you came into this mess from which I'm rescuing you at such great peril."

"That was easy. I wasn't expecting anything of the sort, you see. If you'd said more when you rang me up . . . But I fell for it like a child. There was hardly anyone on the train, and I had a compartment to myself. We must have been near Reading when a man came along the corridor and asked if I had a match. I gave him one and he gave me a cigarette . . . I know I was a fool to take it, but he looked a perfectly ordinary man, and I had no reason to be suspicious . . ."

Simon nodded.

"Until you woke up in a motor-car somewhere?"

"Yes . . . Tied hand and foot, with a bag over my head . . . We drove for a long time, and then I was brought in here. That was only about an hour before you threw stones at my window . . . Oh, Simon, I'm so glad you came!"

The Saint's arm tightened about her shoulders.

"So am I," he said.

He was looking at the door. Clearly, the efficiency of his barricade had been proved, for the attack had paused. Then Marius gave another order.

For a while there was only the murmur of conversation, and then that stopped with the sound of someone coming heavily down the corridor. And Simon Templar caught his breath, guessing that his worst forebodings were to be realised.

An instant later he was justified by a rending crash on the door that was different from all the other thunderings that had smashed upon it before.

"What is it?" asked Patricia.

"They've brought up the meat-axe," said the Saint carelessly, but he did not feel careless at heart, for the noise on the door and the crack that had appeared in one panel told him that an axe was being employed that would not take very long to damage even four inches of seasoned oak.

The blow was repeated.

And again.

The edge of a blade showed through the door like a thin strip of silver at the fourth blow.

A matter of minutes, now, before a hole was cut large enough for the besiegers to fire into the room—with an aim. And when that was done . . .

The Saint knew that the girl's eyes were upon him, and tried desperately to postpone the question he knew she was framing.

"Marius, little pal!"

There was a lull, and then Marius answered.

"Are you going to say," sneered the giant, "that you will save us the trouble of breaking in the door?"

"Oh, no. I just wanted to know how you were."

"I have nothing to complain of, Templar. And you?"

"When there are grey skies," said the Saint, after the manner of Al Jolson, "I don't mind the grey skies. You make them blue, sonny boy . . . By the way, how did you leave my friend?"

Marius's sneering chuckle curdled through the door.

"He is still at Brook Street, in charge of Hermann. You remember Hermann, the man you knocked out? . . . But I am sure Hermann will be very kind to him . . . Is there anything else you wish to know?"

"Nothing at the moment," said the Saint.

Marius spoke in his own language, and the axe struck again.

Then Patricia would no longer be denied. The Saint met her eyes, and saw that she understood. But she showed no fear.

Quite quietly they looked at each other, and their hands came together quite gently and steadily.

"I'm sorry," said Simon in a low voice. "I can never tell you how sorry I am."

"But I understand, Simon," she said, and her voice was still the firm, clear, unfaltering voice that he loved. "The gods haven't forgotten you, after all. Isn't this the sort of end you've always prayed for?"

"It is the end of the world," he said quietly. "Roger was my only reinforcement. If I didn't get back to Brook Street by a certain time, he was to come after me. But, obviously, Roger can't come now . . ."

"I know."

"I won't let you be taken alive, Pat."

"And you?"

He laughed.

"I shall try to take Marius with me. But—oh, Pat, I'd sell my soul for you not to be in it! This is my way out, but it isn't yours . . ."

"Why not? Shouldn't I want to see the last fight through with you?"

Her hands were on his shoulders then, and he was holding her face between his hands. She was looking up at him.

"Dear," he said, "I'm not complaining. We don't live in a magnificent age, but I've done my best to make life magnificent as I see it—to live my ideal of the happy warrior. But you made that possible. You made me seek and fight for the tremendous things. Battle and sudden death—yes, but battle and sudden death in the name of peace and life and love. You know I love you, Pat . . ."

She knew. And if she had never given him the ultimate depth of her heart before, she gave them all to him then, with a gladness in that kiss as vivid as a shout in silence.

"Does anything matter much beside that?" she asked.

"But I've sacrificed you! If I'd been like other men—if I hadn't been so fool crazy for danger—if I'd thought more about you, and what I might be letting you in for . . ."

She smiled.

"I wouldn't have had you different. You've never apologised for yourself before: why do it now?"

He did not answer. Who could have answered such a generosity?

So they sat together, and the battering on the door went on. The great door shook and resounded to each blow, and the sound was like the booming of a muffled knell.

Presently the Saint looked up, and saw that in the door was a hole the size of a man's hand. And suddenly a strange strength came upon him, weak and weary as he was.

"But, by Heaven, this isn't going to be the end!" cried the Saint. "We've still so much to do, you and I!"

He was on his feet.

He couldn't believe that it was the end. He wasn't ready, yet, to pass out—even in a blaze of some sort of glory. He wouldn't believe that that was his hour at last. It was true that they still had so much to do. There was Roger Conway, and Vargan, and Marius, and the peace of the world wrapped up in these two. And adventure and adventure beyond. Other things . . . For in that one adventure, and in that one hour, he had seen a new and wider vision of life, wider even than the ideal of the happy warrior, wider even than the fierce delight of battle and sudden death, but rather a fulfilment and a consummation of all these things—and how should he die before he had followed that vision farther?

And he looked at the door, and saw the eyes of Marius.

"I should advise you to surrender, Templar," said the giant coldly. "If you are obstinate, you will have to be shot."

"That'd help you, wouldn't it, Angel Face? And then how would you find Vargan?"

"Your friend Conway might be made to speak."

"You've got a hope!"

"I have my own methods of persuasion, Templar, and some of them are almost as ingenious as yours. Besides, have you thought that your death would leave Miss Holm without a protector?"

"I have," said the Saint. "I've also thought that my surrender would leave her in exactly the same position. But she has a knife, and I don't think you'll find her helpful. Think again!"

"Besides," said Marius in the same dispassionate tone, "you need not be killed at once. It would be possible to wound you again."

The Saint threw back his head.

"I never surrender," he said.

"Very well," said Marius calmly.

He snapped out another order, and again the axe crashed on the door. The Saint knew that the hole was being enlarged so that a man could shoot through it and know what he was shooting at, and he knew that the end could not now be long in coming.

There was no cover in the room. They might have flattened themselves against the wall in which the door was, so that they could not be seen from outside, but that would make little difference. A few well-grouped shots aimed along the wall by an automatic would be certain of scoring.

And the Saint had no weapon but the captured knife, and that, as he had said, he had given to Patricia.

The odds were impossible.

As he watched the chips flying from the gap which the axe had already made—and it was now nearly as big as a man's head—the wild thought crossed his mind that he might challenge Marius to meet him in single combat. But immediately he discarded the thought. Dozens of men might have accepted, considering the difference in their sizes: the taunt of cowardice, the need to maintain their prestige among their followers, at least, might have forced their hand and stung them to take the challenge seriously. But Marius was above all that. He had one object in view, and it was already proved that he viewed it with a singleness of aim that was above all ordinary motives. The man who had cold-bloodedly shot a way through the body of one of his own gang—and got away with it—would not be likely to be moved by an argument the Saint could use.

Then—what?

The Saint held Patricia in his arms, and his brain seemed to reel like the spinning of a great crazy flywheel. He knew that he was rapidly weakening now. The heroic effort which had taken him to that room and barricaded it had cost him much, and the sudden access of supernatural strength and energy which had just come upon him could not last for long. It was like a transparent mask of glittering crystal, hard but brittle, and behind it and through it he could see the foundations on which it based its tenacity crumbling away.

It was a question, as it had been in other tight corners, of playing for time. And it was also the reverse. Whatever was to be done to win the time must be done quickly—before that forced blaze of vitality fizzled out and left him powerless.

The Saint passed a hand across his eyes, and felt strangely futile. If only he were whole and strong, gifted again with the blood that he had lost, with a shoulder that wasn't spreading a numbing pain all over him, and a brain cleared of the muzzy aftermath of that all-but-knock-out swipe on the jaw, to be of some use to Patricia in her need!

"Oh, God!" he groaned. "God help me!"

But still he could see nothing useful to do—nothing but the forlorn thing that he did. He put Patricia from him and leapt to the door on to part of the barricade, covering with his body the hole that was being cut. Marius saw him.

"What is it now, Templar?" asked the giant grimly.

"Nothing, honey," croaked the Saint, with a breathless little laugh. "Just that I'm here, and I'm carefully arranging myself so that if anyone shoots at me it will be fatal. And I know you don't want me to die yet. So it'll keep you busy a bit longer—won't it?—making that hole big enough for it to be safe to shoot through . . ."

"You are merely being foolishly troublesome," said Marius unemotionally, and added an order.

The man with the axe continued his work.

But it would take longer—that was all the Saint cared about. There was hope as long as there was life. The miracle might happen . . . might happen . . .

He found Patricia beside him.

"Simon—what's the use?"

"We'll see, darling. We're still kicking, anyway—that's the main thing."

She tried to move him by force, but he held her hands away. And then she tore herself out of his grasp, and with dazed and uncomprehending eyes he watched her at the window—watched her raise the sash and look out into the night.

"Help!"

"You fool!" snarled the Saint bitterly. "Do you want them to have the last satisfaction of hearing us whine?"

He forgot everything but that—that stern point of pride—and left his place at the door. He reached her in a few lurching strides, and his hands fell roughly on her shoulders to drag her away.

She shouted again. "Help!"

"Be quiet!" snarled the Saint bitterly.

But when he turned her round he saw that her face was calm and serene, and not at all the face that should have gone with those cries.

"You asked God to help you, old boy," she said. "Why shouldn't I ask the men who have come?"

And she pointed out the window.

He looked, and he saw that the gate at the end of the garden, and the drive within, were lighted up as with the light of day by the headlights of a car that had stopped in the road beyond. But for the din of the axe at the door he would have heard its approach.

And then into that pathway of light stepped a man, tall and dark and trim, and the man cupped his hands about his mouth and shouted:

"Coming, Pat! . . . Hullo, Simon!"

"Norman," yelled the Saint. "Norman—my seraph—my sweet angel!"

Then he remembered the odds, and called again:

"Look out for yourself! They're armed . . ."

"So are we," said Norman Kent happily. "Inspector Teal and his merry men are all round the house. We've got 'em cold."

For a moment the Saint could not speak.

Then—

"Did you say Inspector Teal?"

"Yes," shouted Norman. And he added something. He added it brilliantly. He knew that the men in the house were foreigners—that even Marius, with his too-perfect English, was a foreigner—and that no one but the Saint and Patricia could be expected to be familiar with the more abstruse perversions and defilements possible to the well of native English. And he made the addition without a change of tone that might have hinted at his meaning. He added, "All breadcrumbs and bream-bait. Don't bite!"

Then Simon understood the bluff.

It must have been years since the sedate and sober Norman Kent had played such irreverent slapstick with the tongue that Shakespeare spake, but the Saint could forgive the lapse.

Simon's arm was around Patricia's shoulders, and he had seen a light in the darkness. The miracle had happened, and the adventure went on.

And he found his voice.

"Oh, boy!" he cried, and dragged Patricia down into the temporary shelter of the barricade as the first shot from outside the smashed door smacked over their heads and sang away into the blackness beyond the open window.

14

HOW ROGER CONWAY DROVE THE HIRONDEL, AND NORMAN KENT LOOKED BACK

A second bullet snarled past the Saint's ear and flattened itself in a silvery scar on the wall behind him, but no more shots followed. From outside the house came the rattle of other guns. Simon heard Marius speaking crisply, and then he was listening to the sound of footsteps hurrying away down the corridor. He raised his head out of cover, and saw nothing through the hole in the door.

"They're going to try and make a dash through the cordon that isn't there," he divined, and so it was to prove.

He stood up, and began to tear away the barricade, the girl helping him.

They raced down the corridor together, and paused at the top of the stairs. But there was no one to be seen in the hall below.

Simon led the way downwards. Without considering where he went, he burst into the nearest room, and found that it was the room in which he had fought the opening skirmish. The window through which he had hurled himself was now open and through it drifted the sounds of a scattered fusillade.

He caught up a gun from the floor without halting in his rush to the window.

Outside, on the lawn, with the light behind him, he could see a little knot of men piling into a car. The engine started up a second later.

A smile touched the Saint's lips—the first entirely carefree smile that had been there that night. There was something irresistibly entertaining about the spectacle of that death-or-glory sortie whose reckless daring was nothing but the saying of a loud "Boo" to a tame goose—if the men who made the sortie had only known. But they could not have known, and Marius was doing the only possible thing. He could not have hoped to survive a siege, but a sortie was a chance. Flimsy, but a chance. And certainly the effect of a posse shooting all round the house had been very convincingly obtained. Simon guessed that the rescue party had spared neither ammunition nor breath. They must have run themselves off their legs to maintain that impression of revolver fire coming from every quarter of the garden at once.

The car, with its frantic load, was sweeping down the drive in a moment. Simon levelled his gun and spat lead after it, but he could not tell whether he did any damage.

Then another gun poked into his ribs, and he turned.

"Put it up," said the Saint. "Put it up, Roger, old lad!"

"Well, you old horse-thief!"

"Well, you low-down stiff!"

They shook hands.

Then Norman Kent loomed up out of the darkness.

"Where's Pat?"

But Patricia was beside the Saint.

Norman swung her off her feet and kissed her shamelessly. Then he clapped Simon on the shoulder.

"Do we go after them?" he asked.

The Saint shook his head.

"Not now. Is Orace with you?"

"No. Just Roger and I—the old firm."

"Even then—we've got to get back to Vargan. We can't risk throwing away the advantage, and getting the whole bunch of us tied up again. And in about ten seconds more this place is going to be infested with stampeding villagers thinking the next war's started already. We'll beat it while the tall timber looks easy!"

"What's that on your coat—blood?"

"Nothing."

He led the way to the Hirondel, walking rather slowly for him. Roger went beside him. At one step, the Saint swayed, and caught at Roger's arm.

"Sorry, son," he murmured. "Just came all over queer, I did . . ."

"Hadn't you better let us have a look . . ."

"We'll leave now," said the Saint, with more quietly incontestable iciness than he had ever used to Roger Conway in his life before.

The strength, the unnatural vigour which had carried him through until then, was leaving him as it ceased to be necessary. But he felt a deep and absurd contentment.

Roger Conway drove, for Norman had curtly surrendered the wheel of his own recovered car. Thus Roger could explain to the Saint, who sat beside him in the front.

"Norman brought us here. I always swore you were the last word in drivers, but there isn't much you could teach Norman."

"What was the car?"

"A Lancia. He was stuck at Maidenhead without anything, so the only thing to do was to pinch something. He walked up to Skindles and took his pick."

"Let's have this from the beginning," said the Saint patiently. "What happened to you?"

"That was a bad show," said Roger. "Fatty distracted my attention, and Angel Face laid me out with a kick. Then Skinny finished the job, near enough. Marius got on the phone, but couldn't get Bures. He arranged other things with Westminster double-nine double-nine . . ."

"I met 'em. Four of 'em."

"Then Marius went off with Fatty, leaving Hermann in charge. Before that, I'd been ringing up Norman, and Norman had said he might come up. When the bell rang, I shouted to warn him, and got laid out again. But it wasn't Norman—it was Teal. Teal collared Hermann. I told Teal part of the story. It was the only thing I could think of to do—partly to keep us in Brook Street for a bit in case Norman turned up, and partly to help you. I told Teal to get through to the police at Braintree. Did they miss you?"

"They tried to stop me, but I ran through."

"Then Norman turned up. Took Teal in beautifully—and laid him out with a battle-axe or something off the wall. We left Teal and Hermann trussed up like chickens . . ."

The Saint interrupted.

"Half a minute," he said quietly. "Did you say you rang up Norman?"

Conway nodded.

"Yes. I thought . . ."

"While Marius was there?"

"Yes."

"He heard you give the number?"

"Couldn't have helped hearing, I suppose. But . . ."

Simon leaned back.

"Don't tell me," he said, "don't tell me that we already know that the exchange is not allowed to give subscribers' names and addresses. Don't tell me that Hermann, who's with Teal, mayn't have remembered the number. But what fool wouldn't remember the one word 'Maidenhead'?"

Roger clapped a hand to his mouth.

The murder was out—and he hadn't seen the murder until that moment. The sudden understanding of what he had done appalled him.

"Won't you kick me, Saint? Won't you . . . ?"

Simon put a hand on his arm, and laughed.

"Never mind, Roger," he said. "I know you didn't think. You weren't bred to this sort of game, and it isn't your fault if you trip up. Besides, you couldn't have known that it was going to make any difference. You couldn't have known Angel Face was going to get away, or Teal was going to arrive . . ."

"You're making excuses for me," said Roger bitterly. "And there aren't any. I know it. But it's just the sort of thing you would do."

The hand on Roger's arm tightened.

"Ass," said the Saint softly, "why cry over spilt milk? We're safe for hours yet, and that's all that matters."

Conway was silent, and the Hirondel sped on through the night without a check.

Simon leaned back and lighted a cigarette. He seemed to sleep, but he did not sleep. He just relaxed and stayed quiet, taking the rest which he so sorely needed. No one would ever know what a gigantic effort of will it had cost him to carry on as he had done. But he would say nothing of that to anyone but Roger, who had found him out. He would not have Patricia know. She would have insisted on delaying the journey, and that he dared not allow.

He explored his wound cautiously, taking care that his movements should not be observed from the back. Fortunately, the bullet had passed cleanly through his shoulder, and there were not likely to be any complications. Tomorrow, with his matchless powers of recuperation and the splendid health he had always enjoyed, he should be left with nothing more seriously disabling than a stiff and sore shoulder. The only real danger was the weakness after losing so much blood. But even that he felt he would be able to cope with now.

So he sat back with his eyes closed and the cigarette smouldering, almost forgotten, between his fingers, and thought over the brick that Roger had dropped.

And he saw one certain result of it staring him in the face, and that was that Maidenhead would not be safe for his democracy for very long.

Marius, still at large, wouldn't be likely to lose much time in returning to the attack. And Maidenhead was not a large place, and the number of houses which could seriously be considered was strictly limited. By morning, Marius would be on the job, working with a desperation that would be doubled by the belief that in some way the police had been enleagued against him. In the morning, also, Teal would be rescued, and would start trying to obtain information from Hermann: and how long would Hermann hold out? Not indefinitely— that was certain. In the circumstances, the Powers Higher Up might turn a conveniently blind eye to methods of persuasion which the easy-going officialdom of England would never tolerate in ordinary times: for the affair might be called a national emergency. And once Teal had the telephone number . . .

Exactly. Say tomorrow evening. By which time Marius, with a good start to make up for his lack of official facilities, would also be getting hot on the trail.

The Saint was no fool. He knew that the Criminal Investigation Department, except in the kind of detective story in which some dude amateur with a violin and a taste for exotic philosophies made rings round their hardened highnesses, was not composed entirely of nit-wits. Here and there, Simon did not hesitate to admit, among the men at New Scotland Yard, there was a brain not utterly cretinous. Claud Eustace Teal's, for instance. And Teal, though he might be something of a dim bulb at the spectacular stuff, was a hound for action when he had anything definite to act upon. And there might be more concrete things to act upon than a name and address in a chase of that sort, but, if there were, the Saint couldn't think of them.

Marius also. Well, Marius spoke for himself.

Taken by and large, it seemed as if Maidenhead was likely to become the centre of some considerable activity before the next nightfall.

"But we won't cry over spilt milk, my lads, we won't cry over spilt milk," went Simon's thoughts in a kind of refrain that harmonised with the rush of the big car. "We ought to have the best part of a day to play with, and that's the hell of a lot to me. So we won't cry over spilt milk, my lads—and so say all of us!"

But Roger Conway wasn't saying it.

He was saying, "We shall have to clear out of Maidenhead tomorrow—with or without Vargan. Have you any ideas about that?"

"Dozens," said the Saint cheerfully. "As for Vargan, by tomorrow evening there'll either be no more need to keep him a prisoner, or—well, there'll still be no need to keep him a prisoner . . . As for ourselves, there's my Desoutter at Hanworth. Teal won't have had time to find out about that, and I don't think he'll allow anything to be published about us in the papers so long as he's got a chance of clearing up the trouble without any publicity. To the ordinary outside world we're still perfectly respectable citizens. No one at Hanworth will say anything if I announce that we're pushing off to Paris by air. I've done it before. And once we're off the deck we've got a big cruising range to choose our next landing out of."

And he was silent again, revolving schemes farther ahead.

In the back of the car, Patricia's head had sunk on to Norman's shoulder. She was asleep.

The first pale streaks of dawn were lightening the sky when they ran into the east of London. Roger put the Hirondel through the City as quickly as the almost deserted streets would allow.

He turned off on to the embankment by New Bridge Street, and so they came to pass by Parliament Square on their way westwards. And it was there that Norman Kent had a strange experience.

For some while past, words had been running through his head, so softly that he had not consciously been aware of them—words with which he was as familiar as he was with his own name, and which, nevertheless, he knew he had not heard for many years. Words to a kind of chanting tune that was not a tune . . . And at that moment, as the Hirondel was murmuring past the Houses of Parliament, he became consciously aware of the words that were running through his head, and they seemed to swell and become louder and louder and clearer, as if a great choir took them up, and the illusion was so perfect that he had looked curiously round towards the spires of Westminster Abbey before he realised that no service could be proceeding there at that hour.

"To give light to them that sit in darkness, and in the shadow of death: and to guide our feet into the way of peace . . ."

And, as Norman Kent turned his eyes, they fell upon the great statue of Richard Cœur-de-Lion, which stands outside the House. And all at once the voices died away. But Norman still looked back, and saw Richard Cœur-de-Lion riding there, the last of his breed, huge and heroic against the pale dawn sky, with his right hand and arm hurling up his great sword in a gesture. And for some reason Norman Kent suddenly felt himself utterly alone and aloof, and very cold. But that might have been the chill of the dawn.

15

HOW VARGAN GAVE HIS ANSWER, AND SIMON TEMPLAR WROTE A LETTER

It was full daylight when they came to Maidenhead.

Orace was not in bed. Orace was never in bed when he could be useful, no matter at what unearthly hour that might be. But whether it was because he never went to bed at all, or whether it was because some strange clairvoyance always roused him in time to be ready for all emergencies was his own mysterious secret.

He produced a great dish of sizzling bacon and eggs and a steaming pot of coffee as if by the waving of a magic wand.

Then the Saint gave orders.

"We will sleep till lunch-time," he said. "The difference it'll make to our strength will be worth the waste of time."

He himself was feeling ready to drop.

He took Orace with him to his room, and swore him to silence before he allowed him to see the wound. But Orace, seeing it, said, "Wot the thunderinell—"

Simon fluttered a tired hand.

"Don't swear, Orace," he rambled vaguely. "I didn't swear when it happened. And Miss Patricia doesn't know yet . . . You'll look after Miss Patricia and the boys, Orace, if I conk out. Keep them out of mischief and so forth . . . And if you see Angel Face, you'll shoot him through the middle of his ugly mug, with my compliments, Orace . . ."

He slid sideways off the chair suddenly, but Orace's strong arms caught him as he fell.

Orace put him to bed as tenderly as if he had been a child.

And yet, next morning, the Saint was up and dressed before any of the others. He was rather pale under his tan, and his lean face seemed leaner than ever, but there was still a spring in his step. He had slept like a healthy schoolboy. His head was as clear as his eyes, and a cold shower had sent fresh life tingling through his veins.

"Learn a lesson from me," he said over his third egg. "If you had constitutions like mine, invigorated by my spiritual purity, and unimpaired, like mine, by the dissipation and riotous living that has brought you to the wrecks you are—"

And in this he was joking less than they thought. Sheer ruthless will-power had forced his splendid physique on to the road of an almost miraculously swift recovery. Simon Templar had no time to waste on picturesque convalescences.

He sent Orace out for newspapers, and read them all. Far too much that should have been said was still left unsaid. But he could glean a hint here, a warning there, a confirmation everywhere; until at the end of it he seemed to see Europe lying under the shadow of a dreadful darkness. But nothing was said in so many words. There were only the infuriatingly inadequate clues for a suspicious man to interpret according to his suspicions. It seemed as if the face of the shadow was waiting for something to happen, before which it would not unveil itself. The Saint knew what that something was, and doubted himself for the first time since he had gathered his friends together under him to serve the ends of a quixotic deal.

But still nothing whatever was said in the newspapers about the affair at Esher, and the Saint knew that this silence could only mean one thing.

It was not until three o'clock that he had a chance to discuss Vargan again with Roger and Norman, for it had been agreed that, although Patricia had to know that Vargan was a prisoner, and why he was a prisoner, and although his possible fate had once been mentioned before her, the question should not be raised again in her presence.

"We can't keep him for ever," said Simon, when the chance came. "For one thing, we look like spending a large part of the rest of our lives on the run, and you can't run well with a load of unwilling luggage. Of course, we might get away with it if we found some lonely place and decided to live like hermits for the rest of our days. But, either way, there'd still always be the risk that he might escape. And that doesn't amuse me in the least."

"I spoke to Vargan last night," said Norman Kent soberly. "I think he's mad. A megalomaniac. His one idea is that his invention will bring him world-wide fame. His grievance against us is that we're holding up his negotiations with the Government, and thereby postponing the front-page headlines. I remember he told me he was naming a peerage as part of the price of his secret."

The Saint recalled his lunch with Barney Malone, of *The Clarion*, and the conversation which had reinforced his interest in Vargan, and found Norman's analysis easy to accept.

"I'll speak to him myself," he said.

He did so shortly afterwards.

The afternoon had grown hot and sunny, and it was easy to arrange that Patricia should spend it on the lawn with a book.

"Give your celebrated impersonation of innocent English girlhood, old dear," said the Saint. "At this time of the year, and in this weather, anyone searching Maidenhead for a suspicious-looking house, and seeing one not being used in the way that houses at Maidenhead are usually used, will be after it like a cat after kippers. And now you're the only one of us who's in balk—bar Orace. So you'll just have to give the local colour all by yourself. And keep your eyes skinned. Look out for a fat man chewing gum. We're shooting all fat men who chew gum on sight, just to make sure we don't miss Claud Eustace . . ."

When she had gone, he sent Roger and Norman away also. To have had the other two present would have made the affair too like a kangaroo court for his mood.

There was only one witness of that interview: Orace, a stolid and expressionless sentinel, who stood woodenly beside the prisoner like a sergeant-major presenting a defaulter to his orderly officer.

"Have a cigarette?" said the Saint.

He knew what his personality could do, and, left alone to use it, he still held to a straw of hope that he might succeed where Norman had failed.

But Vargan refused the cigarette. He was sullenly defiant.

"May I ask how much longer you propose to continue this farce?" he inquired. "You have now kept me here three days. Why?"

"I think my friend has explained that to you," said Simon.

"He's talked a lot of nonsense—"

Simon cut the speech short with a curt movement of his hand.

He was standing up, and the professor looked small and frail beside him. Tall and straight and lean was the Saint.

"I want to talk to you seriously," he said. "My friend has appealed to you once. I'm appealing to you now. And I'm afraid this is the last

THE SAINT CLOSES THE CASE

appeal we can make. I appeal to you in the name of whatever you hold most sacred. I appeal to you in the name of humanity. In the name of the peace of the world."

Vargan glared at him short-sightedly.

"An impertinence," he replied. "I've already heard your proposition, and I may say that I've never heard anything so ridiculous in my life. And that's my answer."

"Then," said Simon quietly, "I may say that I've never in my life heard anything so damnable as your attitude. Or can it be that you're merely a fool—an overgrown child playing with fire?"

"Sir—"

The Saint seemed to grow even taller. There was an arrogance of command in his poise, in an instant, that brooked no denial. He stood there, in that homely room, like a king of men. And yet, when he continued, his voice was even milder and more reasonable than ever.

"Professor Vargan," he said, "I haven't brought you here to insult you for my amusement. I ask you to try for the moment to forget the circumstances and listen to me as an ordinary man speaking to an ordinary man. You have perfected the most horrible invention with which science has yet hoped to torture a world already sickened with the beastliness of scientific warfare. You intend to make that invention over to hands that would not hesitate to use it. Can you justify that?"

"Science needs no justification."

"In France, today, there are millions of men buried who might have been alive now. They were killed in a war. If that war had been fought before science applied itself to the perfection of slaughter, they would have been only thousands instead of millions. And, at least, they would have died like men. Does science need no justification for the squandering of those lives?"

"Do you think you can stop war?"

"No. I know I can't. That's not the argument. Listen again. In England today there are thousands of men blind, maimed, crippled for life, who might have been whole now. There are as many again in France, Belgium, Germany, Austria. The bodies that God gave, and made wonderful and intricate and beautiful—torn and wrecked by your science, often made so hideous that men shudder to see them . . . Does science need no justification for that?"

"That is not my business."

"You're making it your business."

The Saint paused for a moment, and then he went on in a voice that no one could have interrupted, the passionate voice of a prophet crying in the wilderness.

"There is science that is good and science that is evil. Yours is the evil science, and all the blessings that good science has given to mankind are no justification for your evil. If we must have science, let it be good science. Let it be a science in which men can still be men, even when they kill and are killed. If there must be war, let it be holy war. Let men fight with the weapons of men, and not with the weapons of fiends. Let us have men to fight and die as champions and heroes, as men used to die, and not as the beasts that perish, as men have to die in our wars now."

"You are an absurd idealist—"

"I am an absurd idealist. But I believe that all that must come true. For, unless it comes true, the world will be laid desolate. And I believe that it can come true. I believe that, by the grace of God, men will awake presently and be men again, and colour and laughter and splendid living will return to a grey civilisation. But that will only come true because a few men will believe in it, and fight for it, and fight in its name against everything that sneers and snarls at that ideal. You are such a thing."

"And you are the last hero—fighting against me?"

Simon shook his head.

"Not the last hero," he said simply. "Perhaps not a hero at all. I call myself a soldier of life. I have sinned as much as any man, and more than most. I have been a hunted criminal. I am that now. But everything I've done has been done for the glory of an invisible ideal. I never understood it very clearly before, but I understand it now. But you . . . Why haven't you even told me that you want to do what you want to do for the glory of your own ideal—for the glory, if you like, of England?"

A fantastic obstinacy flared in Vargan's eyes.

"Because it wouldn't be true," he said. "Science is international. Honour among scientists is international. I've offered my invention first to England—that's all. If they're fools enough to refuse to reward me for it, I shall find a country that will."

He came closer to the Saint, with his head sideways, his faded lips curiously twisted. And the Saint saw that he had wasted all his words.

"For years I've worked and slaved," babbled Vargan. "Years! And what have I got for it? A few paltry letters to put after my name. No honour for everybody to see. No money. I'm poor! I've starved myself, lived like a pauper, to save the money to carry on my work! Now you ask me to give up everything that I've sacrificed the best years of my life to win—to gratify your Sunday School sentimentality! I say you're a fool, sir—an imbecile!"

The Saint stood quite still, with Vargan's bony hands clawing the air a few inches from his face. His impassivity seemed to infuriate the professor.

"You're in league with them!" screamed Vargan. "I knew it. You're in league with the devils who've tried to keep me down! But I don't care! I'm not afraid of you. You can do your worst. I don't care if millions of people die. I hope you die with them! If I could kill you—"

Suddenly he flung himself at the Saint like a mad beast, blubbering incoherently, tearing, kicking . . .

Orace caught him about the middle and swung him off his feet in arms of iron and the Saint leaned against the table, rubbing a shin that he had not been quick enough to get out of the way of that maniacal onslaught.

"Lock him up again," said Simon heavily, and saw Orace depart with his raving burden.

He had just finished with the telephone when Orace returned.

"Get everybody's things together," he ordered. "Your own included. I've phoned for a van to take them to the station. They'll go as luggage in advance to Mr Tremayne, in Paris.

I'll write out the labels. The van will be here at four, so you'll have to move."

"Yessir," said Orace obediently.

The Saint grinned.

"We've been a good partnership, haven't we?" he said. "And now I'm clearing out of England with a price on my head. I'm sorry we've got to . . . break up the alliance . . ."

Orace snorted.

"Ya bin arskin forrit, aintcha?" he demanded unsympathetically. "Ain't I tolja so arfadozen times? . . . Where ya goin' ta?" he added, in the same ferocious tone.

"Lord knows," said the Saint.

"Never bin there," said Orace. "Allus wanted ta, but never adno invitashun. I'll be ready to leave when you are, sir."

He turned smartly on his heel and marched to the door. Simon had to call him back.

"Shake, you darned old fool," said the Saint, and held out his hand. "If you think it's worth it . . ."

"'Tain't," said Orace sourly. "But I'll avta look arfter ya."

Then Orace was gone, and the Saint lighted a cigarette and sat down by the open window, gazing dreamily out over the lawn and the sunlit river.

And it seemed to him that he saw a cloud like a violet mist unrolled over the lawn and the river and the white houses and fields behind, a gigantic cloud that crept over the country like a living thing, and the cloud scintillated as with the whirling and flashing of a thousand thousand sparks of violet fire. And the grass shrivelled in the searing breath of the cloud, and the trees turned black and crumpled in hot cinders as the cloud engulfed them. And men ran before the cloud, men agonised for breath, men with white, haggard faces and eyes glazed and staring, men . . . But the creeping of the cloud was faster than the swiftest man could run . . .

And Simon remembered the frenzy of Vargan.

For the space of two cigarettes he sat there with his own thoughts, and then he sat down and wrote a letter.

To Chief Inspector Teal,
Criminal Investigation Department,
New Scotland Yard,
London, S.W.1.

Dear Old Claud Eustace,
Before anything else, I want to apologise for assaulting you and one of your men at Esher on Saturday, and also to apologise for the way a friend of mine treated you yesterday. Unfortunately, on both occasions, the circumstances did not permit us to dispose of you by more peaceful means.
The story that Roger Conway told you last night was nothing but the truth. We rescued Professor Vargan from the men who first took him—who were led, as Conway

told you, by the celebrated Dr Rayt Marius—and removed him to a place of safety. By the time you receive this, you will know our reason, and, since I have not the time to circularise the Press myself, I hope this explanation will be safe in your hands.

Little remains for me to add to what you already know. We have tried to appeal to Vargan to suppress his invention on humanitarian grounds. He will not listen. His sole thought is the recognition which he thinks his scientific genius deserves. One cannot argue with monomaniacs: therefore, we find ourselves with only one course open to us.

We believe that for this diabolical discovery to take its place in the armament of the nations of Europe, at a time when jealousies and fears and the rumours of wars are again lifting their heads, would be a refinement of "civilisation" which the world could well be spared. You may say that the exclusive possession of this invention would confirm Great Britain in an unassailable supremacy, and perhaps thereby secure the peace of Europe. We answer that no secret can be kept for ever. The sword is two-edged. And, as Vargan answered me by saying, "Science is international"—so I answer you by saying that humanity is also international.

We are content to be judged by the verdict of history, when all the facts are made known.

But in accomplishing what we have accomplished, we have put you in the way of learning our identities, and that, as you will see, must be an almost fatal blow to such an organisation as mine.

Nevertheless, I believe that in time I shall find a way for us to continue the work that we have set ourselves to do.

We regret nothing that we have already done. Our only

regret is that we should be scattered before we have had time
to do more. Yet we believe that we have done much good,
and that this last crime of ours is the best of all.
Au revoir!

Simon Templar ("The Saint").

He had heard, while he wrote, the sounds of Orace despatching luggage, and, as he signed his name, Orace entered with a tray of tea and the report that the van had departed.

Patricia came in through the French windows a moment later. He thought she could never have looked so slim and cool and lovely. And, as she came to him, he swung her up in one arm as if she had been a feather.

"You see," he smiled, as he set her down, "I'm not quite a back number yet."

She stayed close to him, with cool golden-brown arms linked round his neck, and he was surprised that she smiled so slowly.

"Oh, Simon," she said, "I do love you so much!"

"Darling," said the Saint, "this is so sudden! If I'd only known . . ."

But something told him that it was not a time for jesting, and he stopped.

But of course she loved him. Hadn't he known it for a whole heavenly year, ever since she confessed it on the tor above Baycombe—that peaceful Devonshire village—only a week after he'd breezed into the district as a smiling swashbuckler in search of trouble, without the least notion that he was waltzing into a kind of trouble to which he had always been singularly immune? Hadn't she proved it, since, in a hundred ways? Hadn't the very night before, at Bures, been enough in itself to prove the fact beyond question for all time?

And now, in the name of fortune and all the mysteries of women, she had to blurt it out of the blue like that, almost as if . . . "Burn it!" thought the Saint. "Almost as if she thought I was going to leave her!"

"Darling old idiot," said the Saint, "what's the matter?"

. Roger Conway answered, from the Saint's shoulder, having entered the room unnoticed. He answered with a question.

"You've seen Vargan?"

"I have."

Roger nodded.

"We heard some of the noise. What did he say?"

"He went mad, and gibbered. Orace rescued me, and carried him away—fighting like a wild cat. Vargan's a lunatic, as Norman said. And a lunatic said . . . 'No.'"

Conway went to the window and looked up the river, shading his eyes against the sun. Then he turned back.

"Teal's on his way," he said, in a matter-of-fact voice. "For the last half-hour the same energetic bird has been scuttling up and down the river in a motor-boat. We spotted him through the kitchen window, while we were drinking beer and waiting for you."

"Well, well, well!" drawled the Saint, very gently and thoughtfully.

"He was snooping all round with a pair of binoculars. Pat being out on the lawn may have put him off for a bit. I left Norman on the look-out, and sent Orace out for Pat as soon as we heard you were through."

Norman Kent came in at that moment, and Simon took his arm and drew him into the group.

"Our agile brain," said the Saint, "deduces that Hermann has squealed, but has forgotten the actual number of our telephone. So Teal has to investigate Maidenhead generally. That may yet give us another hour or two, but it doesn't alter the fact that we have our marching orders. They're easy. Your luggage has already gone. So, if you beetle off to your rooms and have a final wash and brush-up, we'll be ready to slide. Push on, souls!"

He left them to it, and went to the kitchen in search of Orace.

"Got your bag packed, Orace?"

"Yessir."

"Passport in order?"

"Yessir."

"Fine. I'd like to take you in the Desoutter, but I'm afraid there isn't room. However, the police aren't after you, so you won't have any trouble."

"Nossir."

The Saint took ten five-pound notes from a bulging wallet.

"There's a train to London at 4:58," he said. "Paddington, 5:40. That'll give you time to say good-bye to all your aunts, and catch a train from Victoria at 8:20, which will take you via Newhaven and Dieppe to Paris, where you arrive at 5:23 tomorrow morning at the Gare St Lazare. While you're waiting in London, you'd better tear yourself away from your aunts for as long as it takes you to send a wire to Mr Tremayne and ask him to meet you at the station and protect you from all those wild French ladies you've read about. We'll meet you at Mr Tremayne's . . . Oh, and you might post this letter for me."

"Yessir."

"O.K., Orace. You've just got time to get to the station without bursting a bloodvessel. S'long!"

He went on to his room, and there he found Patricia.

Simon took her in his arms at once.

"You're coming on this getaway?" he asked.

She held tightly to him.

"That's what I was wondering when I came in from the garden," she said. "You've always been such a dear old quixotic ass, Simon. You know how it was at Baycombe."

"And you thought I'd want to send you away."

"Do you?"

"I should have wanted to once," said the Saint. "In the bad old days . . . But now—oh, Pat, dear lass, I love you too much to be unselfish! I love your eyes and your lips and your voice and the way your hair shines like gold in the sun. I love your wisdom and your understanding and your kindliness and your courage and your laughter. I love you with every thought of my mind and every minute of my life. I love you so much that it hurts. I couldn't face losing you. Without you, I just shouldn't have anything to live for . . . And I don't know where we shall go or what we shall do or what we shall find in the days that are coming. But I do know that if I never find more than I've got already—just you, lass!—I shall have had more than my life . . ."

"I shall have had more than mine, Simon . . . God bless you!"

He laughed.

"He has," said the Saint. "You see how it is . . . And I know a gentleman would be strong and silent, and send you out into the night for your own sake. But I don't care. I'm not a gentleman. And if you think it's worth it, to be hunted out of England with me—"

But her lips silenced his, and there was no need to say more. And in Simon Templar's heart was a marvel of thanksgiving that was also a prayer.

16

HOW SIMON TEMPLAR PRONOUNCED SENTENCE, AND NORMAN KENT WENT TO FETCH HIS CIGARETTE-CASE

A few minutes later, the Saint joined Roger Conway and Norman Kent in the sitting-room. He had already started up the Hirondel, tested its smooth running as well as he could, and examined the tyres. The sump showed no need of oil, and there was petrol enough in the tank to make a journey twice as long as the one they had to take. He had left the car ticking over on the drive outside, and returned to face the decision that had to be taken.

"Ready?" asked Norman quietly.

Simon nodded.

In silence he took a brief survey through the French windows, and then he came back and stood before them.

"I've only one preliminary remark to make," he said. "That is—where is Tiny Tim?"

They waited.

"Put yourselves in his place," said the Saint. "He hasn't got the facilities for trailing us that Teal has had. But Teal is here, and wherever old Teal is, Angel Face won't be far behind. Angel Face, being presumably anything but a bonehead, would naturally figure that the smartest thing to do, knowing Teal was trailing us, would be to trail Teal. That's the way I'd do it myself, and you can bet that Angel Face is nearly as rapid on the bounce, in the matter of brainwaves, as we are ourselves. I just mention that as a factor to be remembered during this fade-away act—and because it's another reason for us to solve a certain problem quickly."

They knew what he meant, and met his eyes steadily—Roger Conway grim, Norman Kent grave and inscrutable.

"Vargan will not listen to reason," said the Saint simply. "You heard him . . . And there's no way out for us. We've only one thing to do. I've tried to think of other solutions, but there just aren't any . . . You may say it's cold-blooded. So is any execution. But a man is cold-bloodedly executed by the law for one murder that is a matter of ancient history. We execute Vargan to save a million murders. There is no doubt in any of our minds that he will be instrumental in those murders if we let him go. And we can't take him with us . . . So I say that he must die."

"One question," said Norman. "I believe it's been asked before. If we remove Vargan, how much of the menace of war do we remove with him?"

"The question has been answered before. I think Vargan is a keystone. But even if he isn't—even if the machinery that Marius has set in motion is able to run on without wanting more fuel—even if there is to be war—I say that the weapon that Vargan has created must not be used. We may be accused of betraying our country, but we must face that. Perhaps there are some things even more important than winning a war . . . Do you understand, I wonder?"

Norman looked through the window, and some whimsical fancy, unbidden alien at such a conference, touched his lips with the ghost of a smile.

"Yes," he said, "there are so many important things to think of."

The Saint turned to Roger Conway.

"And you, Roger—what do you say?"

Conway fingered an unlighted cigarette.

"Which of us shall do it?" he asked simply.

Simon Templar looked from Roger to Norman, and he said what he had always meant to say.

"If we are caught," he said, "the man who does it will be hanged. The others may save themselves. I shall do it."

Norman Kent rose.

"Do you mind?" he said. "I've just remembered I left my cigarette-case in my bedroom. I'll be back in a moment."

He went out, and passed slowly and thoughtfully down the little hall to a door that was not his own.

He knocked, and entered, and Patricia Holm looked round from the dressing-table to see him.

"I'm ready, Norman. Is Simon getting impatient?"

"Not yet," said Norman.

He came forward and set his hands on her shoulders. She turned, with a smile awakening on her lips, but the smile died at the sight of a queer light burning in his dark eyes.

"Dear Pat," said Norman Kent, "I've always longed for a chance to serve you. And now it's come. You knew I loved you, didn't you?"

She touched his hand.

"Don't, Norman dear . . . please! . . . Of course I knew. I couldn't help knowing. I'm so sorry . . ."

He smiled.

"Why be sorry?" he answered gently. "I shall never bother you. I wouldn't, even if you'd let me. Simon's the whitest man in the world, and he's my dearest friend. It will be my happiest thought, to know that you love him. And I know how he loves you. You two will go on together until the stars fall from the sky. See that you never lose the splendour of life."

"What do you mean?" she pleaded.

The light in Norman Kent's eyes had in it something like a magnificent laughter.

"We're all fanatics," he said. "And perhaps I'm the most fanatical of us all . . . Do you remember, Pat, how it was I who first said that Simon was a man born with the sound of trumpets in his ears? . . . That was the truest thing I ever said. And he'll go on in the sound of the trumpet. I know, because today I heard the trumpet myself . . . God bless you, Pat."

Before she knew what was happening, he had bent and kissed her lightly on the lips. Then he walked quickly to the door, and it was closing behind her when she found her voice. She had been left with no idea of what he meant by half the things he had said, and she could not let him go so mysteriously.

She called him—an imperative Patricia. "Norman!"

He was back in a moment, almost before she had spoken his name. Something had changed in his face. His finger signed her to silence.

"What is it?" she whispered.

"The last battle," said Norman Kent quietly. "Only a little sooner than we expected. Take this!"

He jerked back the jacket of a small automatic, and thrust it into her hands. An instant later he was rapidly loading a larger gun which he took from his hip pocket.

Then he opened the window noiselessly, and looked out. He beckoned her over. The Hirondel stood waiting on the drive, less than a dozen yards away. He pointed.

"Hide behind the curtains," he ordered. "When you hear three shots in quick succession, it's your cue to run for the car. Shoot down anyone who tries to stop you."

"But where are you going?"

"To collect the troops." He laughed soundlessly. "Good-bye, dear!"

He put her hand to his lips, and was gone, closing the door softly behind him.

It was when he had left the room for the first time that he had heard, through the open door of the sitting-room, the terse command "Put up your hands!" in a voice that was certainly neither Roger's nor Simon's. Now he stood still for a moment outside Patricia's door, listening, and heard the inimitably cheerful accents of Simon Templar in a tight corner.

"You're welcome—as the actress said to the bishop on a particularly auspicious occasion. But why haven't you brought Angel Face with you, sweetheart?"

Norman Kent heard the last sentence as he was opening the door of the kitchen.

He passed through the kitchen and opened another door. A flight of steps showed before him in the light which he switched on. He went down, and a third door faced him—a ponderous door of three-inch oak, secured by two heavy bars of iron. He lifted the bars and went in, closing that third door behind him as carefully as he had closed the first two. The three doors between them should be enough to deaden any sound . . .

Vargan was sitting huddled up in a chair, scribbling with a stump of pencil in a tattered notebook.

He raised his head at the sound of Norman's entrance. His white hair was dishevelled, and his stained and shabby clothes hung loosely on his bones. The eyes seemed the only vital things in a lined face like a creased old parchment, eyes with the dull fire of his madness stirring in them like the pale flickering flame that simmers over the crust of an awakening volcano.

Norman felt a stab of absurd pity for this pitifully crazy figure. And yet he knew that his business was not with the man, but with the madness of the man—the madness that could, and would, let loose upon the world a greater horror than anything that the murderous madness of other men had yet conceived.

And the face of Norman Kent was like a face graven in dark stone.

"I have come for your answer, Professor Vargan," he said.

The scientist sat deep in his chair, peering aslant at the stern dark figure framed against the door. His face twitched spasmodically, and his yellow hands clutched his notebook clumsily into his coat; he made no other movement. And he did not speak.

"I am waiting," said Norman Kent presently.

Vargan passed a shaky hand through his hair.

"I've given you my answer," he said harshly.

"Think," said Norman.

Vargan looked down the muzzle of the automatic, and his lips curled back from his teeth in an animal snarl.

"You are a friend of my persecutors," he croaked, and his voice rose to a shrill sobbing scream as he saw Norman Kent's knuckle whiten over the trigger.

17

HOW SIMON TEMPLAR
EXCHANGED BACK-CHAT, AND
GERALD HARDING SHOOK HANDS

"We were expecting Angel Face," remarked the Saint. "But not quite so soon. The brass band's ordered, the Movietone cameramen are steaming down, the reporters are sharpening their pencils as they run, and we were just going out to unroll the red carpet. In fact, if you hadn't been so sudden, there'd have been a full civic reception waiting for you. All except the mayor. The mayor was going to present you with an illuminated address, but he got lit up himself, while he was preparing it, so I'm afraid he's out of the frolic, anyway. However . . ."

He stood beside Roger Conway, his hands prudently held high in the air.

He'd been caught on the bend—as neatly as he'd ever been caught in the whole of his perilous career. Well and truly bending, he'd been. Bending in a bend which, if he could have repeated it regularly and with the necessary adornments of showmanship, would undoubtedly have made his fortune in a Coney Island booth as The Man with the Plasticene Spine. In fact, when he reviewed that bend with a skinned eye, he could see that nothing short of the miracle which is traditionally supposed to save fools from the consequences of their folly could have saved him from hearing that imponderable inward ping! which informs a man, supple on the uptake, that one of his psychological suspender-buttons has come unstuck.

It struck the Saint that this last adventure wasn't altogether his most brilliant effort. It didn't occur to him to blame anyone else for the various leaks it had sprung. He might, if he had been that sort of man, have put the blame on Roger Conway, for Roger's two brilliant contributions, in the shape of dropping the brick about Maidenhead and then letting Marius escape, could certainly be made out to have something to do with the present trouble, but the Saint just wasn't that sort of man. He could only visualise the adventure, and those taking part in it, as one coherent whole, including himself, and, since he was the leader, he had to take an equal share of blame for the mistakes of his lieutenants, like any other general. Except that, unlike any other general, he kept the blame to himself, and declined to pass on the kick to those under him. Any bricks that were dropped must, in the nature of things, flop on everybody's toes simultaneously and with the same sickening thud: therefore the only intelligent and helpful thing to do was to consider the bricks as bricks and deal with the bricks as bricks, simple and absolute, without wasting time over the irrelevant question of who dropped the brick and why.

And here, truly, was an admirable example of the species brick, a brick colossal and catastrophic, a very apotheosis of Brick, in the shape of this fresh-faced youngster in plus eights, who'd coolly walked in through the French window half a minute after Norman Kent had walked out of the door.

It had been done so calmly and impudently that neither Simon nor Roger had had a chance to do anything about it. That was when they had been so blithely on the bend. At one moment they had been looking through the window at a garden; at the next moment they had been looking through the window at a gun. They hadn't been given a break.

And what had happened to Norman Kent? By rights, he should have been back by that time. He should have been cantering blindfold into the hold-up—and Patricia with him, as like as not. Unless one of them had heard the conversation. Simon had noticed that Norman hadn't closed the door behind him, and for that reason deliberately raised his voice. Now, if Norman and Patricia received their cue before the hold-up merchant heard them coming . . .

"You wouldn't believe me," Simon went on affably, "if I told you how much I've been looking forward to renewing my acquaintance with Angel Face. He's so beautiful, and I love beautiful boys. Besides, I feel that a few more informal chats will make us friends for life. I feel that there's a kind of soul affinity between us. It's true that there was some unpleasantness at our first few meetings, but that's only natural between men of such strong and individual personalities as ours at a first acquaintance. It ought not to last. Deep will call to deep. I feel that we shall not separate again before he's wept on my shoulder and vowed eternal friendship and lent me half a dollar . . . But perhaps he's just waiting to come in when you give him the All Clear?"

A slight frown appeared on the face of the young man with the gun.

"Who is this friend of yours—Angel Face—anyway?"

The Saint's eyebrows went up.

"Don't you know Angel Face, honeybunch?" he murmured. "I had an idea you'd turn out to be bosom friends. My mistake. Let's change the subject. How's dear old Teal? Still living on spearmint and struggling with the overflow of that boyish figure? You know, I can't help thinking he must have thought it very inhospitable of us to leave him lying about Brook Street all last night with only Hermann for company. Did he think it was very rude of us?"

"I suppose you're Templar?"

Simon bowed.

"Right in one, loveliness. What's your name—Ramon Novarro? Or are you After Taking Wuggo? Or are you just one of the strong silent men from the musical comedy chorus? You know: Gentlemen's clothes by Morris Angel and the brothers Moss. Hair by Marcel. Faces by accident. What?"

"As a low comedian you'd be a sensation," said the youngster calmly. "As a clairvoyant, you'd probably make a most successful coal-heaver. Since you're interested, I'm Captain Gerald Harding, British Secret Service, Agent 2238."

"Pleased to meet you," drawled the Saint.

"And this is Conway?"

Simon nodded.

"Right again, son. You really are God's little gift to the General Knowledge Class, aren't you? . . . Speak your piece, Roger, and keep nothing back. You can't bamboozle Bertie. I shouldn't be surprised if he even knew where you hired your evening clothes."

"Same place where he had the pattern tattooed on those pants," said Roger. "Very dashing, isn't it? D'you think it reads from left to right, or up and down?"

Harding leaned one shoulder against the wall, and regarded his captures with a certain reluctant admiration.

"You're a tough pair of wags," he concluded.

"Professionally," said the Saint, "we play twice nightly to crowded houses, and never fail to bring them down. Which reminds me. May we do the same thing with our hands? I don't want you to feel nervous, but this position is rather tiring and so bad for the circulation. You can relieve us of our artillery first, if you like, in the approved style."

"If you behave," said Harding. "Turn round."

"With pleasure," murmured the Saint. "And thanks."

Harding came up behind them and removed their guns. Then he backed away again.

"All right—but no funny business, mind!"

"We never indulge in funny business," said Simon with dignity.

He reached for a cigarette from the box on the table and prepared to light it unhurriedly.

To all outward appearances he was completely unruffled, and had been so ever since Harding's arrival. But that was merely the pose which he habitually adopted when the storm was gathering most thickly; the Saint reserved his excitements for his spare time. He could always maintain that air of leisured nonchalance in any emergency, and other men before Harding had been perplexed and disconcerted by it. It was always the same—the languid affectation of indifference, and that genial flow of idle persiflage that smoked effortlessly off the mere surface of his mind without disturbing the concentrated thought which it concealed.

The more serious anything was, the more extravagantly the Saint refused to treat it seriously. And thereby he was never without some subtle advantage over the man who had the drop on him, for Simon's bantering assurance was so perfectly assumed that only an almost suicidally self-confident opponent could have been left untroubled by a lurking uneasiness. Only a fool or a genius would have failed to jump to the conclusion that such a tranquil unconcern must base itself on a high card somewhere up its frivolous sleeve. And very often the man who was neither a fool nor a genius was right.

But on this occasion the card up the sleeve was very ordinary. The Saint, inwardly revolving every aspect of the interruption with a furious attention, could still find nothing new to add to his first estimate of the deal. Norman Kent remained the only hidden card.

By now, Norman Kent must know what had happened. Otherwise he would have been in the boat with them long ago, reaching down the ceiling while a youngster in plus eights whizzed his Webley. And if Norman Kent knew, Patricia would know. The question was—what would they be most likely to do? And how could Simon Templar, out of touch with them and practically powerless under the menace of Harding's automatic, divine their most probable plan of action and do something in collaboration?

That was the Saint's problem—to reverse the normal processes of strategy and put himself in the place of the friend instead of in the place of the enemy. And, meanwhile, to keep Harding amused . . .

"You're a clever child," said the Saint. "May one inquire how you come to be doing Teal's job?"

"We work in with the police on a case like this," said Harding grimly, "but we don't mind stealing a march on them if we can. Teal and I set out on an independent tour. He took the high road and I took the low road, and I seem to have got there before him. I saw your car outside on the drive, and came right in."

"You should have a medal," said Simon composedly. "I'm afraid I can't give you anything but love, baby, but I'll write to the War Office about you, if you think that might help."

Harding grinned and smoothed his crisp hair.

"I like your nerve," he said.

"I like yours," reciprocated the Saint. "I can see you're a good man gone wrong. You ought to have been one of *us*. There's a place in the gang vacant for you, if you'd care to join. Perhaps you'd like to be my halo?"

"So you are the Saint!" crisped Harding alertly.

Simon lowered his eyelids, and his lips twitched.

"Touché! . . . Of course, you didn't know that definitely, did you? But you tumbled to the allusion pretty smartly. You're a bright spark, sonny boy—I'll tell the cockeyed world."

"It wasn't so difficult. Teal's told everyone that he'd eat his hat if Vargan didn't turn out to be your show. He said he knew your work too well to make any mistake about it, even if it wasn't signed as usual."

Simon nodded.

"I wonder which hat Teal would have eaten?" he murmured. "The silk one he wears when he goes to nightclubs disguised as a gentleman, or the bowler with the beer-stain? Or has he got a third hat? If he has, I've never seen it. It's a fascinating thought . . ."

And the Saint turned his eyes to the ceiling as if he really were fascinated by the thought.

But the Saint thought, "If Bertie and Teal have been putting their heads together, Bertie must know that there's likely to be a third man on the premises. A man already proved handy with the battle-axe, moreover . . . Now, why hasn't Bertie said anything about him? Can it be that Bertie, our bright and bouncing Bertie, is having a moment of mental aberration and overlooking Norman?"

And the Saint said aloud, "However—about that halo job. How does it appeal to you?"

"Sorry, old man."

"Oh, not at all," sighed the Saint. "Don't apologise . . . What else can we do for you? You seem to have everything your own way, so we'll try to oblige. Name your horse."

"Yes, I seem to have rounded you up fairly easily."

So the cunningly hidden question was answered. It was true. Norman Kent, being for the moment out of sight, had fallen for the moment out of mind.

For a fleeting second the Saint met Roger Conway's eyes.

Then—

"What do we do?" asked the Saint amiably. "Stand and deliver?"

The youngster retired to the window and glanced out. Simon took one step towards him, stealthily, but there was an awkward distance between them, and Harding's eyes were only turned away for an instant. Then Harding turned round again, and the Saint was serenely selecting another cigarette.

"Have you got Vargan here?"

The Saint looked up.

"Ah!" said the Saint cautiously.

Harding set his lips.

In the few minutes of their encounter Simon Templar had had time to appreciate in the younger man a quiet efficiency that belied the first impression of youthfulness, combined with a pleasant sense of humour that was after the Saint's own heart. And at that moment the sense of humour was not so evident, but all the efficiency was there, and with it went a certain grimness of resolution.

"I don't know why you took Vargan," he said. "In spite of what we know about your ideas generally, that's still a mystery we haven't solved. Who are you working for?"

"Our own sweet selves," answered the Saint. "You see our lawn's been going all to hell, and none of the weedkillers we've tried seem to do it any good, so we thought perhaps Vargan's electric exterminator might—"

"Seriously!"

Simon looked at him.

"Seriously, if you want to know," said the Saint, and he said it very seriously, "we took Vargan so that his invention should not be used in the war. And that decision of ours still stands."

"That was Teal's theory."

"Dear old Teal! The man's a marvel, isn't he? Just like a blinkin' detective in a story-book . . . Yes, that's why we took Vargan. Teal will get a letter from me in the morning explaining ourselves at length."

"Something about the good of humanity, I suppose?"

"Correct," said the Saint. "Thereby snookering Angel Face, who certainly isn't thinking about the good of humanity."

Harding looked puzzled.

"This man you keep talking about—Angel Face—"

"Tiny Tim," explained Simon.

A light of understanding dawned upon the other.

"A man like an overgrown gorilla—with a face according . . ."

"How beautifully you put it, old dear! Almost the very words I used myself. You know . . ."

"Marius!" snapped Harding.

The Saint nodded.

"It rings the bell," he said, "and your penny will be returned in due course. But you don't surprise me. We knew."

"We guessed Marius was in this—"

"We could have told you."

Harding's eyes narrowed.

"How much more do you know?" he asked.

"Oh, lots of things," said the Saint blandly. "In my more brilliant moments I can run Teal a close race on some tracks. For instance, I wouldn't mind betting my second-best pair of elastic-sided boots that you were followed today—by one of Marius's men. But you mightn't have noticed that."

"But I did!"

Harding's automatic was still coolly and steadily aimed at the Saint's stomach, as it had been throughout the interview—when the aim was not temporarily diverted to Roger Conway. But now there was just a little more steadiness and rigidity in the hand that held it. The change was almost imperceptible, but Simon Templar never missed anything like that. He translated the inflexion in his own way, and when he shifted his gaze back to Harding's eyes he found the interpretation confirmed there.

"I shook off my shadow a mile back," said Harding. "But I don't mind telling you that I shouldn't have come in here alone without waiting for reinforcements if I hadn't seen that somebody was a darned sight too interested in what I was doing. And the same reason is the reason why I want Vargan at once!"

The Saint rested gracefully against the table and blew two smoke-rings of surpassing perfection.

"Is—that—so!"

"That is so," said Harding curtly. "I'll give you two minutes to decide."

"The alternative being?"

"I shall start shooting holes in you. Arms, legs . . . I think you'll tell me what I want to know before that's gone on very long."

Simon shook his head.

"You mayn't have noticed it," he said, "but I have an impediment in my speech. I'm very sensitive, and if anyone treats me unkindly it makes my impediment worse. If you started shooting at me it'd make me stammer so frightfully that I'd take half an hour to get out the first d-d-d-d-damn—let alone answering any questions."

"And," said Harding relentlessly, "I'll treat your friend in the same way."

The Saint flashed Roger Conway a smile.

"You wouldn't breathe a word, would you, old Roger?"

"Let him try to make me!" Conway scoffed.

Simon turned again.

"Honestly, Algernon," he said quietly, "you'll get nothing that way. And you know it."

"We shall see," said Harding.

The telephone stood on a small table beside the window. Still keeping the Saint and Conway covered, he took up the receiver.

"Hullo . . . Hullo . . . Hullo . . ."

Harding looked at his watch, fidgeting with the receiver-hook.

"Fifteen seconds gone . . . Blast this exchange! Hullo . . . Hullo!"

Then he listened for a moment in silence, and after that he replaced the receiver carefully. He straightened up again, and the Saint read his face.

"There was another man in your gang," said Harding. "I remember now. Is he here?"

"Is the line dead?"

"As pork."

"No one in this house would have cut the line," said Simon. "I'll give you my word for that."

Harding looked at him straightly.

"If that's true—"

"It can only be Marius," said the Saint slowly. "Perhaps the man who followed you wasn't so easy to shake off."

Roger Conway was looking out of another window, from which he could see the lawn and the river at the end of the garden. Beyond the Saint's motor-boat another motor-boat rode in mid-stream, but it was not the motor-boat in which he had seen Teal. It seemed to Roger that the two men in the second motor-boat were looking intently towards the bungalow, but he could not be sure.

"Naturally," he agreed, "it might be Marius."

It was then that Simon had his inspiration, and it made him leap suddenly to his feet.

"Harding."

Simon cried the name in a tone that would have startled anyone. Harding would not have been human if he had not turned completely round.

He had been looking through a window, with the table between himself and the Saint for safety, trying to discover what Conway was looking at. But all the time he had been there he had kept the windows in the corner of his eye. Simon had realised the fact in the moment of his inspiration, and had understood it. Norman had not been overlooked. But Harding admitted that he had come alone, and he had to make the best of a bad job. He had to keep covering the two prisoners he had already taken, and wait and hope that the third man would blunder unsuspectingly into the hold-up. And as long as part of Harding's alertness was devoted to that waiting and hoping, Norman's hands were tied. But now . . .

"What is it?" asked Harding.

He was staring at the Saint, and his back was squarely turned to the window behind him. Roger Conway, from the other side of the room, was also looking at the Saint in perplexed surprise. Only the Saint saw Norman Kent step through the window behind Harding.

But Harding felt and understood the iron grip that fell upon his gun wrist, and the hard bluntness that nosed into the small of his back.

"Don't be foolish," urged Norman Kent.

"All right."

The words dropped bitterly from the youngster's lips after a second's desperate hesitation. His fingers opened grudgingly to release his gun, and the Saint caught it neatly off the carpet.

"And our own peashooters," said Simon.

He took the other two automatics from Harding's pocket, restored one to Roger, and stepped back to the table with a gun in each of his own hands.

"Just like the good old story-book again," he remarked. "And here we are—all armed to the teeth. Place looks like an arsenal, and we all feel at home. Come over and be sociable, Archibald. There's no ill-feeling . . . Norman, will you have a dud cheque or a bag of nuts for that effort?"

"I was wondering how much longer it'd be before you had the sense to create a disturbance?"

"I'm as slow as a freight car today," said the Saint. "Don't know what's the matter with me. But all's well that ends well, as the actress used to say, and—"

"Is it?" asked Norman soberly.

"Why?"

"I heard you talking about the telephone. You were right. I didn't cut the line. Didn't think of it. And if the line is dead—"

The sentence was not finished.

No one heard the sound that interrupted it. There must have been a faint sound, but it would have been lost in the open air outside. But they all saw Norman Kent's face suddenly twist and go white, and saw him stagger and fall on one knee.

"Keep away from that window!"

Norman had understood as quickly as anyone, and he got the warning out in an agonised gasp. But the Saint ignored it. He sprang forward, and caught Norman Kent under the arms, and dragged him into shelter as a second bullet splintered the window-frame a few inches from their heads.

"They're here!"

Harding was standing recklessly in the open, careless of what his captors might be doing. The Saint rapped out a command to take cover, but Harding took no notice. Roger Conway had to haul him out of the danger zone almost by the scruff of the neck.

Simon had jerked a settee from its place by the wall and run it across three-quarters of the width of the window opening, and he lay behind it, looking towards the road with his guns in his hands. He saw something move behind the hedge, and fired twice at a venture, but he could not tell how much damage he had done.

There was the old Saintly smile back on the Saint's lips, and the old Saintly light back in his eyes. Against Harding, he hadn't really enjoyed himself. Against Teal, if it had been Teal outside, he wouldn't really have enjoyed himself. But it definitely wasn't Teal outside. Neither Chief Inspector Teal nor any of his men would have started blazing away like that with silenced guns and no preliminary parley. There was only one man in the cast who could conceivably behave like that, and against that man the Saint could enjoy himself thoroughly. He couldn't put his whole heart into the job of fighting men like Harding and Teal, men whom in any other circumstances he would have liked to have for his friends. But Marius was quite another matter. The feud with Marius was over something more than an outlook and a technical point of law. It was a personal and vital thing, like a blow in the face and a glove thrown down . . .

So Simon watched, and presently fired again. This time a cry answered him. And one bullet in reply zipped past his ear, and another clipped into the upholstery of the settee an inch from his head, and the Saintly smile became positively beatific.

"This is like war," said the Saint happily.

"It is war!" Harding shot back. "Don't you realise that?"

Roger Conway was kneeling beside Norman Kent, cutting away a trouser-leg stained with a spreading dark stain.

"What do you mean?" he demanded.

Harding stepped back.

"Didn't you understand? You seemed to know so much . . . But you hadn't a chance to know that. Still, it would have been announced in the lunch editions, and plenty of people knew about it last night. Our ultimatum was delivered at noon today, and they've got till noon tomorrow to answer."

"What country? And what's the ultimatum about?"

Harding answered. The Saint was not very surprised. He had not read between the lines of his newspapers so assiduously for nothing.

"Of course, it's all nonsense, like anything else that any country ever sent an ultimatum to another about," said Harding. "We've put it off as long as we can, but they've left us no choice. They're asking for trouble, and they're determined to have it. Half the Government still can't understand it—they think our friends ought to know better. Just swollen heads, they say. That's why everything's been kept so dark. The Government thought the swelling was bound to pass off naturally. Instead of which, it's been getting worse."

The Saint remembered a phrase from the letter which he had taken from Marius: "Cannot fail this time . . ."

And he understood that the simple word of a man like Marius, with all the power that he represented standing in support behind the word, might well be enough to sway the decisions of kings and councils.

He said, with his eyes still watching the road, "How many people have a theory to account for the swelling?"

"My chief, and a handful of others," said Harding. "We knew that Marius was in it, and Marius spells big money. But what's the use of telling ordinary people that? They couldn't see it. Besides, there was still a flaw in our theory, and we couldn't fill it up—until the show at Esher on Saturday. Then we knew."

"I figured it out the same way," said the Saint.

"Everything hangs on this," said Harding quietly. "If Marius gets Vargan for them, it means war."

Simon raised one gun, and then lowered it again as his target ducked.

"Why have you told me all this?" he asked.

"Because you ought to be on our side," Harding said steadily. "I don't care what you are. I don't care what you've done. I don't care what you're working for. But Marius is here now, and I know you can't be with Marius. So—"

"Somebody's waving a white flag," said the Saint.

He got to his feet, and Harding came up beside him. Behind the hedge, a man stood up and signalled with a handkerchief.

Then Simon saw that the road beyond the hedge was alive with men.

"What would you do here?" he asked.

"See them!" rapped Harding. "Hear what they've got to say. We can still fight afterwards. They will fight! Templar—"

The Saint beckoned, and saw a man rise from his crouched position under the hedge and walk alone up the drive. A giant of a man . . .

"Angel Face himself!" murmured Simon.

He swung round, hands on hips.

"I've heard your argument, Harding," he said. "It's a good one. But I prefer my own. In the circumstances, I'm afraid you'll have to accept it. And I want your answer quickly. The offer I made you is still open. Do you join us for the duration, or have I got to send you out there to shift for yourself? I'd hate to do it, but if you're not for us—"

"That's not the point," said Harding steadfastly. "I was sent here to find Vargan, and I think I've found him. As far as that's concerned, there can't be peace between us. You'll understand that. But for the rest of it . . . Beggars can't be choosers. We agree that Marius must not have Vargan, whatever else we disagree about. So, while we have to fight Marius—"

"A truce?"

The youngster shrugged. Then he put out his hand.

"And let's give 'em hell!" he said.

18

HOW SIMON TEMPLAR RECEIVED

MARIUS, AND THE CROWN PRINCE

REMEMBERED A DEBT

A moment later the Saint was on his knees beside Norman Kent, examining Norman's wound expertly. Norman tried to delay him.

"Pat," whispered Norman; "I left her hiding in your room."

Simon nodded.

"All right. She'll be safe there for a bit. And I'd just as soon have her out of the way while Tiny Tim's beetling around. Let's see what we can do for you first."

He went on with the examination. The entrance was three inches above the knee, and it was much larger than the entrance of even a large-calibre automatic bullet should have been. There was no exit hole, and Norman let out an involuntary cry of agony at the Saint's probing.

"That's all, sonny boy," said the Saint, and Norman loosened his teeth from his lips.

"Smashed the bone, hasn't it?"

Simon stripped off his coat, and tore off the sleeve of his shirt to improvise a bandage.

"Smashed to bits, Norman, old boy," he said. "The swine are using dum-dums . . . A large whisky, Roger . . . That'll be a consolation for you, Norman, old warrior."

"It's something," said Norman huskily.

He said nothing else about it, but he understood one thing very clearly.

No man can run very far or very fast with a thigh-bone splintered by an expanding bullet.

Strangely enough, Norman did not care. He drank the whisky they gave him gratefully, and submitted indifferently to the Saint's ministrations. In the pallor of Norman Kent's face was a strange calm.

Simon Templar also understood what that wound meant, but he did not think of it as Norman did.

He knew that Marius was standing in the window, but he did not look up until he had completed the rough dressing with practised hands that were as gentle as a woman's. He wanted to start some hard thinking before he began to bait Marius. Once well under way, the thinking process would continue by itself underneath the inevitable froth of banter and back-chat, but the Saint certainly wanted to get a stranglehold on the outstanding features of the situation first. And they were a pretty slimy set of features to have to pin down. What with Patricia on the premises to cramp his style, and Norman Kent crippled, and the British Secret Service, as represented by Captain Gerald Harding, a prisoner inside the fort on a very vague parole, and Chief Inspector Teal combing the district and liable to roll up on the scene at any moment, and Rayt Marius surrounding the bungalow with a young army corps that had already given proof enough that it wasn't accumulated in Maidenhead for a Sunday afternoon bunfight—well, even such an optimistic man as the Saint had to admit that the affair had begun to look distinctly sticky. There had been a time when the Saint was amused to call himself a professional trouble-hunter. He remembered that pleasant bravado now, and wondered if he had ever guessed that his prayers would be so abundantly answered. Verily, he had cast his bread upon the waters and hauled up a chain of steam bakeries . . .

He rose at last to his feet with these meditations simmering down into the impenetrable depths of his mind, and his face had never been milder.

"Good afternoon, little one," he said softly. "I've been looking forward to meeting you again. Life, for the last odd eighteen hours, has seemed very empty without you. But don't let's talk about that."

The giant inclined his head.

"You know me," he said.

"Yes," said the Saint, "I think we've met before. I seem to know your face. Weren't you the stern of the elephant in the circus my dear old grandmother took me to just before I went down with measles? Or were you the whatsit that stuck in the how's-your-father and upset all our drains a couple of years ago?"

Marius shrugged. He was again wearing full morning dress, as he had been when the Saint first met him in Brook Street, but the combination of that costume with this new setting, together with the man's colossal build and hideously rugged face, would have been laughably grotesque if it had not been subtly horrible.

He said, "I have already had some samples of your humour, Templar—"

"On a certain occasion which we all remember," said the Saint gently. "Quite. But we don't charge extra for an encore, so you might as well have your money's worth."

Marius's little eyes took in the others—Roger Conway lounging against the book-case swinging an automatic by the trigger-guard,

Norman Kent propped up against the sofa with a glass in his hand, Gerald Harding on the other side of the window with his hands in his pockets and a faint flush on his boyish face.

"I have only just learnt that you are the gentleman who calls himself the Saint," said Marius. "Inspector Teal was indiscreet enough to use a public telephone in the hearing of one of my men. The boxes provided are not very sound-proof. I presume this is your gang?"

"Not 'gang,'" protested the Saint, "not 'gang.' I'm sure saints never go in gangs. But, yes—these are other wearers of the halo . . . But I'm forgetting. You've never been formally introduced, have you? . . . Meet the boys . . . On your left, for instance, Captain Acting Saint Gerald Harding, sometime Fellow of Clark's College, canonised for many charitable works, including obtaining a miserly millionaire's signature to a five-figure cheque for charity. The millionaire was quite annoyed when he heard about it . . . Over there, Saint Roger Conway, winner of the Men's Open Beauty Competition at Noahsville, Ark., in '25, canonised for glorifying the American girl. At least, she told the judge it glorified her . . . On the floor, Saint Norman Kent, champion beer-swiller at the last Licensed Victuallers' and Allied Trades' Centennial Jamboree, canonised for standing free drinks to a number of blind beggars on the Feast of Stephen. The beggars, by the way, were not blind until after they'd had the drinks . . . Oh, and myself, I'm the Simple Simon who met a pieman coming through the rye. Or words to that effect. I can't help feeling that if I'd been christened bootlegger I should have met a bootlegger, which would have been much more exciting, but I suppose it's too late to alter that now."

Marius heard out this cataract of nonsense without a flicker of expression. At the end of it he said, patiently, "And Miss Holm?"

"Absent, I'm afraid," said the Saint. "It's my birthday, and she's gone to Woolworth's to buy me a present."

Marius nodded.

"It is not of importance," he said. "You know what I have come for?"

Simon appeared to ponder.

"Let's see . . . You might have come to tune the piano, only we haven't got a piano. And if we had a mangle you might have come to mend the mangle. No—the only thing I can think of is that you're travelling a line of straw hats and natty neckwear. Sorry, but we're stocked for the season."

Marius dusted his silk hat with a tenderly wielded handkerchief. His face, as always, was a mask.

Simon had to admire the nerve of the man. He still had a long score to settle with Marius, and Marius knew it, but here was Marius dispassionately dusting a silk hat in the very presence of a man who had promised to kill him. It was true that Marius came under a flag of truce, which he would justly expect a man like the Saint to respect, but still Marius gave no sign of recognising that he was in the delicate position of having to convey an ultimatum to a man who, given the flimsiest rag of excuse, would cheerfully shoot him through the stomach.

"You gain nothing by wasting time," said Marius. "I have come in the hope of saving the lives of some of my men, for some will certainly be killed if we are forced to fight."

"How touching!—as the actress said to the bishop. Is it possible that your conscience is haunted by the memory of the man you killed at Bures, ducky? Or is it just because funerals are so expensive these days?"

Marius shrugged.

"That is my business," he said. "Instead of considering that, you would do better to consider your own position. Every telephone line for ten miles has been cut—that was done as soon as we had definitely located you. Therefore there can be no quicker communication with London than by car. And the local police are not dangerous. Even

Inspector Teal is now out of touch with his headquarters, and there is an ambush prepared for him into which he cannot help falling. In addition to that, at the nearest cross-roads on either side of this house, I have posted men in police uniform, who will turn back any car which attempts to come this way, and who will explain away the noise of shooting to any inquisitive persons. It must be over an hour before any help can come to you—and then it can only end in your own arrest. That is, if you are still alive. And you cannot possibly hope to deceive me a second time with the bluff you employed so successfully last night."

"You're sure it was a bluff?"

"If it had not been a bluff I should not have found you here. Do you really think me so ignorant of official methods as to believe that you could possibly have been released so quickly?"

"And yet," said the Saint thoughtfully, "we might have been put here to bait a police trap—for you!"

Marius smiled. The Saint would never have believed that such a face could smile if he had not seen it smile once before. And it smiled with ghastly urbanity.

"Since Inspector Teal left London," said Marius, "he has never been out of sight of my agents. Therefore I have good reason to be convinced that he still does not know where you are. Shall we say, Templar, that this time you will have to think of something more tangible than—er—what was the phrase your friends used?—than breadcrumbs and bream-bait?"

Simon nodded.

"A charming phrase," he murmured.

"So," said Marius, "you may choose between surrendering Vargan or having him taken from you by force."

The Saint smiled.

"Heads you win, tails I lose—what? . . . But suppose the coin falls on its blinkin' edge? Suppose, sweet pet, you got pinched yourself? This isn't Chicago, you know. You can't run little wars of your own all over the English countryside. The farmers might get annoyed and start throwing broccoli at you. I'm not sure what broccoli is, but they might throw it."

Again that ghastly grin flitted across the giant's face.

"You have not understood me. My country requires Vargan and his invention. In order to obtain that, I will sacrifice as many lives as I may be forced to sacrifice, and my men will die here for their country as readily as they would die on any other battlefield."

"Your country!"

The Saint had been lighting a cigarette with a cool and steady hand, and for all that might have been read in the scene by an observer who could not hear the words, they might have been discussing nothing more than the terms of a not-too-friendly golf match—instead of a situation in which the fates of nations were involved . . . At one moment . . . And then the Saint split the thin crust of calm with those two electric words. The voice that spoke them was no longer the Saint's gently mocking drawl. It was a voice of pure steel and rock and acid. It took those three simple syllables, ground and honed a hundred knife-edges around them, fenced them about with a thousand stinging needle-points, and spoke them in a breath that might have whipped off the North Pole.

"Your country!"

"That is what I said."

"Has a man like you a country? Is there one acre of God's earth that a man like you loves for no other reason than that it's his home? Have you a loyalty to anything—except the bloated golden spiders whose webs you weave? Are there any people you can call your people— people you wouldn't sacrifice without a qualm to put thirty pieces of silver into your pocket? Do you care for anything in the world but your own greasy god of money, Rayt Marius?"

For the first time Marius's face changed.

"It is my country," he said.

The Saint laughed shortly.

"Tell us any lie but that, Marius," he said. "Because that one won't get by."

"But it is still my country. And the men outside lent to me by my country for this work—"

"Has it occurred to you," said the Saint, "that we also might be prepared to die for our country—and that the certainty of being imprisoned if we were rescued might not influence us at all?"

"I have thought of that."

"And don't you place too great a reliance on our honesty? Is there anything to stop us forgetting the armistice and holding you as a hostage?"

Marius shook his head.

"What then," he said silkily, "was there to stop my coming here under a white flag to distract your attention while my men occupied the rest of the house from the other side? When the fortune of one's country is at stake one has little time for conventional honesty. A white flag may be honoured on a battlefield, but this is more than a mere battlefield. It is all the battlefields of the war."

Simon was teetering watchfully on his heels, his cigarette canted up between his lips. His hands hung loosely at his sides, but in each of them he held sudden death.

"You'd still be our hostage, loveliness," he said. "And if there's going to be any treachery—"

"My life is nothing," said Marius. "There is a leader out there"—he gestured towards the road—"who would not hesitate to sacrifice me and many others."

"Namely?"

"His Highness—"

Simon Templar drew a deep breath.

"His Highness the Crown Prince Rudolf of—"

"Hell!" said the Saint.

"A short time ago you saved his life," said Marius. "It is for that reason that His Highness has directed me to give you this chance. He also wished me to apologise for wounding you yesterday, although it happened before we knew that you were the Saint."

"Sweetest lamb," said the Saint, "I'll bet you wouldn't have obeyed His Highness if you hadn't needed his men to do your dirty work!"

Marius spread his huge hands.

"That is immaterial. I have obeyed. And I await your decision. You may have one minute to consider it."

Simon sent his cigarette spinning through the window with a reckless flourish.

"You have our decision now," he said.

Marius bowed.

"If you will answer one question," said the Saint.

"What do you want to know?"

"When you kidnapped Vargan, you couldn't take his apparatus with you—"

"I follow your thoughts," said the giant. "You are thinking that even if you surrender Vargan the British experts will still possess the apparatus, which they can copy even if they do not understand it. Let me disillusion you. While some of my men were taking Vargan, others were destroying his apparatus—very effectively. You may be sure nothing was left which even Sir Roland Hale could make workable. I'm sorry to disappoint you—"

"But you don't disappoint me, Angel Face," said the Saint. "On the contrary, you bring me the best news I've had for a long time. If you weren't so unspeakably repulsive, I believe I'd—I'd fling my arms round your bull neck, Angel Face, dear dewdrop! . . . I'd guessed I could rely on your efficiency, but it's nice to know for certain . . ."

Roger Conway interposed from the other side of the room.

He said, "Look here, Saint, if the Crown Prince is outside, we've only got to tell him the truth about Marius—"

Marius turned.

"What truth?" he inquired suavely.

"Why—the truth about your septic patriotism! Tell him what we know. Tell him you're just leading him up the garden for your own poisonous ends—"

"And you think he would believe you?" sneered Marius. "You are too childish, Conway! Even you cannot deny that I am doing my best to place Vargan's invention in His Highness's hands."

The Saint shook his head.

"Angel Face is right, Roger," he said. "The Crown Prince is getting his caviare, and he isn't going to worry why the sturgeon died. No—I've got a much finer lead on the problem than that."

And he faced Marius again.

"It's really truly true, dear one, that Vargan is the key to the whole situation?" he asked softly, persuasively.

"Exactly."

"Vargan is the really truly cream in your coffee?"

The giant twitched his shoulders.

"I do not understand all your idioms. But I think I have made myself plain."

"I was wondering who did it," said Roger sympathetically.

But a new smile was coming to Simon Templar's lips—a mocking, devil-may-care, swashbuckling, Saintly smile. He set his hands on his hips and smiled.

"Then this is our answer," smiled the Saint. "If you want Vargan, you can either come and fetch him or go home and suck jujubes. Take your choice, Angel Face!"

Marius stood still.

"Then His Highness wishes to say that he disclaims all responsibility for the consequences of your foolishness—"

"One minute!"

It was Norman Kent, trying painfully to struggle up on to his sound leg. The Saint was beside him in a moment, with an arm about his shoulders.

"Easy, old Norman!"

Norman smiled faintly.

"I want to stand up, Simon."

And he stood up, leaning on the Saint, and looked across at Marius. Very dark and stern and aloof he was.

And—

"Suppose," said Norman Kent, "suppose we said that we hadn't got Vargan?"

"I should not believe you."

Roger Conway cut in: "Why should we keep him? If we'd only wanted to take him away from you, he'd have been returned to the Government before now. You must know that he hasn't been sent back. What use could we have for him?"

"You may have your own reasons. Ransom, perhaps. Your Government should be prepared to pay well for his safety—"

Norman Kent broke in with a clear, short laugh that shattered Marius's theory more fatally than any of the words that followed could have done.

"Think again, Marius! You don't understand us yet! . . . We took Vargan away for the sake of the peace of the world and the sparing of millions of lives. We hoped to persuade him to turn back from the thing he proposed to do. But he was mad, and he would not listen. So this evening, for the peace of the world . . ."

He paused, and passed a hand across his eyes.

Then he drew himself erect, and his dark eyes gazed without fear into a great distance, and there was no flinching in the light in his eyes.

His voice came again, clear and strong.

"I shot him like a mad dog," he said.

"You—"

Harding started forward, but Roger Conway was barring his way in an instant.

"For the peace of the world," Norman Kent repeated. "And—for the peace of my two dearest friends. You'll understand, Saint. I knew at once that you'd never let Roger or me risk what that shot meant. So I took the law into my own hands. Because Pat loves you, Simon, as I do. I couldn't let her spend the rest of her life with you under the shadow of the gallows. I love her, too, you see. I'm sorry . . ."

"You killed Vargan?" said Marius incredulously.

Norman nodded. He was quite calm.

And, outside the window, the shadows of the trees were lengthening over the quiet garden.

"I found him writing in a notebook. He'd covered sheets and sheets. I don't know what it was about, or whether there's enough for an expert to work on. I'm not a scientist. But I brought them away to make sure. I'd have burnt them before, but I couldn't find any matches. But I'll burn them now before your eyes, and that'll be the end of it all. Your lighter, Saint—"

He was fumbling in his pocket.

Roger Conway saw Marius's right hand leap to his hip, and whirled round with his automatic levelled at the centre of the giant's chest.

"Not just yet, Marius!" said Roger, through his teeth.

The Saint, when he went to support Norman, had dropped one gun into his coat pocket. Now, with one arm holding Norman, he had had to put his other gun down on the arm of the sofa while he searched for his petrol-lighter.

He had not realised that the grouping of the others had so fallen that Conway could not now cover both Harding and Marius. Just two simple movements had been enough to bring about that cataclysmic rearrangement—when Norman Kent stood up and Marius tried to draw. And Simon hadn't noticed it. He'd confessed that he was as slow as a freight car that day, which may or may not have been true, but the fact remained that for a fraction of a second he'd allowed the razor-edge of his vigilance to be taken off. And he saw his mistake that fraction of a second too late.

Harding reached the gun on the arm of the sofa in two steps and a lightning dive, and then he had his back to the wall.

"Drop that gun, you! I give you three seconds. One—"

Conway, moving only his head to look round, knew that the youngster could drop him in his tracks before he had time to more than begin to move his automatic. And he had no need to wonder whether the other would carry out his threat. Harding's grim and desperate determination was sufficiently attested by the mere fact that he had dared to make the gamble that gave him the gun and the strategic advantage at the same time. And Harding's eyes were as set and stern as the eyes of a young man can be.

"Two—"

Suppose Roger chanced his arm? He'd be pipped, for a million. But would it give Simon time to draw? But Marius was ready to draw also . . .

"Three!"

Roger Conway released the gun, even as Harding had had to do not many minutes before, and he had all the sense of bitter humiliation that Harding must have had.

"Kick it over to me."

Conway obeyed, and Harding picked up the gun, and swung two automatics in arcs that included everyone in the room.

"The honour of the British Secret Service!" drawled the Saint, with a mildness that only emphasised the biting sting of his contempt.

"The truce is over," said Harding dourly. "You'd do the same in my place. Bring me those papers!"

The Saint lowered Norman Kent gently, and Norman rested, half-standing, half-sitting, on the high arm of the settee. And Simon tensed himself to dice the last foolhardy throw.

Then a shadow fell on him, and he looked round and saw that the number of the congregation had been increased by one.

A tall, soldierly figure in grey stood in the opening of the window. A figure utterly immaculate and utterly at ease . . . And it is, of course, absurd to say that any accident of breeding makes a man stand out among his fellows, but this man could have been nothing but the man he was . . .

"Marius," spoke the man in grey, and Marius turned.

"Back, Highness! For God's sake—"

The warning was rapped out in another language, but the man in grey answered in English.

"There is no danger," he said. "I came to see why you had overstayed your time-limit."

He walked calmly into the room, with no more than a careless glance and a lift of his fine eyebrows for Gerald Harding and Gerald Harding's two circling guns.

And then the Saint heard a sound in the hall, beyond the door, which still stood ajar.

He reached the door in a reckless leap, and slammed it. Then he laid hold of the heavy book-case that stood by the wall, and with a single titanic heave toppled it crashing over to fall like a great bolt across the doorway. An instant later the table from the centre of the room had followed to reinforce the book-case.

And Simon Templar stood with his back to the pile, breathing deeply, with his head thrown back defiantly. He spoke.

"So you're another man of honour—Highness!"

The Prince stroked his moustache with a beautifully manicured finger.

"I gave Marius a certain time in which to make my offer," he said. "When that time was exceeded, I could only presume that you had broken the truce and detained him, and I ordered my men to enter the house. They were fortunate enough to capture a lady . . ."

The Saint went white.

"I say 'fortunate' because she was armed, and might have killed some of them, or at least raised an alarm, if they had not taken her by surprise. However, she has not been harmed. I mention the fact merely to let you see that my intrusion is not so improvident as you might otherwise think. Are you Simon Templar?"

"I am."

The Prince held out his hand.

"I believe I owe you my life. I had hoped for an opportunity of making your acquaintance, but I did not expect that our meeting would be in such unpropitious circumstances. Nevertheless, Marius should have told you that I am not insensitive to the debt I owe you."

Simon stood where he was.

"I saved your life, Prince Rudolf," he answered in a voice like a whip-lash, "because I had nothing against you. But now I have something against you, and I may take your life for it before the end of the day."

The Prince shrugged delicately.

"At least," he remarked, "while we are discussing that point, you might ask your friend to put away his weapons. They distress me."

Captain Gerald Harding leaned comfortably against the wall, and devoted one of his distressing weapons entirely to the Prince.

"I'm not Templar's friend," he said. "I'm a humble member of the British Secret Service, and I was sent here to get Vargan. I didn't arrive in time to save Vargan, but I seem to have got here in time to save something nearly as valuable. You're late, Your Highness!"

19

HOW SIMON TEMPLAR WENT TO HIS LADY, AND NORMAN KENT ANSWERED THE TRUMPET

For a moment there was an utter silence, and then Marius began to speak rapidly in his own language.

The Prince listened, his eyes narrowing. Apart from that attentive narrowing of the eyes, neither his attitude nor his expression changed at all. The man had an inhumanly sleek superiority to all ordinary emotion.

Simon made no attempt to interrupt Marius's recital. Someone had to explain the situation, and, since Marius had assumed the job, Marius might as well go on with it. The interval would give the Saint another welcome breather. And the Saint relaxed against his barricade and took out his cigarette-case, and began to tap a cigarette thoughtfully against his teeth.

Then the Prince turned to him, and spoke in his sleek velvety voice.

"So! I begin to understand. This man caught you, but you came to an agreement when you found that you were at least united against me. Is that right?"

"But what a brain Your Highness has!" murmured the Saint.

"And he has ended the armistice in his own way without giving you notice?"

"I'm afraid so. I think he got some sort of stag fever when he saw the papers. Anyway, he forgot the spirit of the Eton Boating Song."

"And you have no influence with him?"

"None."

"But your friend"—the Prince indicated Norman Kent—"has the papers?"

"And I've got the friend," said Harding cheerfully. "So what do you all do about it?"

In that instant he stood absolutely alone, dominating the situation, and they all looked at him. He was young, but he had the spirit, that boy! And the Saint understood that Harding could not have helped breaking his parole, even where an older man might have hesitated.

And then Harding no longer stood alone, for in the next instant Norman Kent had usurped the limelight with a compelling movement of his hand that drew every eye.

"I should like to have something to say about this," said Norman Kent.

His voice was always low and measured. Now it was quieter than ever, but every syllable was as sure as a clarion.

"I have the papers," he said, "and Captain Harding has me. Perfectly true. But there is one thing you've all overlooked."

"What is that?"

It was the Prince who spoke, but Norman Kent answered them all. He took one glance out of the window, at the sunlight and the trees and the green grass and a clump of dahlias splashed against the hedge like a wound, and they saw him smile. And then he answered.

"Nothing is won without sacrifice," he said simply.

He looked across at the Saint.

"Simon," he said, "I want you to trust me. Ever since we came together I've done everything you ordered without question. We've all followed you, naturally, because you were always our natural leader. But we couldn't help learning something from your leadership. I've heard how you beat Marius in Brook Street last night—by doing the one thing you couldn't possibly do. And I've heard how Roger used the same principle, and helped us to beat Teal with it—by doing the one thing he couldn't possibly do. It's my turn now. I think I must be very clever today. I've seen how to apply the principle to this in my own way. Because now—here—there is something that no one could do. And I can do it. Will you follow me?"

And Norman's dark eyes, with a queer fanatical light burning in them, met the Saint's clear, sea-blue eyes. For a second's tense stillness . . .

Then:

"Carry on," said the Saint.

Norman Kent smiled.

"It's easy," he said. "You've all appreciated the situation, haven't you? . . . We have you, Prince, and you, Marius, as hostages, but you have as a counter-hostage a lady who is very dear to all but one of us. That in itself would be a deadlock, even if it were not for Captain Harding and his guns."

"You express it admirably," said the Prince.

"On the other hand, Captain Harding, who for the moment is in command, is in a very awkward situation. He is by far the weakest party in a three-cornered fight. Whether the fact that you hold a friend of ours as a hostage would weigh with him is open to doubt. Personally,

I doubt it very much. He's never met the lady—she's nothing more than a name to him—and he has to do what he believes to be his duty. Moreover, he has already given us an example of the way in which his sense of duty is able to override all other considerations. So that we are in a very difficult predicament. As Englishmen, we are bound to take his part against you. As mere men, we would rather die than do anything to endanger the lady whom you have in your power. These two motives alone would be complication enough. But there's a third. As the Saint's friends, who hold to his ideals, we have set ourselves to accomplish something that both you and Captain Harding would do anything to prevent."

"You could not have made a more concise summary," said the Prince.

Again Norman Kent smiled.

"So you will agree that the deadlock only exists because we are all trying to win without a sacrifice," he said. "And the answer is—that the situation doesn't admit of a victory without sacrifice, though there are plenty of means of surrender without the sacrifice of more than honour. But we dislike surrenders."

He took from his pocket three sheets of paper closely written in a small, neat hand, folded them carefully, and held them out.

"Captain Harding—you may take these."

"Norman! Damn you—"

The Saint was crossing the room. His mouth was set in a hard line, and his eyes were as bleak as an arctic sky. But Norman Kent faced him without fear.

"You agreed to let me handle this, Saint."

"I never agreed to let you surrender. Sooner than that—"

"But this isn't surrender," said Norman Kent. "This is victory. Look!"

Harding was beside him. Norman turned, the papers loosely held in his fingers. And Norman looked straight at Roger Conway.

"Roger," he said slowly, "I think you'll understand. Take the papers, Harding!"

Harding dropped one gun into his pocket, and snatched . . .

And then the Saint understood.

Harding was, as Norman had said, alone among many enemies. And for a moment he had only one automatic with which to hold them all. The gun was aimed at Roger Conway, who was nearest, but in order to take the papers Harding had to glance away at right angles to his line of aim, towards Norman Kent and the Saint. Just for a sufficient moment.

And Norman let go the papers as Harding touched them, but then, instead of going back, his hand went forward. It had closed upon Harding's wrist in a flash, fastened there like a vice. And it jerked—one sudden heave into which Norman put all the strength at his command.

The gun in Harding's hand exploded once, but the shot smacked harmlessly up into the ceiling. For Roger Conway had understood in time. He had pounced on Harding's left hand and wrenched away the automatic in the instant of time that was given him, and he had the Prince safely covered with it even as Gerald Harding, yanked off his balance by Norman Kent's superhuman effort, stumbled slap into the Saint's left.

It was all over in a split second, before either the Prince or Marius could have realised what was happening and taken advantage of it.

And then Roger's gun was discouraging the movement of the hand towards the hip that Marius had started too late, and Norman Kent, white to the lips with the agony his supreme attempt had cost him, was leaning weakly against the arm of the sofa. And Gerald Harding was stretched out on the floor like a log, with the Saint stooping over him and collecting the second automatic with one hand and the fallen papers with the other.

"That looks better," said Roger Conway contentedly.

But Norman Kent had not finished.

He was saying, through clenched teeth, "Give me back those papers, Simon!"

The Saint hesitated, with the sheets crumpled in his hand.

"But—"

"At once!" rang Norman's voice imperatively, "You've trusted me so far, and I haven't let you down. Trust me a little more."

He took the papers almost by force, and stuffed them into his pocket. Then he held out his hand again.

"And that gun!"

Simon obeyed. It would have been impossible to refuse. For once, the Saint was not the leader. Perhaps the greatest thing he ever did in all his leadership was to surrender it then, as he surrendered it, without jealousy and without condescension.

But Norman Kent was a man inspired. His personality, which had always been so gentle and reserved, flamed in the room then like a dark fire.

"That's the first thing," said Norman. "And there are only two things more."

The Prince had not moved. Nothing in those few momentous and eventful seconds had provoked the faintest ripple on the tranquil surface of his self-control. He still stood in the position he had taken up when he first entered the room—perfectly at his ease, perfectly calm, perfectly impassive, smoothing his wisp of moustache. Suave and imperturbable, he waited without any visible exertion of patience for the ferment to subside and the embroiled items of it to settle down into their new dispositions. It was not until he appeared satisfied that they had done so that he spoke, with the tiniest of smiles curving his lips.

"Gentlemen," he remarked, "you do not disappoint me. I have heard much about you, and seen a little. The little I have seen tells me that the much I have heard may not be greatly exaggerated. If you should ever wish to forsake your careers of crime, and take service with a foreigner, I should be delighted to engage you."

"Thanks," said Norman curtly. "But this is not a crime. In our eyes, it's a far, far better thing than you will ever do. We'll waste no more time. Prince, do you agree that the situation has been simplified?"

The Prince inclined his head.

"I saw you simplify it."

"And you say that if we give you these papers"—Norman Kent touched his pocket—"we may leave at once, without hindrance?"

"That was my offer."

"Have we any assurance that you'll stand by it?"

The thin eyebrows went up in expostulation.

"I have given my word."

"And apart from that?"

"If the word of a gentleman is not enough for you, may I point out that I have twenty-five men here—some in the garden, some inside the house on the other side of the door which Mr Templar has so adroitly barricaded, and some on the river. I have but to give the signal—they have but to hear my voice—" The sentence ended in a significant shrug. "You are at my mercy. And, after you have given up the papers, what reason could there be for me to detain you further? And, in any case, why should I trouble to offer terms at all, if I did not remember the service you once did me? It is true that Mr Templar has refused to shake hands with me, but I bear him no malice for that. I may be able to understand his feelings. I have already said that I regret the circumstances. But it is the fortune of war. I make the most generous compromise I can."

"And yet," said Norman Kent, "I should like to be sure that there can be no mistake. I have the papers. Let my friends go, with the girl, in the car that's waiting outside. I'll undertake that they won't warn the police, or come back to attack you, and I'll stay here myself, as a hostage, to give you the papers half an hour after they've left. For that half-hour you and Marius must remain here as security for the safe-conduct of my friends—at the end of this gun."

"Highness!"

Marius spoke, standing stiffly to attention.

"Highness, need we have more of this parleying. A word to the men—"

The Prince raised his hand.

"That is not my way, Marius. I owe these gentlemen a debt. And I accept their terms, strange as they seem." He turned back to Norman. "But I need hardly add, sir, that if I find any cause to suspect you of treachery, I shall consider the debt cancelled."

"Of course," said Norman Kent. "That is quite fair."

The Prince stepped to the window.

"Then, if you will permit me—"

He stood in the opening and beckoned, and two men came running. Inside the room, they pocketed their automatics and saluted. The Prince addressed them briefly, and they saluted again. Then he turned and spoke again in English, with a graceful gesture of his sensitive hands.

"Your car is waiting, gentlemen."

Both Roger and the Saint looked at Norman Kent puzzledly, doubtfully, almost incredulously, but Norman only smiled.

"Don't forget that you promised to trust me," he said. "I know you think I'm mad. But I was never saner in my life. I have found the only solution—the only way to peace with honour."

Still Simon Templar looked at him, trying to read what was not to be read.

It tore at his heart to leave Norman Kent there like that. And he couldn't make out what inspiration Norman could be acting on. Norman couldn't possibly mean the surrender. That couldn't possibly be called peace with honour. And how Norman could see any way for himself, alone, hurt and lame as he was . . . But Norman seemed to be without doubt or fear—that was the only thing that could be read in his face, that supernatural confidence and contentment.

And the Saint himself could see no way out, even for the three of them together. The Prince held all the cards. Even if Patricia had been in no danger, and they had shot the Prince and Marius and stood the siege, they must inevitably have been beaten. Even if they had made up their minds to sell their lives in the achievement of their purpose . . . But Norman had not the air of a man who was facing death.

And the Prince's man held Patricia, even as Marius had held her the night before. But the same methods could not possibly be applied this time.

Yet the Saint pleaded: "Won't you let me stay, son? I do trust you, but I know you're wounded—"

Norman Kent shook his head.

"It doesn't matter," he said. "I shall be carried out of here in state."

"When do we see you?" asked Roger.

Norman gazed dreamily into the distance, and what he saw there seemed to amuse him.

"I shall be some time," he said.

And he turned to the Prince.

"May I write a short note?"

"I remind you," said the Prince, "that you remain here as a guarantee of the good behaviour of your friends."

"I agree to that," said Norman. "Give me a pen and paper, Roger."

And once again Marius tried to intervene.

"Highness, you are trusting them too far! This can only be a treachery. If they meant what they said, why should there be any need for all this—"

"It is their way, Marius," said the Prince calmly. "I admit that it is strange. But no matter. You should be a more thorough psychologist, my friend. After what you have seen of them can you believe that two of them would leave the third to face his fate alone while they themselves escaped? It is absurd!"

Norman Kent had scribbled one line. He blotted it carefully, and folded the sheet.

"And an envelope, Roger."

He placed the sheet inside and stuck down the flap.

Then he held out his hand to Roger Conway.

"Good luck, Roger," he said. "Be good."

"All the best, Norman, old man."

They gripped.

And Simon was speaking to the Prince.

"It seems," said Simon, "that this is au revoir, Your Highness!"

The Prince made one of his exquisitely courteous gestures.

"I trust," he replied, "that it is not adieu. I hope to meet you again in better days."

Then the Saint looked at Marius, and for a long time he held the giant's eyes. And he gave Marius a different good-bye.

"You, also," said the Saint slowly, "I shall meet again."

But, behind the Saint, Norman Kent laughed, and the Saint turned.

Norman stretched out one hand, and the Saint took it in a firm grasp. And Norman's other hand offered the letter.

"Put this in your pocket, Simon, and give me your word not to open it for four hours. When you've read it, you'll know where you'll see me again. I'll be waiting for you. And don't worry. Everything is safe with me. Good hunting, Saint!"

"Very good hunting to you, Norman."

Norman Kent smiled.

"I think it will be a good run," he said.

So Simon Templar went to his lady.

Norman saw Roger and Simon pass through the window and turn to look back at him as they reached the garden, and he smiled again, and waved them a gay good-bye. A moment afterwards he heard the rising drone of the Hirondel and the soft crunching of tyres down the drive.

He caught one last glimpse of them as the car turned into the road—the Saint at the wheel, with one arm about Patricia's shoulders, and Roger Conway in the back, with one of the Prince's men riding on the running-board beside him. That, of course, would be to give them a passage through the guards at the cross-road . . .

And then they were gone.

Norman sat down on the sofa, feeling curiously weak. His leg was numb with pain. He indicated decanter, siphon, glasses, and cigarette-box with a wave of his automatic.

"Make yourselves at home, gentlemen," he invited. "And pass me something on your way. I'm afraid I can't move. You ought to stop your men using soft-nosed bullets, Marius—they're dirty things."

It was the Prince who officiated with the whisky and lighted Norman a cigarette.

"War is a ruthless thing," said the Prince. "As a man I like and admire you. But as what I am, because you are against my country and myself, if I thought you were attempting to trick me I should kill you without compunction—like that!" He snapped his fingers. "Even the fact you once helped to save my life could not extenuate your offence."

"Do you think I'm a fool?" asked Norman, rather tiredly.

He sipped his drink, and the hands of the clock crawled round.

Five minutes.

Ten.

Fifteen.

The Prince sat in an armchair, his legs elegantly crossed with a proper regard for the knife-edge crease in his trousers. In one hand he held a glass; with the other he placidly smoked a cigarette through a long holder.

Marius paced the room like a caged lion. From time to time he glanced at Norman with venom and suspicion in his slitted gaze, and seemed about to say something, but each time he checked himself and resumed his impatient promenade—until the Prince stopped him with a languid wave of his cigarette-holder.

"My dear Marius, your restlessness disturbs me. For Heaven's sake practise some self-control."

"But, Highness—"

"Marius, you repeat yourself. Repetition is a tedious vice."

Then Marius sat down.

The Prince delicately stifled a yawn.

Harding, on the floor, groaned, and roused as if from a deep sleep. Norman leaned over and helped him to come to a sitting position. The youngster opened his eyes slowly, rubbing a tender jaw muzzily. He would never know how the Saint had hated having to strike that blow.

Norman allowed him to take in the situation as best he could. And he gave him a good look at the automatic.

"Where are the others?" asked Harding hazily.

"They've gone," said Norman.

In short, compact sentences he explained what had happened.

Then he addressed a question to the Prince.

"What is Captain Harding's position in this affair?"

"If he does not allow his sense of duty to override his discretion," answered the Prince carelessly, "we are no longer interested in him."

Harding scrambled unsteadily to his feet.

"But I'm damned well interested in you!" he retorted. And he turned to Norman with a dazed and desperate entreaty. "Kent—as an Englishman—you're not going to let these swabs—"

"You'll see in seven minutes," said Norman calmly.

Harding wavered before the level automatic in Norman's hand. He cursed, raved impotently, almost sobbed.

"You fool! You fool! Oh, damn you! . . . Haven't you any decency? Can't you see—"

Norman never moved, but his face was very white. Those few minutes were the worst he had ever spent. His leg was throbbing dreadfully. And Harding swore and implored, argued, pleaded, fumed, begged almost on his knees, lashed Norman Kent with words of searing scorn . . .

Five minutes to go.

Four . . . three . . . two . . .

One minute to go.

The Prince glanced at the gold watch on his wrist, and extracted the stub of a cigarette from his long holder with fastidious fingers.

"The time is nearly up," he murmured gently.

"Oh, for God's sake!" groaned Harding. "Think, Kent, you worm! You miserable—abject—crawling—coward! Give me a gun and let me fight—"

"There's no need to fight," said Norman Kent.

He put one hand to his pocket, and for a second he thought that Harding would chance the automatic and leap at his throat. He held up the crumpled sheets, and both the Prince and Marius rose—the Prince with polished and unhurried elegance, and Marius like an unleashed fiend.

Somehow Norman Kent was struggling to his feet again. He was very pale, and the fire in his eyes burned with a feverish fierceness. His wounded leg was simply the deadened source of a thousand twinges of torment that shot up the whole of his side at the least movement, like long, jagged needles. But he had a detached stubborn determination to face the end on his feet.

"The papers I promised you!"

He pushed them towards Marius, and the giant grabbed them with enormous, greedy hands.

And then Norman was holding out his gun, butt foremost, towards Harding. He spoke in tense, swift command.

"Through the window and down the garden, Harding! Take the Saint's motor-boat. It's moored at the end of the lawn. The two men on the river shouldn't stop you—"

"Highness!"

It was Marius's voice, shrill and savage. The giant's face was hideously contorted.

Norman thrust Harding behind him, covering his retreat to the window.

"Get out!" he snarled. "There's nothing for you to wait for now . . . Well, Marius?"

The Prince's voice slashed in with a deadly smoothness: "Those are not Vargan's papers, Marius?"

"An absurd letter—to this man himself—from one of his friends!"

"So!"

The word fell into the room with the sleek crispness of a drop of white-hot metal. Yet the Prince could never have been posed more gracefully, nor could his face have ever been more serene.

"You tricked me, after all!"

"Those are the papers I promised you," said Norman coolly.

"He must have the real papers still, Highness!" babbled Marius. "I was watching him—he had no chance to give them to his friends . . ."

"That's where you're wrong!"

Norman spoke very, very quietly, almost in a whisper, but the whisper held a ring of triumph like a trumpet call. The blaze in his dark eyes was not of this world.

"When Harding grabbed Templar's gun—you remember, Marius?—I had the papers in my hands. I put them in Templar's pocket. He never knew what I did. I hardly knew myself. I did it almost without thinking. It was a sheer blind inspiration—the only way to spoof the lot of you and get my friends away. And it worked! I beat you . . ."

He heard a sound behind him, and looked round. Harding had started—he was racing down the lawn, bent low to the ground like a greyhound. Perhaps there were silenced guns plopping at him from all round the house, but they could not be heard, and he must have been untouched, for he ran on without a false step, swerving and zigzagging like a snipe.

A smile touched Norman's lips. He didn't mind being left alone now that his work was done. And he knew that Harding could not have stayed. Harding also had work to do. He had to find help—to deal with Marius and intercept Simon Templar and the precious papers. But Norman smiled, because he was sure the Saint wouldn't be intercepted. Still, he liked the mettle of that fair-haired youngster . . .

His leg hurt like blazes.

But the Saint had never guessed the impossible thing. That had been Norman Kent's one fear, that the Saint would suspect and refuse to leave him. But Norman's first success, when he had tricked Harding with the offer of the papers, had won the Saint's faith, as it had to win it. And Simon had gone, and Patricia with him. It was enough.

And in the fullness of time Simon would find the papers, and he would open the letter and read the one line that was written there. And that line Norman had already spoken, but no one had understood.

"Nothing is won without sacrifice."

Norman turned again, and saw the automatic in Marius's hand. There was something in the way the gun was held, something in the face behind it, that told him that this man did not miss. And the gun was not aimed at Norman, but beyond him, at the flying figure that was nearing the motor-boat at the end of the lawn.

That gentle far-away smile was still on Norman Kent's lips as he took two quick hops backwards and to one side, so that his body was between Marius and the window.

He knew that Marius, blind, raging mad with fury, would not relax his pressure on the trigger because Norman Kent was standing directly in his line of fire, but Norman didn't care. It made no difference to him. Marius, or the Prince, would certainly have shot him sooner or later. Probably he deserved it. He had deliberately cheated, knowing the price of the revoke. He thought no more of himself. But an extra second or two ought to give Harding time to reach comparative safety in the motor-boat.

Norman Kent wasn't afraid. He was smiling.

It was a strange way to come to the end of everything, like that, in that quiet bungalow by the peaceful Thames, with the first mists of the evening coming up from the river like tired clouds drifted down from Heaven, and the light softening over the cool, quiet garden. That place had seen so much of their enjoyment, so much comradeship and careless laughter. They had been lovely and pleasant in their lives . . . He wished his leg wasn't giving him such hell. But that would be over soon. And there must be many worse ways of saying farewell to so full a life. It was something to have heard the sound of the trumpet. And the game would go on. It seemed as if the shadows of the peaceful evening outside were the foreshadowings of a great peace over all the world.

PUBLICATION
HISTORY

The Saint Closes the Case occupies a peculiar position in the Saint canon. The novel evolved from two stories first published in *The Thriller*, a weekly magazine that Leslie Charteris wrote for very early on in his career. These two adventures were "The Creeping Death," from issue 23, which was first published on 13 July 1929, and "Sudden Death," which appeared in issue 40, published on 9 November 1929. The novel itself came out in May 1930 as *The Last Hero*. It was the first Saint adventure published by Hodder & Stoughton, and they declared on the cover, "Hodder & Stoughton present Leslie Charteris for the first time in their lists. His work is in fact most uncommon and most uncommonly good . . ."

The novel sold well, so they followed it up just a couple of months later with another Saint book, *Enter the Saint*. It has a similar heritage to *The Saint Closes the Case*, for it was based on work that first appeared in *The Thriller* magazine, but in this case they were kept as short stories rather than being adapted into a novel.

With the benefit of over eighty years of hindsight, you have to question the wisdom of calling the third book in the series *Enter the Saint*, for over the years many publishers and readers have assumed it is the first Saint book. There is a case to be made for that assumption, given that Charteris prefaced many early editions with this introduction:

> Since The Last Hero, *many people have asked me how the Saint came by the reputation that he already had at the beginning of that story, and what cause there was for so many to fear him and some few to love him as they did. It is in the hope of pleasing these people that I have put together these tales of some of his earlier exploits . . .*

Regardless, although *The Saint Closes the Case* was chronologically the first Saint book published by Hodder, in terms of the canon it makes more sense to consider it as the third book in the series. It is also the first of the trilogy of stories featuring Rayt Marius, with *The Avenging Saint* and *The Saint's Getaway* completing the set. Even Charteris would later acknowledge this logic and encourage readers to start with *Enter the Saint*.

When he came to adapt the magazine stories into a novel, Charteris made some significant changes. Since Norman Kent was originally killed at the end of the first story in *The Thriller*, Charteris rewrote the ending and used the second original story as filler for the middle of the novel. He made a few other minor changes and took out one slightly larger section from the first story. In this expunged section the Saint is shot outside his Brook Street dwelling by the villains. The bullet went "slap through the right lung," and he had "one rib chipped." Treated by his neighbour Dr Terry Mannering (hero of Charteris's first novel, *X Esquire*) "for four days the Saint hovered between life and death," but in "an almost miraculously swift convalescence," was cured in three weeks.

Much like *Enter the Saint*, this novel was almost continuously in print through the first half of the Saint's career. Hodder printed on average one hardback edition a year until the early 1950s. The novel was serialized in the March 1931 edition of the American magazine *Detective Classics*, and then published shortly afterwards by the Doubleday Crime Club.

A Danish edition appeared in 1936 under the title *Sankt Jørgen og dragen*, published as part of a small series of Saint adventures by Berglingske Forlag. The title literally translates as "St George and the dragon." In early translations the Saint, for reasons unknown, was called St George. By the time of mass Danish translations in the 1960s, he'd been rechristened Helgenen. In Sweden it was called *Helgonet i härnad*, published by Aktiebolaget Skoglunds Bokförlag in 1938.

A German edition (*Der letzte Held*) appeared in 1933, whilst the Spanish got to read about *El último héroe* in November 1934. Editions have also appeared in other languages; Poland and Hungary became the most recent converts in the 1990s.

Unusually for the adventures of the Saint, this novel has only been adapted once, as part of a short run of radio plays, starring Paul Rhys as Simon Templar. It was broadcast on BBC Radio 4 in 1995.

ABOUT THE AUTHOR

I'm mad enough to believe in romance. And I'm sick and tired of this age—tired of the miserable little mildewed things that people racked their brains about, and wrote books about, and called life. I wanted something more elementary and honest—battle, murder, sudden death, with plenty of good beer and damsels in distress, and a complete callousness about blipping the ungodly over the beezer. It mayn't be life as we know it, but it ought to be.

—Leslie Charteris in a 1935 BBC radio interview

Leslie Charteris was born Leslie Charles Bowyer-Yin in Singapore on 12 May 1907.

He was the son of a Chinese doctor and his English wife, who'd met in London a few years earlier. Young Leslie found friends hard to come by in colonial Singapore. The English children had been told not to play with Eurasians, and the Chinese children had been told not to play with Europeans. Leslie was caught in between and took refuge in reading.

"I read a great many good books and enjoyed them because nobody had told me that they were classics. I also read a great many bad books which nobody told me not to read . . . I read a great many popular scientific articles and acquired from them an astonishing amount of general knowledge before I discovered that this acquisition was supposed to be a chore."[1]

One of his favourite things to read was a magazine called *Chums.* "The Best and Brightest Paper for Boys" (if you believe the adverts) was a monthly paper full of swashbuckling adventure stories aimed at boys, encouraging them to be honourable and moral and perhaps even "upright citizens with furled umbrellas."[2] Undoubtedly these types of stories would influence his later work.

When his parents split up shortly after the end of World War I, Charteris accompanied his mother and brother back to England, where he was sent to Rossall School in Fleetwood, Lancashire. Rossall was then a very stereotypical English public school, and it struggled to cope with this multilingual mixed-race boy just into his teens who'd already seen more of the world than many of his peers would see in their lifetimes. He was an outsider.

He left Rossall in 1924. Keen to pursue a creative career, he decided to study art in Paris—after all, that was where the great artists went—but soon found that the life of a literally starving artist didn't appeal. He continued writing, firing off speculative stories to magazines, and it was the sale of a short story to *Windsor Magazine* that saved him from penury.

He returned to London in 1925, as his parents—particularly his father—wanted him to become a lawyer, and he was sent to study law at Cambridge University. In the mid-1920s, Cambridge was full of Bright Young Things—aristocrats and bohemians somewhat typified in the Evelyn Waugh novel *Vile Bodies*—and again the mixed-race Bowyer-Yin found that he didn't fit in. He was an outsider who preferred to make his own way in the world and wasn't one of the privileged upper class. It didn't help that he found his studies boring and decided it was more fun contemplating ways to circumvent the law. This inspired him to write a novel, and when publishers Ward Lock & Co. offered him a three-book deal on the strength of it, he abandoned his studies to pursue a writing career.

When his father learnt of this, he was not impressed, as he considered writers to be "rogues and vagabonds." Charteris would later recall that "I wanted to be a writer, he wanted me to become a lawyer. I was stubborn, he said I would end up in the gutter. So I left home. Later on, when I had a little success, we were reconciled by letter, but I never saw him again."[3]

X Esquire, his first novel, appeared in April 1927. The lead character, X Esquire, is a mysterious hero, hunting down and killing the businessmen trying to wipe out Britain by distributing quantities of free poisoned cigarettes. His second novel, *The White Rider*, was published the following spring, and in one memorable scene shows the hero chasing after his damsel in distress, only for him to overtake the villains, leap into their car . . . and promptly faint.

These two plot highlights may go some way to explaining Charteris's comment on *Meet—the Tiger!*, published in September 1928, that "it was only the third book I'd written, and the best, I would say, for it was that the first two were even worse."[4]

Twenty-one-year-old authors are naturally self-critical. Despite reasonably good reviews, the Saint didn't set the world on fire, and Charteris moved on to a new hero for his next book. This was *The Bandit*, an adventure story featuring Ramon Francisco De Castilla y Espronceda Manrique, published in the summer of 1929 after its serialisation in the *Empire News*, a now long-forgotten Sunday newspaper. But sales of *The Bandit* were less than impressive, and Charteris began to question his choice of career. It was all very well writing—but if nobody wants to read what you write, what's the point?

"I had to succeed, because before me loomed the only alternative, the dreadful penalty of failure . . . the routine office hours, the five-day week . . . the lethal assimilation into the ranks of honest, hard-working, conformist, God-fearing pillars of the community."⁵

However his fortunes—and the Saint's—were about to change. In late 1928, Leslie had met Monty Haydon, a London-based editor who was looking for writers to pen stories for his new paper, *The Thriller*—"The Paper with a Thousand Thrills." Charteris later recalled that "he said he was starting a new magazine, had read one of my books and would like some stories from me. I couldn't have been more grateful, both from the point of view of vanity and finance!"⁶

The paper launched in early 1929, and Leslie's first work, "The Story of a Dead Man," featuring Jimmy Traill, appeared in issue 4 (published on 2 March 1929). That was followed just over a month later with "The Secret of Beacon Inn," starring Rameses "Pip" Smith. At the same time, Leslie finished writing another non-Saint novel, *Daredevil*, which would be published in late 1929. Storm Arden was the hero; more notably, the book saw the first introduction of a Scotland Yard inspector by the name of Claud Eustace Teal.

The Saint returned in the thirteenth issue of *The Thriller*. The byline proclaimed that the tale was "A Thrilling Complete Story of the Underworld"; the title was "The Five Kings," and it actually featured Four Kings and a Joker. Simon Templar, of course, was the Joker.

Charteris spent the rest of 1929 telling the adventures of the Five Kings in five subsequent *The Thriller* stories. "It was very hard work, for the pay was lousy, but Monty Haydon was a brilliant and stimulating editor, full of ideas. While he didn't actually help shape the Saint as a character, he did suggest story lines. He would take me out to lunch and say, 'What are you going to write about next?' I'd often say I was damned if I knew. And Monty would say, 'Well, I was reading something the other day . . .' He had a fund of ideas and we would talk them over, and then I would go away and write a story. He was a great creative editor."⁷

Charteris would have one more attempt at writing about a hero other than Simon Templar, in three novelettes published in *The Thriller* in early 1930, but he swiftly returned to the Saint. This was partly due to his self-confessed laziness—he wanted to write more stories for *The Thriller* and other magazines, and creating a new hero for every story was hard work—but mainly due to feedback from Monty Haydon. It seemed people wanted to read more adventures of the Saint . . .

Charteris would contribute over forty stories to *The Thriller* throughout the 1930s. Shortly after their debut, he persuaded publisher Hodder & Stoughton that if he collected some of these stories and rewrote them a little, they could publish them as a Saint book. *Enter the Saint* was first published in August 1930, and the reaction was good enough for the publishers to bring out another collection. And another . . .

Of the twenty Saint books published in the 1930s, almost all have their origins in those magazine stories.

Why was the Saint so popular throughout the decade? Aside from the charm and ability of Charteris's storytelling, the stories, particularly those published in the first half of the '30s, are full of energy and joie de vivre. With economic depression rampant throughout the period, the public at large seemed to want some escapism.

And Simon Templar's appeal was wide-ranging: he wasn't an upper-class hero like so many of the period. With no obvious background and no attachment to the Old School Tie, no friends in high places who could provide a get-out-of-jail-free card, the Saint was uniquely classless. Not unlike his creator.

Throughout Leslie's formative years, his heritage had been an issue. In his early days in Singapore, during his time at school, at Cambridge University or even just in everyday life, he couldn't avoid the fact that for many people his mixed parentage was a problem. He would later tell a story of how he was chased up the road by a stick-waving typical

English gent who took offence to his daughter being escorted around town by a foreigner.

Like the Saint, he was an outsider. And although he had spent a significant portion of his formative years in England, he couldn't settle. As a young boy he had read of an America "peopled largely by Indians, and characters in fringed buckskin jackets who fought nobly against them. I spent a great deal of time day-dreaming about a visit to this prodigious and exciting country."[8]

It was time to realise this wish. Charteris and his first wife, Pauline, whom he'd met in London when they were both teenagers and married in 1931, set sail for the States in late 1932; the Saint had already made his debut in America courtesy of the publisher Doubleday. Charteris and his wife found a New York still experiencing the tail end of Prohibition, and times were tough at first. Despite sales to *The American Magazine* and others, it wasn't until a chance meeting with writer turned Hollywood executive Bartlett McCormack in their favourite speakeasy that Charteris's career stepped up a gear.

Soon Charteris was in Hollywood, working on what would become the 1933 movie *Midnight Club*. However, Hollywood's treatment of writers wasn't to Charteris's taste, and he began to yearn for home. Within a few months, he returned to the UK and began writing more Saint stories for Monty Haydon and Bill McElroy.

He also rewrote a story he'd sketched out whilst in the States, a version of which had been published in *The American Magazine* in September 1934. This new novel, *The Saint in New York*, published in 1935, was a significant advance for the Saint and Leslie Charteris. Gone were the high jinks and the badinage. The youthful exuberance evident in the Saint's early adventures had evolved into something a little darker, a little more hard-boiled. It was the next stage in development for the author and his creation, and readers loved it. It became a bestseller on both sides of the Atlantic.

Having spent his formative years in places as far apart as Singapore and England, with substantial travel in between, it should be no surprise that Leslie had a serious case of wanderlust. With a bestseller under his belt, he now had the means to see more of the world.

Nineteen thirty-six found him in Tenerife, researching another Saint adventure alongside translating the biography of Juan Belmonte, a well-known Spanish matador. Estranged for several months, Leslie and Pauline divorced in 1937. The following year, Leslie married an American, Barbara Meyer, who'd accompanied him to Tenerife. In early 1938, Charteris and his new bride set off in a trailer of his own design and spent eighteen months travelling round America and Canada.

The Saint in New York had reminded Hollywood of Charteris's talents, and film rights to the novel were sold prior to publication in 1935. Although the proposed 1935 film production was rejected by the Hays Office for its violent content, RKO's eventual 1938 production persuaded Charteris to try his luck once more in Hollywood.

New opportunities had opened up, and throughout the 1940s the Saint appeared not only in books and movies but in a newspaper strip, a comic-book series, and on radio.

Anyone wishing to adapt the character in any medium found a stern taskmaster in Charteris. He was never completely satisfied, nor was he shy of showing his displeasure. He did, however, ensure that copyright in any Saint adventure belonged to him, even if scripted by another writer—a contractual obligation that he was to insist on throughout his career.

Charteris was soon spread thin, overseeing movies, comics, newspapers, and radio versions of his creation, and this, along with his self-proclaimed laziness, meant that Saint books were becoming fewer and further between. However, he still enjoyed his creation: in 1941 he indulged himself in a spot of fun by playing the Saint—complete with monocle and moustache—in a photo story in *Life* magazine.

In July 1944, he started collaborating under a pseudonym on Sherlock Holmes radio scripts, subsequently writing more adventures for Holmes than Conan Doyle. Not all his ventures were successful—a screenplay he was hired to write for Deanna Durbin, "Lady on a Train," took him a year and ultimately bore little resemblance to the finished film. In the mid-1940s, Charteris successfully sued RKO Pictures for unfair competition after they launched a new series of films starring George Sanders as a debonair crime fighter known as the Falcon. But he kept faith with his original character, and the Saint novels continued to adapt to the times. The transatlantic Saint evolved into something of a private operator, working for the mysterious Hamilton and becoming, not unlike his creator, a world traveller, finding that adventure would seek him out.

"I have never been able to see why a fictional character should not grow up, mature, and develop, the same as anyone else. The same, if you like, as his biographer. The only adequate reason is that—so far as I know—no other fictional character in modern times has survived a sufficient number of years for these changes to be clearly observable. I must confess that a lot of my own selfish pleasure in the Saint has been in watching him grow up."[9]

Charteris maintained his love of travel and was soon to be found sailing round the West Indies with his good friend Gregory Peck. His forays abroad gave him even more material, and he began to write true-crime articles, as well as an occasional column in *Gourmet* magazine.

By the early '50s, Charteris himself was feeling strained. He'd divorced his second wife in 1943 and got together with a New York radio and nightclub singer called Betty Bryant Borst, whom he married in late 1943. That relationship had fallen apart acrimoniously towards the end of the decade, and he roamed the globe restlessly, rarely in one place for longer than a couple of months. He continued to maintain a firm grip on the exploitation of the Saint in various media but was writing little himself. The Saint had become an industry, and Charteris couldn't keep up. He began thinking seriously about an early retirement. Then in 1951 he met a young actress called Audrey Long when they became next-door neighbours in Hollywood. Within a year they had married, a union that was to last the rest of Leslie's life.

He attacked life with a new vitality. They travelled—Nassau was a favoured escape spot—and he wrote. He struck an agreement with *The New York Herald Tribune* for a Saint comic strip, which would appear daily and be written by Charteris himself. The strip ran for thirteen years, with Charteris sending in his handwritten story lines from wherever he happened to be, relying on mail services around the world to continue the Saint's adventures. New Saint books began to appear, and Charteris reached a height of productivity not seen since his days as a struggling author trying to establish himself. As Leslie and Audrey travelled, so did the Saint, visiting locations just after his creator had been there.

By 1953 the Saint had already enjoyed twenty-five years of success, and *The Saint Detective Magazine* was launched. Charteris had become adept at exploiting his creation to the full, mixing new stories with repackaged older stories, sometimes rewritten, sometimes mixed up in "new" anthologies, sometimes adapted from radio scripts previously written by other writers.

Charteris had been approached several times over the years for television rights in the Saint and had expended much time and effort during the 1950s trying to get the Saint on TV, even going so far as to write sample scripts himself, but it wasn't to be. He finally agreed a deal in autumn 1961 with English film producers Robert S. Baker and Monty Berman. The first episode of *The Saint* television series, starring Roger Moore, went into production in June 1962. The series was an immediate success, though Charteris himself had his reservations. It reached second place in the ratings, but he commented that "in that distinction it was topped by wrestling, which only suggested to me that the competition may not have been so hot; but producers are generally cast in a less modest mould." He resented the implication that the TV series had finally made a success of the Saint after twenty-five years of literary obscurity.

As long as the series lasted, Charteris was not shy about voicing his criticisms both in public and in a constant stream of memos to the producers. "Regular followers of the Saint saga . . . must have noticed that I am almost incapable of simply writing a story and shutting up."[10] Nor was he shy about exploiting this new market by agreeing to a series of tie-in novelisations ghosted by other writers, which he would then rewrite before publication.

Charteris mellowed as the series developed and found elements to praise too. He developed a close friendship with producer Robert S. Baker, which would last until Charteris's death.

In the early '60s, on one of their frequent trips to England, Leslie and Audrey bought a house in Surrey, which became their permanent base. He explored the possibility of a Saint musical and began writing some of it himself.

Charteris no longer needed to work. Now in his sixties, he supervised the Saint from a distance whilst continuing to travel and indulge himself. He and Audrey made seasonal excursions to Ireland and the south of France, where they had residences. He began to write poetry and devised a new universal sign language, Paleneo, based on notes and symbols he used in his diaries. Once Paleneo was released, he decided enough was enough and announced, again, his retirement. This time he meant it.

The Saint continued regardless—there was a long-running Swedish comic strip, and new novels with other writers doing the bulk of the work were complemented in the 1970s with Bob Baker's revival of the TV series, *Return of the Saint.*

Ill-health began to take its toll. By the early 1980s, although he continued a healthy correspondence with the outside world, Charteris felt unable to keep up with the collaborative Saint books and pulled the plug on them.

To entertain himself, Leslie took to "trying to beat the bookies in predicting the relative speed of horses," a hobby which resulted in several of his local betting shops refusing to take "predictions" from him, as he was too successful for their liking.

He still received requests to publish his work abroad but had become completely cynical about further attempts to revive the Saint. A new Saint magazine only lasted three issues, and two TV productions— *The Saint in Manhattan*, with Tom Selleck look-alike Andrew Clarke, and *The Saint*, with Simon Dutton—left him bitterly disappointed. "I fully expect this series to lay eggs everywhere . . . the only satisfaction I have is in looking at my bank balance."[11]

In the early 1990s, Hollywood producers Robert Evans and William J. Macdonald approached him and made a deal for the Saint to return to cinema screens. Charteris still took great care of the Saint's reputation and wrote an outline entitled *The Return of the Saint* in which an older Saint would meet the son he didn't know he had.

Much of his time in his last few years was taken up with the movie. Several scripts were submitted to him—each moving further and further away from his original concept—but the screenwriter from 1940s Hollywood was thoroughly disheartened by the Hollywood of the '90s: "There is still no plot, no real story, no characterisations, no personal interaction, nothing but endless frantic violence . . ." Besides, with producer Bill Macdonald hitting the headlines for the most un-Saintly reasons, he was to add, "How can Bill Macdonald concentrate on my Saint movie when he has Sharon Stone in his bed?"

The Crime Writers' Association of Great Britain presented Leslie with a Lifetime Achievement award in 1992 in a special ceremony at the

House of Lords. Never one for associations and awards, and although visibly unwell, Leslie accepted the award with grace and humour ("I am now only waiting to be carbon-dated," he joked). He suffered a slight stroke in his final weeks, which did not prevent him from dining out locally with family and friends, before he finally passed away at the age of eighty-five on 15 April 1993.

His death severed one of the final links with the classic thriller genre of the 1930s and 1940s, but he left behind a legacy of nearly one hundred books, countless short stories, and TV, film, radio, and comic-strip adaptations of his work which will endure for generations to come.

I was always sure that there was a solid place in escape literature for a rambunctious adventurer such as I dreamed up in my youth, who really believed in the old-fashioned romantic ideals and was prepared to lay everything on the line to bring them to life. A joyous exuberance that could not find its fulfilment in pinball machines and pot. I had what may now seem a mad desire to spread the belief that there were worse, and wickeder, nut cases than Don Quixote.

Even now, half a century later, when I should be old enough to know better, I still cling to that belief. That there will always be a public for the old-style hero, who had a clear idea of justice, and a more than technical approach to love, and the ability to have some fun with his crusades.[12]

---

1 *A Letter from the Saint*, 30 August 1946
2 "The Last Word," *The First Saint Omnibus*, Doubleday Crime Club, 1939
3 *The Straits Times*, 29 June 1958, page 9

4 Introduction by Charteris to the September 1980 paperback reprint of *Meet—the Tiger!* (Charter), the last ever print edition.

5 *The Saint: A Complete History*, by Burl Barer (McFarland, 1993)

6 PR material from the 1970s series *Return of the Saint*

7 From "Return of the Saint: Comprehensive Information" issued to help publicise the 1970s TV show

8 *A Letter from the Saint*, 26 July 1946

9 Introduction to "The Million Pound Day," in *The First Saint Omnibus*

10 *A Letter from the Saint*, 12 April 1946

11 Letter from LC to sometime Saint collaborator Peter Bloxsom, 2 August 1989

12 Introduction by Charteris to the September 1980 paperback reprint of *Meet—the Tiger!* (Charter).

WATCH FOR THE SIGN
OF THE SAINT!

THE SAINT CLUB

*And so, my friends, dear bookworms, most noble fellow
drinkers, frustrated burglars, affronted policemen, upright
citizens with furled umbrellas and secret buccaneering
dreams that seems to be very nearly all for now. It has been
nice having you with us, and we hope you will come again,
not once, but many times.*

*Only because of our great love for you, we would like
to take this parting opportunity of mentioning one small
matter which we have very much at heart . . .*

—*Leslie Charteris,* The First Saint Omnibus *(1939)*

Leslie Charteris founded The Saint Club in 1936 with the aim of
providing a constructive fanbase for Saint devotees. Before the War, it
donated profits to a London hospital where, for several years, a Saint
ward was maintained. With the nationalisation of hospitals, profits
were, for many years, donated to the Arbour Youth Centre in Stepney,
London.

In the twenty-first century, we've carried on this tradition but have
also donated to the Red Cross and a number of different children's
charities.

The club acts as a focal point for anyone interested in the adventures of Leslie Charteris and the work of Simon Templar, and offers merchandise that includes DVDs of the old TV series and various Saint-related publications, through to its own exclusive range of notepaper, pin badges, and polo shirts. All profits are donated to charity. The club also maintains two popular websites and supports many more Saint-related sites.

After Leslie Charteris's death, the club recruited three new vice-presidents—Roger Moore, Ian Ogilvy, and Simon Dutton have all pledged their support, whilst Audrey and Patricia Charteris have been retained as Saints-in-Chief. But some things do not change, for the back of the membership card still mischievously proclaims that . . .

The bearer of this card is probably a person of hideous antecedents and low moral character, and upon apprehension for any cause should be immediately released in order to save other prisoners from contamination.

To join . . .

Membership costs £3.50 (or US$7) per year, or £30 (US$60) for life. Find us online at www.lesliecharteris.com for full details.

Made in the USA
Middletown, DE
20 October 2022

13152293R00168